Troubled Times for Tilly

Kay Seeley

Copyright © 2025 Kay Seeley

All rights reserved.

Enterprise Books

ISBN-978-1-914592-19-5

*To my family with
love and thanks*

Kay Seeley's books

Novels

The Water Gypsy
Troubled Times for Tilly (A Water Gypsy Book)
The Watercress Girls
The Guardian Angel

The Hope Series
A Girl Called Hope (Book 1)
A Girl Called Violet (Book 2)
A Girl Called Rose (Book 3)

Fitzroy Hotel Series
One Beat of a Heart
A Troubled Heart
A Heart full of Hope

All Kay's novels are also available in Large Print

Box Sets (ebook only)
The Victorian Novels Box Set
The Hope Series Box Set

Short Stories
The Cappuccino Collection
The Summer Stories
The Christmas Stories

Chapter One

Fierce fury burned inside Tilly, stealing her breath. She couldn't believe what she was hearing. Martha had been so excited about going to the Ball and now, thanks to some man's cruel judgement, her dreams lay in shatters. Whoever he was, that man should be horsewhipped, in Tilly's opinion. Joey's parentage had never been a problem before. Of course, there were rumours and gossip, Joey's fine features, soft blond hair and slim build being so different from Sam's dark curls and muscular physic, but Tilly and Sam never worried about it. They loved him, he was theirs.

In Tilly's world people were judged by who they were, not by how much money their fathers had. Still, she knew very well the maliciousness and spite of the well-to-do. Hadn't she experienced it all her life?

She recalled how Captain Charles Thackery had changed her life and opened a door to a world in which she'd never truly belonged. She'd paid dearly for it too. Now history threatened to repeat itself and she didn't want her daughter, Martha, to go through what she went through. Martha deserved better and as for Joey...

She loved her son, of course she did. She didn't blame him for what happened, but couldn't help wishing they'd never seen that wretched invitation two months ago...

Tilly's hands had trembled as she held the gold-edged card, a sick feeling churning in her stomach. The words danced before her eyes. *Mr & Mrs Crowe are invited to witness the passing out parade of their son, Joseph Edmund Thackery.*

Thackery! She shuddered. Sir Montague had insisted on the name when he arranged Joey's enrolment at the Royal Naval College. It was the name on his birth certificate. They'd never kept the circumstances of his birth from Joey. It had never been an issue, Sam treated the children all the same, but now...everything suddenly felt different.

Across the breakfast table Sam's voice was steady. "Big day for the lad," he said, "We'll go of course."

Tilly swallowed the lump that rose in her throat. A shiver ran down her spine as she placed the card on the table. "I suppose..." She shrugged and glanced down at her plate. Of course she wanted to be there. She'd always been proud of her eldest son, proud beyond measure, but...

"But?" Sam's eyebrows raised.

She glanced up. He'd always been able to read her thoughts. She took a breath. "I expect Sir Montague will be there." As she said it the memory of him filled her mind: his grey hair, his face as creased as a walnut, and the accusation in his piercing blue eyes that still haunted her. It had been...what...nearly nineteen years since that awful day Joey's true parentage had been revealed to all the world. Another shiver ran down her spine.

When they'd made the agreement, all those years ago, she'd thought that was what his father would have wanted. She'd been young and naive and seduced by the glamour, ease and comfort that comes with money.

She'd never foreseen that he'd grow up and grow away from her. That hurt. All the summers he spent with his paternal family, she missed him but comforted herself with the knowledge that it was good for him, for his security, his future.

Sir Montague had been true to his word over the years and paid for Joey's education. She'd been true to hers and let him spend time with his paternal family. Joey had opportunities she and Sam could never provide, but over the years she'd come to wonder if it was all worthwhile.

Sam reached out and put his hand over hers. "Joey will want you to be there," he said. "And I'll be proud to stand by your side. Don't let the past ruin the present."

Tilly nodded. Sam was right. Solid, reliable Sam. He'd been her anchor, and no boy could wish for a better father than he'd been to Joey. Tears filled her eyes as a kaleidoscope of memories spun through her brain. She recalled the day Joey was born. She hadn't wanted him. He was the result of a brief liaison between a young, naive soldier going to fight for his country and a poor lost girl trying to escape her past. But as soon as she held the tiny, scrawling scrap with his red, screwed up face in her arms her heart had melted. She knew she'd do anything to protect him. And she had, up until that fateful day.

"Goodness, there's a chill in the air this morning," Martha, Tilly's eldest daughter, said as she burst into the room, bringing a blast of cool air with her. "Any tea in that pot? I'm gasping."

"You're out early," Tilly said, glad of the distraction. "I'll get Mrs Conway to bring some fresh." She reached out to pull a bell rope hanging by the curtain next to where she was sitting.

"I wanted to get to the market to pick up some silks." Martha pulled a small brown paper wrapped package from her pocket. "These will be just what I need to finish the blouse I'm working on." She opened the package to show her mother. Tilly smiled. At seventeen Martha was a beauty. As well as her dark as night curls and emerald eyes she'd inherited her sewing skills, something that warmed Tilly's heart.

"I'll leave you to it," Sam said, rising from his chair. He picked up the invitation. "Don't worry. I'll see to this."

Tilly went to complain, but he silenced her protest with a kiss. "I won't be late," he said. He turned to Martha. "If you're free on Saturday you might take your mother shopping. I fear she will be in need of a new hat." Familiar laughter danced in his soft brown eyes and Tilly's heart turned over. In his presence she felt loved and protected, as though nothing bad could ever happen. How she wished that were true.

"A new hat?" Martha said, surprise lifting her voice, just as Sam left and Mrs Conway, the cook, came in carrying a tray of tea and toast.

Tilly shook her head, but couldn't quite smother the chuckle that rose to her lips. "It's nothing."

"Have the others eaten?" Martha asked, biting into a slice of buttered toast.

"Yes. Harry left at crack of dawn to catch the tide and I sent Katy and George off to get ready for school. I said I'd walk with them this morning. I have some errands to run."

Martha nodded. "Are we shopping on Saturday, then? I could do with something new."

Tilly tutted. "We'll see," she said.

As soon as she'd finished breakfast, Tilly fetched her coat and hat and chivvied her two youngest children to hurry up. At ten and twelve, they were perfectly capable of walking to school on their own, but Tilly enjoyed being out in the early morning. It reminded her of far off, carefree days when she was young and lived on the canals.

A light breeze polished her cheeks to a rosy glow as they walked, but the early spring sunshine would soon warm the street. Katy, the eldest of the two, skipped along, full of chatter and excitement for the day ahead, while George stomped along, quietly by his mother's side. Tilly smiled. He had her father's taciturn ways and was happier with his head in a book than among people.

She nodded to neighbours she knew as they passed, but the invitation preyed on her mind. She was proud of Joey, of course she was. He'd grown into a fine young man. Two years at sea had hardened him and now he'd passed his exams he'd be an officer, like his father and grandfather before him.

Now she had cause to wonder. Would he have been happier messing about on the boats, like Harry with all the freedom that allowed? Sam had done well over the years. He now had three boats on the river which bought them a fair-sized house, too far east to be fashionable and high enough to give a good view of the river. They enjoyed a standard of living she'd only ever been able to dream about, but it was nothing compared to Sir Montague's wealth. He owned half of Warwickshire.

She shook her head and recalled what Ruby, a work-worn kitchen maid, had said to her once many years ago: *Things in the past is best left in the past.* She chuckled at the memory. She was right but it didn't stop her worrying about her son, who'd grown up straddled between two different worlds and didn't really belong in either of them.

Upstairs Martha put the silks she'd brought into her sewing basket. She'd have enough to finish the blouse she was working on. She hoped to finish it before Joey came home.

He'd written to say he would be home in summer, and she looked forward to seeing him. Life was always more exciting when he was around and Ma and Pa smiled more. He was her big brother who looked out for her when they were growing up. She couldn't remember when or how she knew Pa wasn't Joey's birth father. It was something she was conscious of, but it wasn't talked about, still, it might explain the mysterious benefactor he mentioned when she asked about his summer visits to Warwickshire. She missed him when he was away. Why didn't he work on the river like young Harry? She knew he enjoyed privileges she'd never enjoy: a better school and summer trips away – she didn't begrudge him that. She couldn't blame Ma and Pa for wanting the best for him, after all he was their eldest son and he'd have to earn a living. She guessed he wasn't cut out for working on the river like Pa and Harry.

He was popular too. She recalled the day on his last leave when he'd offered to accompany her into town on Saturday where she was meeting friends for lunch. He had to call in at an office near the docks, so they walked together. When they arrived, all her friends gathered round in a frenzy to fawn over him. She couldn't think why. Probably the uniform. I suppose it is impressive compared to the rough and ready boys who work on the docks, she thought. They can hardly string a sentence together and would rather cut their throats than be seen in polite conversation with a girl. She chuckled. She still found it irritating when they asked about him, as though she had any say in what he did.

She closed her sewing basket and grabbed her hat and coat. If she hurried, she could catch the early bus and walk along by the river in the sunshine enjoying the clamour of the morning as she made her way to the office where she worked. She often imagined what it would be like to work on the river, something she'd wanted to do when she left school. She'd helped in long summer holidays when she was young and, at ten, could haul and tie up a boat faster and firmer than young Harry, two years her junior, but strong and stocky like Pa. Her mother wouldn't hear of it. She told her that life on the water was hard and relentless and enrolled her in secretarial school, it being thought more ladylike, and, Martha supposed, enable her to get a job where she was more likely to meet an eligible young man who'd want to marry her. Sam's partner had arranged her job in the shipping office. She didn't intend to stay there for the rest of her life, but the money was good, the people bearable and the work undemanding. She had no cause for complaint.

She called good morning, to the doorman as she entered the building. "Lovely day," she said. "Shame to spend it indoors."

He nodded a good morning and smiled. No point being miserable, she thought. The office supervisor, Miss Todd, was already at her desk when Martha arrived in the office. She knew she would be. Miss Todd, known as Toddy to her friends, and, rather unkindly as Toady by

Martha's fellow clerks, had steel grey hair and a face to match. Stern and pernickety, she was a dyed in the wool supporter of 'standards', although prone to fits of flutter when Mr Bartholomew, the senior partner, came into the office.

Martha went to her desk and pushed her bag into a drawer. A pile of shipping manifestos sat on her desk ready to be typed up and sent out. She sighed and began. As she worked thoughts of Joey were never far from her mind. She'd been shocked when, at sixteen, he signed up to go to sea.

"To see the world," he said. She envied him that. It sounded like an adventure. When he enrolled in naval college, she wasn't sure it was his idea. It was as though Joey's life had been mapped out for him a long time ago and he had no real say in it.

The whistle for lunch brought her out of her reverie. She gathered up the papers she'd typed and picked her bag out of the drawer. She took the papers to the front of the room, adding them to the pile on the desk. On fine days she'd have lunch by the river with the other girls and today was a particularly fine day.

Chapter Two

Late in the afternoon, Tilly set out the children's tea. They were always ravenous when they returned from school. She'd sent them out into the garden and could hear Katy skipping. George would be reading a book or examining some insect or worm he'd discovered. She smiled. When she was their age she'd worked on the boat, polishing brass and hauling coal. She started when she heard the front door close and footsteps in the hall. Thinking it must be Sam come home early, she hurried out to meet him and gasped when she saw Joey, a bunch of flowers in one hand and his cap in the other.

"Joey! What on earth. Why didn't you tell us you were coming? Oh...this is a lovely surprise..."

He pushed the flowers into her hand and kissed her cheek. "Thought I'd surprise you." He stepped back, his eyes shining with youthful vitality. "You look wonderful. Haven't aged a day. How do you do it, Ma?"

Tilly blushed and laughed. "Get away with you." She hugged him, brushing his cheek with hers. It felt good, having him home again. "How long are you staying?"

He grinned. "Not long. A flying visit I'm afraid, but long enough to stay overnight if that's all right?"

"Of course it is. Come on in. Katy and George are in the garden. They'll be excited to see you." She opened the back door and the afternoon sun flooded in. Katy and George stopped what they were doing and rushed to greet their older brother, their faces wreathed in smiles.

"My goodness, you've grown so much since I saw you last," Joey said. "I'm not sure the presents I've brought will be suitable at all."

"Presents?" Katy's eyes lit up.

He swung his kit bag down from his shoulder and produced two packages wrapped in brown paper. "Let me see," he said. "This is for George." He handed him one of the parcels, "and this must be for Katy."

Excited, they unwrapped their parcels. George whooped as he held the model sailing ship in his hands. "Can we sail it?"

Katy's eyes opened wide when she saw the book entitled *What Katy Did*. "Is this about me?"

"It's about someone like you," Joey said. "I hope you enjoy it. And, yes, George. We can sail the boat but only on the pond over the park."

"Well," Tilly said. "I suppose you're too excited to eat your tea now. Come in, Joey, I'll put these flowers in water. We can have a cup of tea, and you can tell me your plans."

He followed her into the kitchen where she filled the kettle and put it on the stove. "How's Pa?" he asked. "Still working on the river all the hours God sends?"

Tilly paused. How was Sam? Older, more worried, going grey? "You'll see for yourself soon enough," she said. As she spoke, she heard the front door close. "Oh, that sounds like him now."

Sam appeared at the kitchen door. He dropped his bag when he saw Joey. His face lit with a grin. "The prodigal son returns," he said. He grabbed Joey by his outstretched hand and pulled him into his embrace. "It's good to see you, son."

"Good to be home," Joey said. "I wanted to make sure you were both coming to the passing out parade. You did get the invitation, didn't you?" He glanced at Tilly.

"Yes. We got it and we couldn't be more proud of you. Well done, son." Sam clapped him on the back. "We're looking forward to it aren't we, Tilly?"

Tilly's heart hadn't stopped fluttering from the excitement of seeing her eldest son, how she wished she could hold him in her arms like she did when he was little and never let him go. It had taken her a few minutes to get used to the fact that Joey was home, looking so grown up and, she had to admit, handsome. The words, so like his father, ran through her mind but she pushed them away.

The past is best left in the past, she thought, but her heart told her that there were some things you couldn't leave behind. "Looking forward it...er? Yes," she said trying to convince herself as much as Joey.

"I suppose you'll be signing up to a ship now and off sailing the seas again," Sam said. He didn't get an answer as Martha's arrival interrupted them.

She shrieked when she saw Joey and rushed into his arms. He chuckled and allowed her to hug him. "How long are you staying?" she asked. "Please say it's for ages."

Joey shrugged. "I don't know about that." He pulled away. "We're just missing Harry. Will he be home soon?"

"He'll be home for dinner," Sam said. "He's gone with one of the boats into the yard. A problem with the paddles. I hope they can fix it overnight or one of our trips will have to be cancelled." Tilly saw the worry flash across his face. "Still, what about your plans?" he said.

"Oh, nearly forgot." Joey picked up his kit bag, dove his hand into it and brought out a small brown paper wrapped parcel for Martha. "I hope you like it," he said.

Martha's eyes widened and shone with delight as she tore off the paper to reveal a small square box. She gasped as she opened it. Tilly gasped too as she saw the pink and pearl cameo brooch nestling amid the tissue paper. It was exactly the same as the cameo brooch upstairs at the back of her dressing table drawer, the brooch the Captain had given her on her seventeenth birthday. The same brooch she'd given to Joey's father before he sailed for South Africa which was returned to her by Sir Montague Thackery all those years ago.

"Are you all right?" Sam moved towards Tilly. "You look quite pale."

Tilly forced a smile. "The excitement, I expect." She turned to Joey. "Where did you get it?" The words were out of her mouth before she could stop them.

"A small shop in town. Why? Is there anything wrong?"

"Oh. Sorry." A wave of guilt washed over her. "I didn't mean – I mean – it's beautiful. So clever of you, Joey." She turned away to get another cup out of the cupboard. She couldn't bear for them to see her face. Her eyes would betray her, they always did.

"It's beautiful," Martha said, holding it up so the light shone through it.

"It's made of shell," Joey said. "It reminded me of the sea."

"Why don't you all go through to the drawing room," Tilly said, anxious to be alone to compose herself. "I'll bring the tea." To her great relief they didn't need second telling. She busied herself making the tea, forcing her mind away from the memories crowding her brain.

By the time she'd made the tea and cut some of the cake Mrs Conway had left for them, she felt more in control of herself. A cameo brooch, she thought. Why that, after all the years?

Over tea and cake, Sam, Martha and Joey chatted, but Tilly's mind was elsewhere. It wasn't long before the subject came round to the passing out parade. "And that's not all," Joey said. "There's to be a Celebration Ball for the officers passing out."

Tilly's ears pricked up. "A ball?" she said, a wave of horror washing over her.

"Don't worry, Ma. I'm not expecting you and Pa to trip the light fantastic. But I thought perhaps, Martha..."

"Martha?"

"Yes. If that's all right with you and Pa."

"Me!"

Tilly saw the excitement in Martha's face and her heart crunched at the disappointment ahead of her. She glanced at Sam who beamed with happiness.

"Please say yes, Ma. Please, please say I can go. I've never been to a ball and never likely to get the chance again. Please say yes."

Seeing Martha's excitement and the pride on Sam's face, she didn't have the heart to say no.

After tea Katy and George had homework and Joey wanted to hear about Sam's business. It being such a lovely afternoon they sat in the garden overlooking the river. Martha fiddled with the cameo she'd been given, wondering the best way to wear it. Tilly left them to it and went to prepare dinner.

Mrs Conway had prepared a meat and potato pie for them. Tilly hoped it would be enough for their unexpected visitor.

"I'm sure there is, Ma," Martha said, "seeing that she always makes enough to feed an army on the march."

That was true. There was always plenty left over which Tilly usually had for lunch the next day. "I expect you're used to much grander fare in the officers' mess," she said as she served it out.

"Nothing beats home cooking." Joey rubbed his hands together. "I've missed Mrs C's pies."

Tilly tried to relax but anxiety churned her stomach. Don't be so silly, she told herself – it's Joey come home – but the feeling of dread didn't go away.

Over dinner Joey talked about his life at college and his fellow officers, sharing anecdotes about the pranks they played, the fun they had and some of the scrapes he'd got into. He kept everyone laughing and the time passed quickly. It soon became clear to Tilly the sort of people he mixed with. They had the same air of confident entitlement that she remembered from years ago and the ease and comfort that comes with money. She shook the memory of the past away.

"I expect you'll be off on your travels again soon," Sam said

Joey shrugged. "I've talked too much about me," he said. "I want to hear what you've all been up to. You're working on the river now, eh Harry?"

Harry was happy to talk about his work on the boats with the others chipping into the conversation. Martha, bouncing with excitement, wanted to talk about the ball she'd been invited to and Joey asked Katy about school. Overall, it was a happy reunion, but Tilly still feared for Joey's future.

Then there was the ball Martha was so excited about. "Don't worry, I'll look after her," Joey said, but how would Martha feel when she saw the very different life Joey led? There'd be questions about Sir Montague's patronage. That was a subject she had no wish to revisit.

After dinner, when she was alone with Sam, she again expressed her worries. "He's changed," she said. "He's not the boy he was, helping you on the river, mucking in, always with a cheeky smile on his face. I worry for what's to become of him."

"He's grown up, that's all. And grown into a fine young man you should be proud of if I'm any judge."

"I am proud of him," Tilly said. "It's just the people he mixes with. You heard what they get up to. All sons of the well-to-do whose families can afford to bail them out if they get into any trouble. It's a different world and one we'll never be part of."

Sam pulled her into his arms and smoothed away her fears. "You have to trust him, Till. Trust that things will turn out for the best."

Tilly hoped so.

Chapter Three

Martha rose early next morning and hurried down to breakfast. She wanted to catch Joey before he left. When he was ready to leave she offered to walk with him. "We're going the same way," she said, although they weren't. Still, it gave her a chance to talk to him. She wanted to know all about the ball she'd been invited to and she hadn't missed how he changed the subject whenever anyone asked about his plans. She doubted Ma had missed that either.

Joey said his goodbyes and that he'd look out for them at the passing out parade. Martha was quick to latch on to him as he left.

Out in the morning sunshine they walked along by the river. Slanting rays of light shimmered on the rippling waves, the water slapping the sides of the boats moored along the bank the only sound. Martha breathed it all in, relishing the freshness of the morning. That was what she loved about walking by the river, it was different every day. Some days the sky would be grey and dark clouds shadowed the water making it murky and dull, but on others diamonds sparkled in the sunlight.

"Do you miss it?" she asked. "The river?"

"A bit I suppose," he said. "The sea is much fiercer, vast and dangerous. It swallows you up."

They walked in silence for a while, anticipation bubbling inside Martha. "So, tell me about this ball," she said. "Will it be very grand? Who will be there? What are they like? What should I wear?" She'd spent half the night imagining the extravagantly elegant gowns she'd seen in Ma's fashion magazines and speculating on patterns, colours and fabrics. The thought of wearing something so beguiling thrilled her.

He smiled. "Yes, it will be very grand. I'm sure Ma can sort you out something to wear and as for the people – well, they're just people like any other people."

"Will your mysterious benefactor be there?"

Joey frowned. "He's not mysterious. His name is Sir Montague Thackery. We're related."

Martha gasped. "Related?" She frowned. "You mean he's your father, your natural father?"

Joey laughed. "No, of course he's not." He paused in thought. "Sir Montague sees something in me that no one else sees. I appreciate all he's done for me but Pa's the only father I've ever known and I couldn't wish for better."

Martha was curious now and wanted to know more. "Sir Montague, eh? Sounds like a bit…" she flicked her nose indicating he was toffee-nosed. "A toff was he? How much do you know about him?"

"Only what Ma's told me. He was a Thackery and part of her life before she married Pa. I think he was a decent man, at least Ma says he was." He smiled at her. "You're my family – you, Harry, Katy, George, Ma and Pa. When I'm at home I'm plain Joe Crowe, at college and in Warwickshire I'm Joseph Thackery, but I'm still me."

"It must be odd, being two people."

He laughed. "No. I'm used to it."

"So, what are your plans? What are you going to do when you've 'passed out'?" She glanced at him. "What is it that's you're not telling us?"

He chuckled, warmth gleamed in his eyes. "You always were too nosy for your own good," he said.

"So, you are planning something?"

"I can't talk about it yet. There's nothing definite but it will be a bit of a change." He glanced at her, as the bus drew up. "You'll have to wait and see, like everyone else." He laughed as he jumped on. "And don't worry, you'll be the belle of the ball."

Martha smiled and waved as the bus pulled away. It was good to see him and the conversation had given her much to think about.

Although it was a month away, as the day of the parade drew nearer Tilly could think of a thousand reasons not to go. But, it was for Joey, so, she'd put on a brave face and do her best to make him proud. She still worried for Sam, who always thought the best of everyone. She knew first-hand of the hypocrisy, maliciousness and spite of the well-to-do, never missing a chance to humiliate someone who they regarded as 'trade' and beneath them. Sam didn't. She feared he'd be walking defenceless into a lion's den. Then a voice in her head told her that Sam could take care of himself, she had nothing to worry about. Still a niggle of fear wormed its way into her thoughts.

Then there was Martha. Her concern for Martha was even greater than her fear for Sam. For over a week now she had talked of nothing but the blessed ball. What should she wear, who would she meet, what would they be like? Only last night she'd mentioned it again. Tilly shook her head in frustration, then she remembered the excitement she'd felt when she was that age and was taken out for the first time dressed in silk. How could she deny Martha the same opportunity to see a different way of life?

Nothing in Martha's wardrobe would be suitable for a ball. The nearest she possessed to an evening gown was the elaborately frilled dress Tilly had made for her seventeenth birthday party. Even Tilly's wardrobe wouldn't help. Her most glamorous outfits were the gowns she wore to the Watermans' Dinners or Ladies Nights. They were eye-catching, well-made and quite extravagant for those occasions, but nothing like the sort of gowns the ladies at the Celebration Ball would be wearing. Martha would need something new.

"We can go shopping on Saturday," she said when Martha came home that evening. "I still know several of the Spitalfields silk weavers and the haberdashers in Commercial Street. I'm sure they'll help us out."

Martha beamed at the prospect. "What about you?" she said. "Won't you need something new for the parade?"

Tilly recalled Sam's remark about a new hat. She supposed he was right, she too would need a new outfit.

Saturday morning Tilly and Martha visited Spitalfields to buy the material for Martha's dress. Tilly hoped the people there would remember her. She'd never forget them, nor how helpful they'd been when she worked as a dressmaker. It had been many years since she'd stitched through the night to produce gowns suitable for a society ball. Even then the gowns she'd sewn would never have been seen in the drawing rooms of polite society. The girls she made dresses for had no status, other than that which depended on the position and wealth of the men who accompanied them.

Her heart crunched at the memory of those days, and the girls she knew, who were always hoping for a better life. Still, she prided herself on keeping up to date with fashion through the society pages in newspapers and magazines, assessing the women's outfits. It was a game she never tired of. She'd never lost the skill of creating something spectacular at minimum cost or her eye for style either

Inside, the warehouse supervisor greeted her like an old friend. "Good heavens," she said. "If it isn't Mary Tilson. It's been a while," she said.

Tilly laughed, her spirits lifting at the woman's greeting. Of course, she would remember her as Mary Tilson, a name she'd used years ago to hide her identity. "It's Tilly Crowe now," she said, "but I'm glad to see you."

The woman nodded, as though a change in identity was an everyday occurrence. "I'm glad to see you looking so well. The years have been kind to you." Tilly's heart warmed. "Come into the office. I'd love to hear what you've been up to."

After tea and a chat Tilly said they'd need to look at patterns.

"Patterns over here." The warehouse supervisor showed them to a shelf lined with huge pattern books. Tilly took one down and together they went through it.

Martha loved them all, but Tilly's eye was more focussed on the practicalities. She'd be the one making it. In the end they settled for a scoop necked gown with puffed sleeves and a boned bodice tapering to a tiny waist. The full skirt skimmed the hips and flared out in a cascade frills and ruffles. An overskirt fell from the waist, gathered into pleats at the back to form a train embellished with a huge bow. A stiffened linen underskirt gave the dress its shape and several petticoats would provide the volume.

Once the pattern was decided they went into the enormous warehouse area where shelves lined the walls bearing bolts of silk in every colour and hue of the rainbow. Tilly chatted to the supervisor, while Martha picked out two bolts of silk in shades of pink.

"Beautiful," Tilly said, handling the lighter pink silk. "This will make up well for the bodice and overskirt, with the darker pink for the underskirt and ruffles."

"What about the trimmings?" the supervisor said.

"Pearls and lace," Tilly said.

"Excellent." The supervisor beamed.

Tilly thanked her and they left with their purchases. A visit to several haberdashery shops in Commercial Road completed their shopping before they had lunch in a small café near the station.

Monday morning Martha couldn't wait to take some snippets of the material to work to show her friends. They'd be so jealous, she thought. She was running late and just managed to squeeze into the office as the starting bell rang, earning her a frosty look from Miss Todd. Breathless she took her place at her typewriter, but her mind was still on the ball and the dress she would wear. What would Joey think of it? She hoped he'd be suitably impressed.

Halfway through the morning Miss Todd was called into Mr Bartholomew's office. Martha and the other girls exchanged glances, the clack of typewriters slowed, a welcome respite from the constant noise.

Ten minutes later Miss Todd returned, red in the face, several strands of hair had come adrift from the tortoise shell clip she always wore. Martha thought she looked particularly perturbed. "Miss Crowe," she called. "Have you finished the manifest for the *Carnarvon Castle* yet?"

Her glare sent a chill down Martha's spine. "Yes, Miss Todd." Martha tore the page out of her typewriter. "All done."

"Take it up to Mr Bartholomew. Now please." Her tone brooked no argument.

"Yes, Miss Todd." Martha put the page she'd just typed into a brown cardboard folder with some other papers, picked them up and hurried out. When she arrived at Mr Bartholomew's office she hesitated outside the door as she heard raised voices coming from within. She took a breath, not sure whether to interrupt. As she lifted her arm to knock, the door flew open and a man rushed out, pushing past her, sending the folder she was holding out of her hand to fall in a cascade of papers to the floor. Shocked, she gasped and stared at his retreating back. It looked very much like Victor Landridge, her father's partner. It took her several seconds to recover her composure. Her heart still racing she stooped and picked up the scattered papers. She still felt shaky when she went into the office. Mr Bartholomew looked up.

"Ah, Miss Crowe. Is that the manifest?"

"Yes, Mr Bartholomew. Miss Todd asked me to bring it up."

He took the proffered folder, staring at Martha as though he was about to say something. A chill ran down her spine. She glanced at the door through which her father's partner had just departed. "Was that...?"

"That'll be all." Mr Bartholomew said, glancing down at the papers, now spread out on the desk in front of him.

Martha bit her lip and backed away. She was sure it was him and even surer that his visit meant trouble.

Chapter Four

Tilly woke in a sweat of doubt and apprehension on the day of the passing out parade. The worry of it had tormented her mind for weeks and now it was finally here. She'd hardly slept, visions of the day ahead spun through her brain. The naval college was a part of Joey's life that had been closed to her and Sam. It was a world away from life on the river. She'd had her fill of officers and knew from her past that, despite their fine manners and country ways, underneath it all they were mere men with all their faults and foibles. Now Joey would be one of them. How would he feel, seeing her and Sam there, compared to the wealth and position of his classmates' families?

Joey had been sixteen when he asked about his natural father. "He was a Thackery, an officer and a fine gentleman," Tilly told him. "It wasn't nothing, if that's what you think. I really felt for him." Tears had sprung to her eyes at the memory. She'd bit her lip and pressed her tongue to the roof of her mouth to stop them falling. "He was kind, honest and filled with courage. A brave man who was willing to lay down his life for his country, a man to be proud of and a credit to his family." She paused. "I loved him," she'd hesitated, "in a way." She took a breath. "He was foolish enough to think he could marry me. We were young, so young – too young."

Joey didn't speak. He stood and paced the room. Perhaps it was too much to take in, Tilly thought, being told you were born a bastard. A shiver of fear ran through her. What was he thinking? Was he picturing her, his mother, having a meaningless tumble with a faceless stranger? Her heart trembled. It had been a relief to talk about it, after keeping silent for so many years. Tilly thought everything was all right, then Joey signed up to a ship and went to sea and Tilly's heart broke.

Sickness swirled inside her at the memory. No matter how many times she told herself that Joey would be pleased and proud to see them, she couldn't quite believe it.

She rose early and spent an hour getting ready, changing her outfit twice and then back again. She didn't want to let Joey down. In the end she decided on a discreet navy-blue tailored suit with leg of mutton sleeves and gold braid over a pale lavender blouse, frilled and pleated with pearl buttons to give a feminine touch. She teamed it with a jaunty hat with matching ribbons and feathers. A spray of her favourite perfume, smelling of honeysuckle, jasmine and roses, completed the outfit. She took a breath and gazed in the mirror. A broad smile stretched her lips. You'll do, Tilly Crowe, she thought. You'll do.

Downstairs, Sam waited. His smile stretched even wider than hers. "You look wonderful," he said. "As beautiful as the day I married you."

Her heart swelled with gratitude. At least she could rely on Sam to be there whatever happened. He'd always be beside her. She smiled. "I'm not sure that's true," she said. "But thank you for saying it."

Martha too had dressed with care. She'd wangled an invitation from Joey, saying she'd be proud to be there and managed to get a day off from work for the occasion, provided she made up the hours by working through her lunch hour and late the following week. Tilly had been against it, but Sam, as usual, gave in to her.

"She's part of his family," he said. Martha could twist her father round her little finger, a skill she'd possessed since she was born. Tilly had complained on more than one occasion that Sam indulged her. He'd laughed. "A father's privilege," he said, and the matter was closed.

Outside the sun shone bright and clear. Cotton wool clouds floated across a summer blue sky. Birds chirped in the trees and a soft breeze rustled the leaves. Butterflies fluttered in Tilly's stomach. "The whole Thackery family will be there," she said.

"What family?" Sam said. "There's only Lady Thackery and the aunt. I'm sure Joey would want his real family there."

Tilly sighed. She hoped he was right. She appreciated the opportunities and education provided by Sir Montague but couldn't help hoping that her son hadn't left his roots behind. Looking out of the Hackney carriage window now, as they made their way to the college, she wondered. Did she really know her son as well as she thought?

"They've got a fine day for it anyway," Sam said. He paused in thought. "You know, I must have passed the naval college a hundred times on the boat, but, never in my wildest dreams did I ever think I'd be invited in." He turned to Tilly. "What about you?"

Tilly nodded. She too had passed it many times. "I've only seen it from the water," she said. "I've often thought it the most impressive part of the river. Imposing and inspirational. Apparently, Nelson's body was brought here. Did you know that?"

Sam grinned. "I did. And a lot more. You'd be surprised."

Martha leaned forward to glance out, but they turned a corner and the sight was lost.

The cab drew up at the gates. Sam held out the invitation and they were waved through. Inside they were dropped off at a spot in front of the mews. They dismounted the carriage and joined the procession of people making their way along a pathway between solid stone buildings steeped in history. A mix of astonishment, wonder and deep respect surged through Tilly at its scale and magnificence. The multi-columned architecture, the impressive buildings, the space and vastness stunned her as she gazed around. Bees buzzed around a row of sweet chestnut trees set around manicured lawns that stretched to the river. Even Martha appeared humbled by the majesty of it. "It's even bigger than the Royal Dock," she muttered.

When they reached the parade ground, they were ushered to a stand, already half filled, which had been erected for the visitors. Sam squeezed Tilly's hand as they followed the line of people taking their seats. He stood back so Tilly and Martha could go in first. She was pleased to see they were in the middle of a row where they would have an excellent view. Although substantial buildings flanked the parade ground, if she stretched her neck, she could just see the river.

She settled down next to a large man in a rough tweed suit over a yellow waistcoat. He had a ruddy complexion accentuated by his high collar. He nodded as she sat down, gazing around, not sure what to expect.

"Your first time?" the man asked.

"Yes." Tilly took in his bluff appearance, his greying, curly hair and heavy sideburns. "Not yours then?"

A grin stretched across his face. "No. But most likely my last. I'm here to watch my grandson. You?"

"My son." Suddenly it all became very real. Before it had felt like a fantasy, but now she was here she could see the enormity of what Joey had done. He'd be an officer in the Royal Navy.

"Lawton Matherson," the man next to her said and held out his hand. His hand was rough, a working man's hand. Tilly wondered what he was doing there. He must have done well to be able to pay his grandson's way through college.

"Tilly Crowe," Tilly said. "And this is my husband Sam and my daughter, Martha."

Sam reached across to shake the man's hand. "Pleased to meet you," he said.

"Likewise."

"Have you come far?" Tilly asked, guessing from his accent that he was from the North. She saw him as a 'my money's as good as theirs' kind of man. She could imagine him saying, 'Don't let 'em put you down, lad. My money's as good as theirs.'

"Oldham," he said. "Wool and textile country." He smiled at Tilly. "I have a factory there." He paused and sniffed, then nodded at her. "If you don't mind my saying, that's a very nice suit you're wearing. Quality isn't it. I can always tell."

Tilly blushed. She'd run the suit up the previous evening from a piece of cloth that she'd had lurking in her sewing basket for several years. She'd been pleased with the result and his compliment, endorsing her choice, delighted her. "Thank you."

He sat back and they watched as the stand filled. She was spared any further conversation by the sound of a bugle heralding the start of the parade.

Tilly watched entranced. The parade began with a procession led by the Master of the College, followed by the professors and tutors in ceremonial gowns. After them the patrons and benefactors of the college took their places in the raised stand behind a dais at the far end of the parade ground. Tilly spotted Sir Montague with his wife and a woman in her forties, she guessed to be Joey's widowed aunt. He looked more frail than she remembered and walked with a cane. Lady Thackery helped him up the steps.

Once the dignitaries were seated the cadets marched onto the parade ground. Soon the air filled with sound of marching feet and occasional shouted orders, as they carried out their well-practised drills. Tilly watched, fascinated and thrilled by their precision as they performed several close-order formations. She tried to pick Joey out, but in their uniforms and with their caps on, they all looked exactly the same. She sat enthralled as each of the cadets' names were called and they marched up to receive their diplomas. She clapped loudest when Joey's name was called, even though it was Thackery. By the end of the parade, her heart was so swollen with pride she was surprised there was room for it in her chest. Sam too glowed with pleasure.

"Good show," Mr Matherson said, clapping along with everyone else. "They always put on a good show."

They waited while the dignitaries left, then stood to follow as the stand emptied. The hum of conversation filled the air as they made their way to the Officers' Mess where refreshments were being served. The clock on the tower chimed twelve as they entered the impressive building. They were guided through a door on the left into a large, ornately decorated hall.

Inside the midday sun streamed through tall stained-glass windows along the length of one wall, sending prisms of rainbow colours over the proceedings. Portraits of naval heroes graced the other long wall. The high vaulted ceiling gave a sense of spaciousness and light, enhanced by gilded chandeliers reflecting the sunlight.

Martha gasped at the opulence. "It's very grand, isn't it?" she whispered to Tilly.

"In here, it is," Tilly said. "I don't expect the classrooms and barracks are as luxurious."

Waiters stood at the door with trays holding glasses of sherry. Sam took one, so did Martha. Tilly shook her head and moved on. The room soon became crowded. Lawton Matherson followed them in. "Can I get you anything?" he asked, indicating the long table set out with sweetmeats and cake. "It'll be a bit of a crush, but worth it."

Tilly gasped. "Thank you, no. I don't think I could eat anything."

"I could," Sam said. "What about you, Martha?"

"Yes please, if they have that delicious chocolate cake Joey talks about."

"Perhaps a glass of lemonade," Mr Matherson persisted. "Nice and cool."

"Thank you," Tilly said. "That would be lovely."

Sam passed Tilly his glass and went with Lawton to queue for the food. Tilly glanced around. The women were all fashionably dressed, many in printed cotton and muslin summer dresses, all were beautifully coiffured, and perfumed, with splendid hats. The men mainly wore dark suits, but a few were in uniform.

She was pleased to see there was no sign of Sir Montague or his family who would apparently be dining with the other dignitaries in a different hall.

A woman, wearing an enormous hat decorated with scarlet dyed ostrich plumes, was making her way towards where they were standing. Gesticulating wildly as she talked, the hat bobbed to and fro in mesmerising rhythm. Despite the excellence of the tailoring, the fashionably cut burgundy suit she wore still managed to look garish. "Phew it's so hot," Tilly heard her say as she drew closer, waving her gloved hand in front of her face. The room was becoming crowded and siffling. "Do you mind?"

Tilly turned. The woman was standing in front her, staring. Then Tilly realised she was standing in front of an open window. "Oh sorry." She stepped aside, edging away from her, drawing Martha with her. As she did so, Sam and Lawton returned with plates of pastries and cake.

"Should we take it outside?" Lawton said. "There's a lovely garden and benches where we can sit in the shade."

"Wonderful," Tilly said, greatly relieved. "Lead the way."

Chapter Five

Tilly had enjoyed the parade more than she'd expected. Watching the men in their uniforms, the precision of the drills, the ceremony and pageantry, brought home to her what Joey had become part of. She felt as though she'd been swept away to a different world, the world Joey inhabited. She'd been dizzy with pride when they went out into the garden to wait for him.

She hardly listened to Sam talking to Mr Matherson, her thoughts were only on what she'd say to Joey when she saw him again. She didn't have long to wait. He came out with a crowd of other newly qualified officers. Mr Matherson was the first to stand to greet them.

"Rob, my boy." He held out his hand, "Congratulations."

The young lad with Joey, who was not as tall as him, but stocky with sandy hair, grinned and shook his grandfather's hand. "Thanks, Gramps."

"Come and join us." Mr Matherson indicated the group. "These are my new friends, Mr and Mrs Crowe and their daughter, Martha."

Rob nodded. "Pleased to meet you."

Joey, standing next to Rob, grinned. "Ma, Pa, I see you've already met Rob's grandfather. Rob's been a great friend. I doubt I'd have passed mathematics without his help."

Sam held out his hand and Rob shook it. Tilly nodded. "Pleased to meet you."

Martha jumped up. "Any friend of Joey's is a friend of mine," she said.

"Congratulations, son," Sam said shaking Joey's hand. "We're all so very proud of you."

Tilly stood to hug Joey; tears welled in her eyes.

Mr Matherson invited them all to lunch at Simpson's in Piccadilly. "You must come," he said. They serve the best roast sirloin this side of the Atlantic."

Tilly wasn't so sure, and went to demure, but Sam said, "Thank you. We'd be delighted."

Tilly took a breath and managed a smile, but a feeling of dread fell over her.

An hour later they were seated around a table studying menus. The restaurant was dark with panelled walls and hushed silence. Amber lamps glowed, giving off not much light. It smelled of cigars and money. A masculine sort of place, Tilly thought. A place where men felt at home and relaxed as they discussed business and stroked each other's egos.

Once they'd ordered, the men choosing the roast beef and Tilly and Martha going for the grilled Dover sole, Tilly relaxed. Might as well sit back and enjoy it, she thought. It wasn't often these days they enjoyed such luxury.

The waiter brought the wine and poured it. Mr Matherson tapped his glass. "I want to raise a toast to these lads," he said. "They've passed the academic part of their education, now they must choose their professional paths, but first let's drink to their continued good fortune."

Everyone around the table picked up their glass. "To Rob and Jojo," Mr Matherson said.

"Rob and Jojo," they echoed.

Jojo? Tilly thought. Of course. A simple Joe would be too commonplace for Sir Montague and his wife.

"I'm glad we're here all together," Joey said. "Rob and I have something to tell you."

Tilly's heart sank.

"Rob and I both did well in engineering," he said, "and…" he paused. "You tell them, Rob."

Rob grinned. "Well, the Navy have been testing oil-burning boilers to replace coal. Now they're putting the new boilers into the first ships and we've both applied to be assigned to the project." He turned to Tilly. "It's shore based so we won't be going to sea, at least not for a while."

A wide smile spread across Joey's face. "It's based in Woolwich Docks, Ma, so we'll be close to home."

Tilly's heart lifted at the news. Joey wasn't going to sea again, well, not for the time being. "I'm delighted," she said, "if it means we'll be seeing more of you."

"Me too," Sam said. "An engineer, eh? That's something new."

"Rob's the engineer," Joey said, "but I want to learn. It's the future. We have automobiles driven by petroleum engines. Why not ships?"

Tilly smiled. She saw the passion in his eyes. Boatman's passion, she thought.

"Burning oil in ships?" Sam said. "Not sure about that, but if the Navy think it's all right, I suppose I can't argue."

Lawton Matherson, nodded. "I knew you had a brain, Rob and a penchant for mechanical things. I wish you both well."

Liveried waiters brought their food and, from the look of it Lawton was right, the beef was rare and succulent and their fish thick and delicately soft. They drank wine and, in good spirits, talked about the boys' future.

So, Tilly thought, Joey's not going to sea again. I wonder what Sir Montague thinks about that.

After lunch they each went their separate ways, the boys back to the college, Mr Matherson to his hotel, Sam had to call in at his office and Tilly and Martha went home. Martha, who'd said very little over lunch, went straight up to her room. Tilly sensed her excitement about the ball that evening. She sighed. She still had reservations about it. She tried to comfort herself with the thought that Joey would take care of her, but it didn't help.

Sam and the rest of the family came home for dinner. Tilly called Martha down. "You must eat something," she said. "You can't go dancing on an empty stomach."

"I can't eat a thing," Martha said. "I'm too excited. What do you think it will be like?"

"I'm sure it will be everything you hope it is," Tilly said, not at all sure. Her experience of going to a ball had not ended well. "At least have something."

Martha nibbled some cheese and water biscuits while the rest of the family ate their meal.

After dinner Tilly helped her get ready. She brushed her ebony hair into a cluster of curls and pinned pink silk roses into them, leaving a cascade of ringlets to fall on her elegant shoulders. Martha needed only the lightest touch of make-up. Excitement sparked her jade green eyes and her satin soft cheeks already glowed with health.

The dress, when it was finished was everything Martha could have hoped for. Tilly had embroidered the corset bodice with pearls and added lace to the deep ruffles at the neck and hem. The pink silk shimmered as

35

Martha moved. "Oh, it's wonderful," she said as she twirled around. "You're so clever, Ma. Thank you."

Tilly beamed with pleasure. She had to admit the dress was a triumph and Martha looked more beautiful than she'd ever seen her. Tears stung her eyes. Her daughter had grown into a beauty. It was a long time since she'd made anything so exquisite and she was glad she hadn't lost the knack, but it was Martha's grace and elegance that made it so breathtaking.

Martha had only just finished dressing when Tilly heard Joey and Rob arrive to collect her. "They're here," Martha gasped. "Do I look all right?"

"You look wonderful." Tilly's voice marbled with pride. "Joey is lucky to have such a beautiful sister." She paused. "There's just one thing missing. She went to her dressing table drawer and pulled out a small velvet bag. "I've kept this for years in case we ever needed something to sell, but I think it's fairly safe for you to wear it now." She tipped the bag up and an emerald necklace fell into her hand. It was the necklace Captain Thackery had given her. Seeing it again brought a clench to her stomach. She had no need of it now.

Downstairs Sam had shown the boys into the parlour and given them each a drink. Tilly went in first. A bubble of pride and pleasure filled her chest when she saw the look on the boys' faces as Martha followed her in.

Joey stepped forward first, his eyes gleaming with admiration. He put his drink down and held out his hand. Martha took it and twirled around to show him the dress. "Will I do?" she said.

"You look amazing," Joey said. "You'll be the most beautiful girl in the room."

Rob nodded. "Wonderful," he said. Tilly caught the catch in his voice. "May I claim the first dance?"

Martha giggled.

"After me," Joey said.

Tilly helped Martha into the black velvet evening cape she'd made for her. "Now you boys take care of her," she said as she waved them off, her heart in her mouth.

Chapter Six

Martha sat silent as the cab rattled over the cobbles on the way to the college. She could hardly speak for the thrill of it, sitting between the boys, so dashing in their dress uniforms. The boys chatted easily throughout the journey. Rob, attempting to put her at her ease, asked Martha what she was most looking forward to. She didn't know what to say, everything so far had been magical. She wanted to capture every detail and preserve it in her mind, she was hardly likely to be invited to such an event in the future.

"I don't know," she said. "The dancing I suppose." She went on to tell them about the last dance she'd been to, where her feet were trodden on so many times, by the end of the evening she thought her toes must be broken.

Rob laughed. "Well, I can assure you that won't be the case tonight. It's well known that naval officers are extremely light on their feet."

The cab drove up to the door where they were greeted by two naval cadets who checked their invitations. The hall of the building was huge. Martha swallowed as she gazed around, marvelling at its breathtaking magnificence, and the history permeating its walls. She had seen some of the buildings that morning at the passing out parade, but this part of the college was even more striking. A thrill ran through her.

Another cadet directed Martha to the cloakroom where she left her cape. A glow of satisfaction warmed her when she saw the gowns the other women were wearing. They were elaborately adorned with ribbons, lace, sequins and beads, but to her mind none were as elegant and stylish as hers. She held her head high as they climbed the steps to the ante room, where they joined the queue waiting to be announced. The room was surprisingly small, the navy, red and gold decorations making it appear even smaller. Nerves jangled her stomach and her heart hammered so loudly she wondered if Joey and Rob could hear it.

When their names were called, she took a breath and stepped forward, feeling like a queen, with Joey on one side and Rob on the other. It felt odd hearing Joey called Sub-Lieutenant Thackery, and herself Miss Martha Crowe. As they descended the short staircase into the ballroom, she stifled the gasp that reached her throat. She thought it would be grand, but she'd never imagined anything so spectacular. The light from crystal chandeliers reflected in gilded mirrors around the room, dancing on white and gold panelled walls and glasses set out on white clothed tables around the floor. People milled about, settling down amid the hum of conversation. A flush of pleasure washed over her. This was going to be the best night of her life.

A tall, dark-haired man, immaculate in his naval dress uniform, beckoned them over. Two women were sitting at the table next to him.

"Delahaye's here already," Rob said. "I suppose we ought to join him."

Joey nodded and they walked across to the table. The tall man stood and put out his hand. Joey shook it. "Good evening, Theo," he said. "May I introduce my sister Martha, Martha, this is Theodore Delahaye and his sister, Ellen."

"Martha." Theo's eyebrows arched, his voice questioning. "How delightful." He picked up Martha's gloved hand, raising it to his lips. "Charmed," he said. The look in his eyes intrigued Martha. It was as though he was summing her up, but for what purpose, she couldn't decide.

Ellen, still sitting, smiled.

"Good evening, Ellen," Joey said. "Good to see you again."

Ellen nodded and Martha noticed a slight blush as it crept up her cheeks. She hadn't missed the slight softening in Joey's voice either.

"I think you've met my friend, Constance Beaumont," Ellen said. "She's staying with us for the summer."

"Connie," Joey nodded.

"Now we know each other, should I get us a drink?" Rob said. "Martha, what's your pleasure?"

"Champagne," Joey, said, "all round. This is a celebration after all."

Rob went to the bar to order the drinks.

"Excuse us, ladies. Business to attend to," Theo said, pulling Joey along with him as he followed Rob. Martha gazed around, taking in the scene as people were announced and descended into the ballroom. Most were couples, the men in uniform, although there were a few groups with older men and women. A few of the older men sported tailcoats with high collar shirts and white ties. The women were all dressed in extravagant silks and satins. Her eyes widened at the lavish opulence. Martha guessed they were there to chaperone the young ladies.

"So, you're Jojo's sister," Constance said. "He's never mentioned you." She turned to Ellen. "We didn't know he had a sister, did we?"

Ellen shook her head but didn't speak. She seemed to be staring at Martha, as though trying to work out where she might fit in.

"You weren't at Lady Thackery's birthday bash, were you?" Constance continued. "I didn't see you there."

"No," Martha said, feeling uncomfortable as it became clear they were a part of Joey's life that she knew nothing about, and a part of his life that knew nothing about her. "I'm afraid I wasn't."

"What about the Boxing Day Hunt? Did you miss that too? Jojo caused quite a sensation there, didn't he, Ellen?"

"He did." Ellen looked as though she was still summing Martha up. Was she friend or foe?

"And then there was Ascot, the opera and Henley. He's kept us quite entertained throughout the Season." Martha saw hostility in her eyes but couldn't understand why.

"Perhaps she wasn't old enough to come out?" Ellen said.

Constance smirked.

"I'm actually old enough to do anything I wish," Martha said, refusing to allow them to intimidate her. "It's just that I find these things quite a chore." She turned to glance around again and was saved any further inquisition by Rob's return, followed by a waiter carrying an ice bucket on a stand with two bottles of champagne. He placed it next to Martha and opened one of the bottles, pouring champagne into the glasses set out on the table.

Theo, following behind, produced a bottle of rum, which he poured into three glasses. "Champagne for the ladies," he said, "but personally I prefer something a little stronger. How about you, Jojo?" He picked up one of the glasses and handed it to Joey.

Joey glanced at Martha. He put the rum glass back on the table and picked up one of the glasses of champagne. "I think I'll stick to this tonight," he said. "I want to keep a clear head."

Theo's eyebrows went up, his expression one of shock. "Come on, Jojo. Navy tradition. One won't hurt." It sounded like a threat.

Joey shrugged and put the champagne back. He picked up the rum and tossed it back, slamming the glass on the table. "There. Satisfied?"

Theo laughed. He gulped back his own drink and refilled the glass. As he did so another man joined them. A little older than Theo and Joey, his portly build spoke of a penchant for good food and wine. "Tubs," Theo called. "Glad you could make it."

The man he'd called Tubs grinned. "Wouldn't miss it for the world," he said. He turned to the lady with him. "This is my cousin Abigail Abbot. I know you'll make her feel welcome."

Abigail, a girl about Martha's age with a pale face and bright auburn curls, smiled.

Tubs continued, "That old reprobate over there is Theo Delahaye, that's his sister Ellen and her friend, Constance...er..."

"Beaumont," Constance said. "Hello."

"Yes. Jojo Thackery and..." He glanced at Martha.

"Martha Crowe," she said. "Jo...Jojo's sister."

"Really?" Tubs' eyes widened in surprised. "Pleased to meet you."

As he spoke the band struck up for the first dance. "Ah. I think that's us," Joey said, holding his hand out to Martha. She took a breath. So it begins, she thought.

Joey was a good dancer and Martha too was light on her feet. "Inherited from the boatmen," she said once when someone complimented her on the nimbleness of her feet.

She enjoyed the dance, spinning around with Joey, and soon felt part of the sea of silk and satin whirling around the floor. She noticed the jewellery the other women wore. She'd never seen so many sparkling diamonds.

Rob claimed her for the second dance and Joey danced with Ellen. Rob wasn't as light on his feet as Joey, but the strength in his broad shoulders and his warm compliments more than made up for it in Martha's opinion. She danced the third dance with Theo, who complimented her on her dress and lightness of feet. "Nimble footedness obviously runs in your family," he said. She glowed with pleasure. It was something she was proud of. Then he mentioned her dress. "What a beautiful dress," he said. "Almost as beautiful as the person wearing it. No wonder Jojo kept you hidden." Martha found his words as glib as his feet were light. Tubs took her onto the floor for the next dance and she found his jovial conversation adequately compensated for his lack of finesse.

By the time the supper interval was called just before midnight, Martha's feet were aching but her heart was singing. It had been wonderful spinning around the floor losing herself to the rhythm of the music. She'd danced with each of the men in turn, then Rob and Tubs and Theo and Rob again. Joey danced most often with Ellen who blushed and smiled, her eyes shining with pleasure at his attention. Martha wasn't daft. She could see Joey was besotted, and Ellen enjoyed being adored. She wondered what Theo thought about it. Throughout the evening she'd noticed the growing tension between the two men. Perhaps that was the reason.

"Should we get something to eat?" Rob asked as he led her off the floor when the interval was announced. "They've put on quite a spread."

Martha looked around, breathless from the energetic polka they'd just danced. The doors to the supper room were open and people were making their way in there. She glanced at the table where Joey, Ellen, Constance and Theo had already taken their seats. "I think I'll just sit down first, if you don't mind," she said. "Perhaps later, when the queue has died down."

"Of course." Rob held out a chair for her. Then she noticed Joey had a glass of rum in his hand, as did Theo. Judging from the number of empty bottles tipped up in the ice bucket, Martha guessed they'd had quite a few.

A few minutes later Tubs arrived back at the table carrying two plates piled high with chicken legs, rolls of beef, ham and pork, pies and sandwiches. Abigail followed, also carrying two plates of what looked like delicious cakes and pastries.

"I thought you lot would be too tired and emotional to get the ladies anything to eat, so I got to the head of the queue," Tubs said placing the plates on the table. Abigail did the same. Tubs collared a waiter to bring them some plates.

Joey rose unsteadily from his seat, holding his glass aloft. His hair was awry, and his eyes slightly glazed. "You, sir, are a gentleman," he said.

Theo also rose with some difficulty. His words were slurred as he spoke, but everyone heard them. "A gentleman, indeed," he said. "Unlike you, Thackery. You are a bastard, and your mother was a whore."

Martha gasped, reeling in shock. She couldn't believe her ears. The next thing she saw was Joey, face aflame, eyes bulging, land a punch on Theo's jaw. Theo flew through the air crashing to the floor amid an upturned table and several chairs. Joey grabbed his collar and lifted him up, his fist curled for a second punch just as Tubs and another man grabbed him and pulled him off. Theo lay prostrate amid the wreckage. The women screamed, their faces livid with horror. Rob grabbed Martha's arm and pulled her away as Tubs and the other man marched a protesting Joey out of the ballroom.

Martha could hardly breathe. Her mind struggled to take in what was happening. The whole room had descended into chaos. Several waiters hurried over and tried, without success, to right the table and chairs. All around her people were staring, shocked into silence, looks of horror on their faces. She'd seen drunken fights before at the docks. The boatmen's rucks were legendary, but she'd never expected anything of the sort from the well off, highly educated men she was mixing with tonight.

"Did you hear what he said?" she asked Rob, breathless with shock as he guided her towards the door.

"He was drunk," Rob said, rushing her out. "No one will believe it. It's the drink talking."

Martha's brain was buzzing. Half of her wanted to go back and punch Theo herself, but the other half wanted to be anywhere but there. What had started out as the best evening of her life had turned into the worst.

Chapter Seven

"Come on. I'll take you home," Rob said. His voice had a note of urgency to it.

"Home?" Martha stared at him, confused. "But Joey…"

Rob shook his head. "Jojo can take care of himself. You don't need to be here."

"But I…" Tears filled her eyes. Why had it all gone so wrong? She bit her lip to stop the tears from falling and nodded. Rob waited while she went to get her cape. In the cloakroom she sat and took a breath, replaying the last few minutes over in her mind. She still couldn't believe what had happened. A man she'd never met had cast aspersion about her mother and Joey had shut him up. She was pretty sure her mother wasn't a whore, but why had he said it? Supposing they all believed it? Sickness churned in her stomach. Suddenly it all became too much. She sat, head in hands, sobbing. Her dream evening had turned into a nightmare.

After a while, she stopped. She sniffed. She was a Crowe and just as good as anyone. These people meant nothing to her. As far as she could see they were drunks and wasters. Other women were beginning to come in for their coats and pointedly ignoring her, so she supposed the party was well and truly over. She collected her cape.

Rob was waiting for her. "Ah," he said. "I was worried about you." He took her arm and led her outside. "I'll get a cab."

"No," she said. "I'd rather walk for a while, if you don't mind. The fresh air will clear my head."

Rob nodded and together they made their way to the river. They walked in silence for a several minutes. The warmth of the day lingered, the full moon shone bright in the night sky, where a thousand stars twinkled. A soft breeze ruffled the waves, the air filled with the sound of lapping water. Any other time Martha would have thought it romantic, but she was too heartsick to feel anything. She'd seen a different side to Joey, and she wasn't sure she liked it.

"It's not true," she said eventually. "What Theo said about my mother."

Rob looked horrified. "No. Of course it's not. We all know that. It's just Theo's idea of a joke."

"Not much of a joke."

"No. He shouldn't have said anything, not in front of you."

That shocked her. "You mean it would be all right if I wasn't there?"

"No. No. Of course not." Rob's face flushed. "It's just...you know...men's humour."

"Hmm." There's no smoke without fire, she thought, and Joey's parentage wasn't something that was talked about at home. Perhaps they knew something she didn't. "How much do they know about Joey?" she asked. "His background?"

Rob sighed. It was several seconds before he spoke. He glanced at the river as they walked as though wondering what to say. After a while he said, "Once when Jojo, or Joey as you call him," he smiled at her, "was drunk...he'd had a bad day and was feeling sorry for himself, crying in his beer, complaining about his sponsor and how he'd never wanted to join the Navy anyway...you know the sort of thing." He glanced at her as though to check her reaction. She nodded. "Well, he said it was only because they were related but he didn't know how or who his father was." He paused. "Theo egged him on to tell him more...a sympathetic ear but...well...it wasn't out of kindness." She heard the bitterness in his voice.

"What do you mean?"

Rob sighed again. "Jojo is a great guy, I like him a lot and count him as a friend, but he's easily led and Theo is a bully who enjoys humiliating people. That's all."

"What will happen to Joey? What will they do to him?"

"A court martial at the very least. Loss of rank, dismissal, prison even. Assaulting a fellow officer, conduct unbecoming, they could throw the book at him if they've a mind to."

Martha gasped, horrified. "Will they?"

Rob shrugged. "Jojo's got a temper on him. He's been in fights before. That won't help."

"That'll be the boatman blood in him," Martha said. "Boatmen like a fight better than their dinner. They won't really put him prison, will they?" Fear squeezed her heart.

"It depends how influential his sponsor is and who speaks up for him. I will, of course and some of the others who know what Theo's like, but..." He shrugged again.

A cold breeze blew up from the river and Martha shivered. "I think I'd like that cab now," she said.

Rob found a cab and Martha was glad of the close intimacy inside. The evening had turned into one of horror and she still couldn't understand it, despite replaying it in her mind over and over again. Rob's presence was a comfort. "You're a good friend, Rob," she said. "I hope Joey appreciates that."

When they arrived Rob said he'd rather not go in with her. "I'm not sure I can face your parents," he said. "What will you tell them?"

"The truth," Martha said. "There's no point telling them anything else."

Rob nodded. "I'll go back and see what I can do to salvage Jojo's naval career." He waited until he saw her safely inside, then the cab turned and took him back to the college.

Indoors Ma had waited up for her, as she knew she would. She came to greet her with a broad smile and a face lit with hope. "How was it? Did you enjoy yourself?"

The weight of expectation was too much for Martha. "Oh, Ma. It was awful." She broke down in tears. Tilly hugged her. She held her until the crying stopped. Martha could feel her mother's mounting anger.

"Do you want to talk about it?"

Martha shook her head. "I just want to go to bed. I'll tell you about it in the morning."

Tilly nodded.

The next morning, being Saturday and the busiest day on the river for tourists and day trippers, Sam left early with Harry. The boat in the yard hadn't been fixed and Tilly knew Sam was worried about it.

After breakfast Katy said she had arranged to meet a friend at the market, so Tilly gave her a shilling to spend. George had some books to go back to the library, so they left together. Tilly saw them out, with the usual warning about being careful and making sure they were back for tea. She closed the door behind them with a sigh. They were growing up and beginning to have lives of their own.

She decided to let Martha sleep in, as she'd had a late night and, from what she could gather, a troubled one. She couldn't help wondering what had happened. Martha had been so excited about going to the ball, why had it all gone so wrong? She sighed. Martha would tell her about it when she felt up to it. I suppose I'd better catch up with the household accounts, she thought.

She collected the ledger, the cash box, invoices and receipts and took them into her sitting room, her favourite room in the house. It caught the morning sun, and the view of the river in the distance always delighted her. It was the place where she spent most of her time, sewing, reading or just looking out of the window watching the world go by. She made herself a pot of tea and poured a cup before she began.

About eleven o'clock she closed the ledger and went to make herself a fresh pot of tea. She'd just taken it through when the doorbell rang. I bet George has forgotten his key again, she thought, not expecting Katy back until much later. She caught her breath when she opened the door. In front of her on the step was the largest basket of flowers she'd ever seen. A riot of colourful roses, carnations, pinks, hydrangeas, lupins, delphiniums, asters, peonies, lilies, and other extravagant blooms, overflowed the basket and perfumed the air. A messenger stood nearby. "Miss Martha Crowe?" he enquired.

"Er. No. That's my daughter." She stared at the flowers. "It's all right. I'll take them in."

The messenger handed her an envelope addressed to Martha. Tilly found sixpence in her pocket and tipped him. "Thank you, ma'am." He touched his cap as he left.

Tilly didn't know what to think. An admirer perhaps, but after Martha's reaction when she got home Tilly thought that unlikely. She picked up the basket and, as she carried it in, Martha came down the stairs, still in her nightgown and slippers with a wrap around her, her hair tousled and her eyes half-closed from sleep. "Was that the door?" She stared at the flowers. "Gracious. Someone must love you, Ma. Is it your anniversary?" She frowned.

"No. These are for you."

"For me?" Martha followed her into the room and sank onto a chair. "Who'd be sending me flowers?"

Tilly handed her the envelope. "Tea?"

"Please."

Tilly went to get another cup. When she returned Martha was sitting with a letter in her hand. She noticed a couple of tickets had fallen to the floor. She picked them up. They were for the opera at Covent Garden. She laid them on the table, poured the tea and waited for Martha to speak.

Martha, her jaw clenched, her lips a thread of red, tore the letter in half and put it back in the envelope. She picked up the tickets, tore them in half too stuffing them in with it. Then she picked up the pen Tilly had been using, crossed out her name and wrote another. She pushed the envelope into the flowers. "Please see they're returned," she said, handing Tilly the pen.

Tilly handed her the tea. "Of course, if that's what you want," she said. "But I think you'd better tell me what happened last night."

Tilly's anger grew as Martha related the events of the evening. Tears shone in Martha's eyes as she spoke, her face creased with pain. Tilly gasped and clapped her hands over her mouth when she heard what Theo had said. She couldn't believe what she was hearing. A cauldron of rage burned inside her. She didn't know what to think. It wasn't so much the insult, she'd been called a lot worse on the boats, but hearing it from her daughter's lips…

"I'm sorry, Ma. I thought you should know. I couldn't believe what he said."

Tilly shook her head as she tried to imagine the scene. He was probably drunk, she thought, lashing out for some unknown reason, some slight, or feeling he'd been undermined. Men were like that. She'd known girls who made a very good living from just that occupation, most of whom relied on patrons like Theo Delahaye. She wasn't sure if it was the mind-blowing hypocrisy or the moral ineptitude that angered her most. She didn't blame Joey for hitting him, the fellow deserved it, but all the same…Inside she burned with rage, but she wasn't going to let Martha see it. It would only make her feel worse, so she'd make light of it, but she'd never forget.

Her jaw clenched and her fists curled. "Some people see whoring as an honourable profession," she said, forcing a note of jollity into her voice to lift the mood.

Martha obviously didn't agree. "But why would he say it?"

"He was lashing out. People do when they feel powerless or out of control. Theo Delahaye must have problems in his life we know nothing about."

"How can you say that, Ma? How can you be so forgiving? I wanted to thrash him to a pulp myself."

Tilly thought horsewhipping a more appropriate punishment, but said, "I may have felt the same had I been there, but, in the cold light of day they're just words, love. I've been called far worse than that." She smiled. "People can only hurt you if you let them. I don't know this man from Adam, and, from the sound of it I wouldn't want to. Why should I let his drunken outburst spoil even a minute of my day?"

"What about Joey?"

"Joey?" Tilly's heart turned over at the thought of her eldest son in trouble.

"He was protecting our honour, Ma. Rob said he could go to prison."

"Prison? Surely not." Tilly gasped. She stood and paced the floor, her mind in a whirl. Protecting our honour, what a pointless thing to do. A man had died protecting her honour, a distant memory brought into sharp focus. She shook it off. "Perhaps it won't be as bad as that," she said, returning to sit next to Martha to reassure her. A desperate fear circled her stomach. "They'll know the circumstances. He can't be the first cadet who's got into a drunken brawl with a friend."

"Rob said he'd been in fights before."

Tilly sat silent. She couldn't relate what she was hearing with the kind, gentle Joey she knew and loved. What had happened to him? What had changed him?

"It was Theo, Ma. Egging him on, pouring him drinks, challenging him. And his sister Ellen, playing up to him. Joey's besotted."

Ah! A woman. She should have guessed, but it didn't lighten the stone of dread forming inside her. She forced a smile to her lips. "What was that letter?"

"Oh that? Theo, sending drivelling apologies. As though I'd ever forgive him."

"If he's apologised it means he's taking some of the responsibility. Perhaps they won't charge Joey after all."

"Do you really think so?"

Tilly nodded, more in hope than expectation.

"I'm still sending the flowers back."

"Quite right," Tilly said. "Now. Why don't you get dressed and we'll go into town for a slap-up lunch. Put this behind us."

Martha smiled. "Good idea," she said.

"Oh, and perhaps don't mention anything to Pa. He's enough on his plate."

Martha shrugged. "If you say so, although he'll want to know about Joey."

"About the fight, yes. But not the reason for it."

Martha nodded and went to get dressed.

While Martha dressed, Tilly cleared away her accounts and the tea things, but thoughts of Joey were never far from her mind. She recalled the ball she'd been to where she met his father, and the night they'd spent together. For all the wrongness of it she couldn't regret those days, nor could she regret the time she spent with him, brief as it was. It gave her Joey, the one bright light in those darkest of days. Now Joey was grown up did he deserve the whole truth, instead of only part of it? What about Martha and the others? How would they feel? They knew as much as Joey. Did they deserve the whole truth too? Perhaps now was the time to tell it.

Chapter Eight

Once Martha was out of the house the happenings of the previous evening shrunk into perspective. The sun shone, the streets were full of people going about their business. The atmosphere was one of hustle and bustle. Everything looked normal and ordinary, as though nothing had changed. The world hadn't come to an end. Had she overreacted? Ma had brushed the insult off as lightly as she brushed crumbs from the tablecloth. Was she giving too much credence to a drunken outburst? Rob had said Theo was a bully. She'd known bullies at school. She'd never let them intimidate her, why should what Theo thought or said be of any consequence to her? Then she thought of Joey, who'd always fallen on his feet. Perhaps Ma was right, it wouldn't be as bad as Rob had predicted. With that hope warming her heart she cheered up as they caught the bus into town. They'd taken the flowers to the local florist to be returned. As if he could buy her forgiveness with a few bunches of flowers, she thought.

Twenty minutes later they were settled in a small, cosy restaurant in a side street off the Strand, perusing the menu.

"It wasn't all bad last night," she said. "At first it was wonderful, being whirled around the floor, seeing the women in their elegant gowns and fabulous jewellery. It was like being in the middle of a glittering rainbow. Oh, Ma, you wouldn't believe the extravagance."

Tilly smiled. "I can imagine," she said. "It's good that you got to see it at least."

"I did."

They ordered their meals and over lunch Martha went on to tell Tilly about the evening in minute detail, from the ornate opulence of the building to the silks, satins, diamonds, and graceful elegance of the dancers. "If it hadn't been for Theo and Joey getting drunk it would have been the perfect evening," she said. "Why do they do it, Ma? Why do they drink so much?"

"To make them feel better than they are, I suppose. To give them courage or drown their sorrows, who can tell. It's not the drink that's the problem, it's the demons it releases we have to be aware of."

"Well, I wish they wouldn't," Martha said. "I can't see the point of it myself."

Tilly smiled. "No," she said. "You wouldn't."

They'd just finished their main course and were looking at the dessert menu when Martha became aware of raised voices from two men sitting at a table in the corner. She watched them over Tilly's shoulder. After a few minutes one of them jumped up. "Damn you," he shouted and swept the glasses, cutlery and plates off the table before storming out. The commotion made Tilly turn her head.

"What on earth…"

Martha gasped, trepidation churned her stomach. "That was Victor Landridge," she said. "I saw him a few days ago at work. He stormed out of Mr Bartholmew's office as though the devil himself was after him." Panic rose in her throat. "I'd forgotten about it until now. Do you think we should tell Pa?"

Consternation crossed Tilly's face and Martha saw anxiety in her eyes. "It's probably nothing," she said, but Martha guessed she was seriously concerned.

They decided to skip dessert. Outside, they were each lost in their own thoughts as they made their way to the market. Martha bought some silks for her embroidery and Tilly bought a length of linen to make into petticoats.

When they arrived home a messenger stood on the doorstep, waiting for them. "He's been here over an hour," George said.

"I have to wait for a reply," the man said. "Package for Miss Martha Crowe."

Martha took the package inside. Nerves jangled her stomach as she hung up her coat and hat. Her fingers trembled as she tore off the brown paper to reveal a gold embossed box. Her hand flew to her mouth to capture her breath when she opened it. Inside, nestled in velvet lay the most exquisite diamond necklace she'd ever seen. There were earrings too. She handed the box to Tilly and opened the envelope. The card inside read: *To show I'm serious. Please allow me to apologise in person. Theo.*

She turned the card over. There was nothing on the other side. She took the box back and touched the necklace, unable to believe she held something so exquisite. "They're diamonds," she whispered. "Real diamonds."

"I'd expect nothing less," Tilly said. "What are you going to do?"

"Well, I can hardly send them back, can I?" She glanced at the messenger, still waiting. "Tell him I'll be in Victoria Park by the bandstand tomorrow around eleven. I won't be there for long though."

The messenger nodded and hurried off.

Martha glanced at Tilly, sensing her disapproval. "What else could I do?" she said. She sure as hell wasn't going to send the diamonds back.

Tilly banged around in the kitchen trying to suppress her anger. Mrs C had prepared the vegetables for dinner and a piece of beef sat in the larder ready to go into the oven. Sam and Harry had yet to return from work. Katy and George were playing in the garden and Martha was upstairs, admiring her new acquisition and trying to work out what she would wear for her outing the next day.

Diamonds, Tilly thought. Of all things. She'd almost fainted when she saw the necklace and earrings nestling in blue velvet. Whatever was the man thinking? Well, it was obvious what he was thinking. What quicker way to turn a girl's head than giving her diamonds? Of course, Theo Delahaye could afford them. To him it would be no more than pocket money, but they would have cost more than Sam earned in a year. They could never afford to give Martha anything so spectacular. When would she have a chance to wear them? Never. She could hardly expect Martha to return them, despite the impropriety of the gift. How could she? Would she have done so when she was Martha's age?

Then she recalled the emerald necklace she'd clipped around Martha's neck. It had been a gift from the Captain on her eighteenth birthday. Since those far off days she'd never had cause to wear it, but had kept it against misfortune. It was something she could sell if she ever needed to. She took a breath to calm herself. The past was the past, it was of no consequence now, but how easily things drop into your lap when you have money, she thought.

She was about to put the meat into the oven when she heard the front door close. A swell of relief washed over her. Sam was home. He'd know what to do. He had a way of putting things into perspective. Talking things over with him always made her feel better. She waited for him to come into the kitchen as he always did when he returned home. She heard footsteps, but he failed to appear, so she went to look for him. She found him in his study riffling through some paperwork. His appearance shocked her. She'd never seen him looking so perturbed.

"Is something the matter?"

He glanced up. "Oh, it's probably nothing. It's just...well..." He sighed. "The *Maggie May* hasn't been fixed because the bill for the last repair hasn't been paid." He looked stricken. "I don't understand it. It's probably a mix up, but I can't find Victor to sort it out."

The look on his face pushed Tilly's concerns about Martha to the back of her mind. The *Maggie May* was Sam's first boat, named after his mother. The fact it wasn't running would seriously affect his business. "We saw Victor in the restaurant at lunchtime," Tilly said. "Or rather Martha did. Come to think of it..."

"Where? Which restaurant?" A deep frown creased Sam's brow.

"The Orange Grove, but he didn't stay. He rushed out in a temper."

Sam shook his head and continued his search. "I've tried his home and his office, he's not there. I've asked all around..." He stopped and gazed at Tilly, as though trying to make up his mind whether to speak. "I'm worried, Till. It seems some of the other bills haven't been paid either. If Victor's..." He shook his head again.

"It's unthinkable. I've known him for years. There'll be a good reason, I just need to speak to him."

Tilly's heart sank. Sam always thought the best of everyone. He ran the boats, but Victor managed the finance and admin. If he'd…No, that was too awful to contemplate. "How bad is it?"

Sam shrugged and sank into his chair. "The yard won't take a cheque and the bank won't open until Monday. I have the takings from the weekend, but that'll only pay for the last bill. I still can't get *Maggie May* back afloat."

He looked so distraught Tilly's heart went out to him. "Is there anything I can do? I have some savings…"

"No, Till. It's down to me, not you. You know you mean the world to me and, whatever happens I'll look after you and the children. Nothing is more important than that." He managed a brief smile. "Come here." He pulled her onto his lap, put his strong arms around her and kissed her with all the passion she remembered from their early days. This was the man she loved without reservation and she'd be damned if she'd let Victor Landridge make a fool of him.

Chapter Nine

Dinner that evening was a subdued affair. Sam and Harry both ate in silence and appeared distracted. If there was trouble, the dinner table wasn't the place to discuss it. Martha too said little. Tilly guessed her disapproval of the gift she'd received was obvious and Martha didn't want to discuss it. Only Katy and George chatted about their day, mostly Katy, but Tilly was the only one taking any notice.

Sam and Harry went out as soon as dinner finished. Katy went to her room to play with the cut-out doll and its clothes she'd bought in the market and, Tilly speculated, to eat the sweets she'd also bought. George was building a ship out of cardboard, optimistically hoping to sail it on the pond in the park.

Once she'd cleared the dishes away, Tilly decided it was time to talk to Martha. She went upstairs and tapped on her door. There was no reply, so she went in to see Martha gazing at the diamonds, a look of wonder on her face.

"Beautiful, aren't they?" Tilly said, taking the box from her. "And dangerous."

"Dangerous?"

"It's what they represent. Isn't it? Money and power." She took the necklace from the box and held it up so it sparkled in the evening light streaming through the window. "They're the hardest substance known to man. See how they sparkle in the light, so delicate and yet – uncrushable." She put the necklace back in the box and handed it to Martha. "You need to think carefully about accepting such a gift. What strings does it have attached?"

Martha huffed and closed the lid as though tired of looking at it. "It's an apology," she said. "He wants forgiveness. It's an option. I'm interested to hear what he has to say, that's all."

"So, you will go to the park tomorrow?"

"I've said I would."

Tilly sighed. She loved Martha with all her heart and didn't want to upset her, but she was naive if she thought that was all he wanted. She knew from experience it wouldn't be. "I don't like the idea of you going alone," she said. "Perhaps you could take Katy and George. They'd love a day at the park."

Martha gasped, her eyes blazed, her voice rose to a crescendo. "Take Katy and George! I'm nearly eighteen, Ma. I don't need a chaperone, and if I did it wouldn't be Katy and George. I'd look a fool." She jumped up, put the box in her dressing table drawer, slamming it shut. When she turned around her face was twisted with anger, her jaw clenched. Tears shone in her eyes. "You obviously don't trust me. I'm sorry you think so badly of me, but I'm going to meet this man and see what he has to say for himself. He's Joey's friend. I owe him a chance to apologise."

"I'm sorry, I didn't mean...Of course I trust you...but..."

"But you think I'd be so easily swayed, that I'd fall for fine words and expensive gifts. That I'd ever forgive what he said. You don't know me at all."

"Oh Martha, I do. I know and love you, but I also know about temptation and how easy it is to forget your resolve and be taken in."

Martha glared at her. "You're talking about your life, Ma. Not mine." There was a harshness to her voice that Tilly had never heard before. The jibe about her life pierced her heart.

"Do what you will," she said. "Whatever happens I'll be here for you. Remember that." With that she turned and swept out, her pulse racing. Memories of her past filtered through her brain. She was in no position to preach. She'd told herself she had no option, she'd even convinced herself it was always love, but knew different now. Who was she to judge? Emotion churned her stomach and clenched her fist. She'd take Katy and George to the park in the morning. She wouldn't interfere with Martha and Theo Delahaye, but she'd be nearby to pick up the pieces in case it all went wrong.

Martha fumed. She could have kicked herself. That remark about Ma's life was mean and uncalled for. She'd felt a stab of remorse when she saw the hurt on her mother's face. She'd wanted to take it back but her pride wouldn't let her. Guilt lay heavy on her heart. Ma was right of course. It was foolish beyond belief to think that Theo didn't have an ulterior motive for the gift and the meeting. She'd said he was Joey's friend, but she wasn't sure that was true. Rob said he took pleasure in humiliating Joey. She'd found him arrogant and condescending, so, why was she willing to meet him in the park?

She bit her lip as she sat on the bed, trying to make sense of it. Perhaps he wanted to humiliate her too. Some sort of revenge for Joey's interest in Ellen, or merely to show he could. The more she thought about it the more anxious she became. Was he somewhere, chuckling about her speedy acceptance of his offer? Delighted in the idea of manipulating her to his wishes.

How stupid she'd been, for what? A gift he could well afford. Whatever his reason, it wasn't worth falling out with her mother over.

She hardly slept that night, thoughts of the morning ahead turning into vivid dreams of Theo and what sort of vengeance might be wrought against her, what expectations he might have and what obligation she was under having accepted the gift. By morning she was a sweat of trepidation. She kept telling herself it was stupid, he was only a man, flesh and blood. He had no hold over her. She could deal with the likes of him, but her heart still trembled.

She rose early and dressed quickly, not wanting a confrontation with her mother. She chose to wear her pink summer suit, trimmed with blue over the white blouse she'd embroidered with forget-me-nots, with her cameo brooch pinned at the throat. She brushed her hair to an ebony shine and pinned it up in the latest fashion. She sprayed on a spritz of the perfume Ma had bought her last Christmas. It smelled of lilac and apple blossom. The day promised to be warm, with sunny spells, perfect for a walk in the park. She wished she was meeting Rob, not Theo, then chided herself for her foolishness. He'd been kind to her because she was a damsel in distress and he was a gentleman, no other reason. Silly to think otherwise.

She took a breath to prepare herself for the ordeal. She twisted her lips, biting them in thought. Eventually she took out the box with the necklace in, opened it and gazed again at the glittering diamonds nesting there. She sighed. It was a most inappropriate gift, but such a beautiful one. She should return it, or at least offer to. Doing so would be a grand gesture, but she wasn't sure she could do it. Sighing again, she placed the box in her bag. "I'll never have the occasion to wear them," she said to herself.

She'd hoped to slip out before anyone else was up, but Sam and Harry were already downstairs having breakfast before they left to catch the tide.

"Ooo, look at madam, all dressed up," Harry said, eyes wide with surprise. "Special occasion, is it?"

Martha blushed. "None of your business," she said, helping herself to some coffee.

"Oh, come on. It's not like you to be up and about on a Sunday. New fella, is it?"

She pulled a face and tapped her nose.

Harry laughed. Sam looked round. "Morning, Martha. You look nice. Going out?"

"Just to the park. It's such a lovely day, I thought I'd make the most of it."

"Good. Well, have fun." He put his empty cup down. "Come on, lad. Things to do."

Martha breathed a sigh of relief as they left. She made herself a sandwich to take with her and slipped out. Morning sun glinted on the buildings lining the shore as she walked along by the river. The vastness and the open sky calmed her, her fears fell away. A soft breeze rippled the waves rocking the boats moored along the bank. She breathed in the fresh air and smell of the tide. She nodded to the men going about their business. The familiar clamour of the docks reached her ears, a tranquil peace fell over her. This was her world and she wasn't going to allow anyone, or anything to spoil it.

Tilly awoke with a start. She hadn't slept well. Sam had been distracted all the previous evening and the look of deep concern in his eyes when he went out after dinner troubled her. "You shouldn't have waited up," he said when he returned, kissing her lightly, "but I'm glad you did."

Tilly smiled and made some cocoa. It was their ritual. Whenever things looked bad, and over the years there had been many ups and downs, Tilly made cocoa and they talked late into the night to sort things out. From the anxiety on Sam's face and the way his hair had been ruffled, he'd run his fingers through it if he was distressed, she guessed he was deeply troubled.

"How bad is it?" she asked.

He shrugged. "I don't know. I can't find Victor and the rumour is that one of his businesses is in trouble. A lot of his suppliers haven't been paid. It's not just us, it's more widespread than that. I won't know more until the bank opens on Monday."

Tilly swallowed. "You don't think he's…? She couldn't say the words.

"What? Embezzled the money?" Sam's voice rose in a crescendo of fear and horror. "No, not Victor. We're partners. He'd have told me if he was in trouble."

Tilly doubted that.

"No. It'll be cash flow or something, a mistake. An error. Don't worry." His smile was unconvincing.

Tilly sighed. She hadn't dared think the worst. After all Sam's hard work and the years of struggle to get where they were, it would break his heart.

It wasn't until she got downstairs that she realised that Martha had gone out already. She hadn't heard her go. Damn, she thought, the memory of the argument fresh in her mind. She'd hoped to be able talk her out of going alone to the park. Now there was no chance to do that. She went out into the hall and called up the stairs, "Katy, George, breakfast. Hurry up. It's a lovely day. Who wants to go for a picnic in the park?"

"Me," "Me," she heard, followed by footsteps and scrambling to get dressed.

Chapter Ten

Martha arrived at the park at least an hour before she needed to be there. She didn't want to look too eager, so she found a bench overlooking the bowling green and sat and ate her sandwiches. Nerves churned her stomach but she was determined to remain cool and calm. As much as she regretted her hasty acceptance of Theo's invitation to meet, she couldn't help being intrigued by it. She'd danced with him a couple of times but hadn't got the measure of the man. She wasn't sure what she expected.

The day turned sultry and time dragged. She watched the bowling for a while, until she got bored. She strolled to where the children played on the swings and people walked their dogs. She wandered along by the flowerbeds where roses scented the air, then took a walk by the canal under the trees, glad to be in the shade. She ambled along where boats rocked on their moorings, admiring their ornate paintwork and shiny brass fittings. They wouldn't be moored for long. It was a while before she heard the church clock strike the third-quarter-hour. The sound of a brass band tuning up drifted across on a breeze as she headed towards the rows of deckchairs where people sat enjoying the morning sunshine. She couldn't see him. Perhaps he's not coming, she thought. She wasn't sure if she was pleased or disappointed.

"I wasn't sure you'd come," a voice behind her said.

She spun round, heart leaping. Close up and in daylight, with his fine features and strong bone structure, he really was annoyingly good looking. Sunlight glinted on his dark, smooth as a raven's wing hair. He had an elegance about him and a sense of unhurried ease, a hint of humour gleamed in his impenetrable aquamarine eyes.

"I said I would."

He nodded. "So you did." He offered his arm. "Should we walk?"

At that moment the band struck up with an inconvenient blast of sound. She declined his arm but strode off, away from the bandstand, the music fading as they walked. "You said you wanted to apologise," she said. "Are you apologising for your remarks about my family, or the fact that you provoked a fight with my brother that ruined my evening and possibly his career?" She hoped she sounded unimpressed, but wasn't sure she'd managed it.

He took a few moments before he answered. "Both. What I said was unforgivable. The worst kind of barrack-room banter which had no place in mixed company. I can only put it down to having over indulged in the devil drink. Not much of an excuse, I know, but I regret having upset you. I allowed my feelings to control my actions. It was ungentlemanly and dishonourable."

Was that it? A bubble of rage stirred her insides. "You were drunk, ill-mannered and offensive. Pray, what feelings would provoke such behaviour? Jealously, annoyance, aggravation perhaps at my brother paying too much attention to your sister? Or are you merely a bully who hates people to enjoy themselves?"

He gasped, visibly shocked at her forthrightness. "You don't think much of me, do you?"

"I don't think of you at all. I only agreed to meet you out of curiosity and a desire to see you squirm while you made your grovelling apology. Even that disappoints me."

He stopped and stared at her, his hand over his mouth, his eyes shining with something that looked like wonder, or could have been disbelief. "My God," he said. "You really are something. Jojo said you were fierce, but I never imagined..." He shook his head and continued to stare at her. She felt herself blush and inwardly cursed. "I guess you weren't disappointed with the jewellery I sent."

She dived her hand into her bag and brought out the box. "Here, take it back. It's beautiful, but quite inappropriate."

"You don't mean that."

"I do." She stared at him. She'd made the gesture, but in her heart she hoped he wouldn't take it.

"No. It would be a sin to deprive the stones of the chance to adorn the prettiest neck in London." As he spoke, his tone casually seductive, he stared into her eyes and ran his finger down her neck, sending a shiver of delight down her spine. "Keep it. No strings."

Her heart pounded. She pushed the box back into her bag. "If that's all."

"No. Please." He grabbed her arm. "Can we begin again? I really am sorry. I never meant to upset you. It was the drink..."

She pulled her arm away and began walking. Maybe he's not so bad, she thought, but wasn't prepared to let him off so easily. "They say that you can tell a person's true nature by how he acts when he's in his cups," she said.

"Jojo punched me. I wasn't there for a fight. Not that I didn't deserve it. I'm sorry Jojo's suffering for it. More sorry perhaps than he is."

"What do you mean?"

"I mean he never wanted to join the Navy in the first place. He hates routine and discipline. His heart's not in it."

At the mention of Joey, Martha's heart hardened. "Are you saying you've done him a favour? That he'd prefer a spell in prison and a dishonourable discharge to a life at sea?"

"All I'm saying is, that it's possibly not the catastrophe you think it is. A life at sea is one of great sacrifice. Not everyone's cut out for it."

Martha recalled Rob saying something along the same lines. She remembered Joey's application for an onshore posting. Was it true? Was Joey looking for a way out? The thought that Theo might be right irritated her even more than his patronising manner. They walked in silence for a while, worries about Joey's predicament buzzing through her brain.

"You were right about his interest in my sister," Theo said after a few moments. "It's to be discouraged."

Martha took a breath, hit by a sudden realisation. Anger that had been simmering inside her flared. "So, you didn't want to meet me to apologise at all, but to persuade me to crush Joey's hopes in that direction?"

Theo sighed. "For his own good. Even you must see how hopeless it is. My sister has expensive tastes. A sub-lieutenant's salary wouldn't pay for her pet poodle's treats, let alone her preferred lifestyle."

"Surely that's Ellen's decision to make."

He smiled. He really was the most insufferable snob, and patronisingly arrogant with it.

"Ellen will play along for a while, enjoying the attention," he said. "But she'd never settle for less than an Earl. It's a hopeless infatuation that'll come to nothing, however, it could harm her reputation."

Her reputation! So that's what he was worried about. Unfortunately, Martha saw the sense of what he was saying. She'd seen it for herself, but Joey's love life was none of her business. "If that's what you're worried about perhaps you should speak to her, not me."

"I was hoping you'd speak to Jojo."

She almost laughed out loud. "You want me to do your dirty work? Sorry to disappoint you. I came here expecting an apology, not a lecture on the unsuitability of my family to mix with yours."

She was about to walk away when he grabbed her arm. "I'm sorry," he said. "I did want to apologise. I never meant for you to be upset. I spoke out of turn and for that I'm sorry." His voice softened and she saw what she thought was regret in his eyes, or it could have been hope. Perhaps he was genuinely contrite.

"Please don't judge me too harshly. I know I spoke out of turn," he said. "Perhaps I can make amends. Dinner, or a show?"

She shook her head and was about to say no when she caught a glimpse of something that brought her to a stop. Katy was on the grass turning cartwheels. Beyond that she saw George with his boat and her mother sitting on a blanket near the pond. Of all the...Theo's transgressions evaporated into insignificance when she saw what she thought of as her mother's betrayal. She took his arm and led him back the way they'd come. "You're not worried about your reputation then? Being seen with the daughter of a – what did you call my mother?"

He groaned and put his hands over his face. "Don't remind me. I feel bad enough as it is."

The church bell sounded midday. Martha couldn't believe an hour had gone.

"Is that the time?" Theo sounded as surprised as she was. "Much as I regret it, I'm afraid I have to go. Duty calls. May I see you home?"

"No, thank you. I'd like to stay a while and listen to the band."

"If you're sure."

She nodded.

"Please say I may have the pleasure of your company again soon."

"Maybe."

He picked up her hand and brushed it against his lips. "I look forward to it." Then he was gone and the magic of the morning went with him. She realised she'd enjoyed the encounter. It was rare to meet a man willing to speak so openly. She had to admire him for that. She sighed. I suppose I'd better go and make peace with Ma, she thought. At least she'll be happy to see I've survived the encounter.

Chapter Eleven

Sunday evening Tilly prepared tea for herself, Katy and George. Martha still hadn't returned, and Sam and Harry would be out until late working on the boats. Worries about Martha circled her brain while she worked. She was pleased she'd come to her and told her about the conversation with Theo Delahaye, but she couldn't help wondering if there was something she hadn't told her. She sighed. Headstrong and impulsive, Martha was growing up. Had she been the same at that age? Probably, she thought. Sam, who doted on Martha, would say she was being overly protective and that Martha was well able to take care of herself, but it didn't stop her worrying.

Her reflections were interrupted by the arrival of a messenger with a note. Puzzled, Tilly took the envelope. It was addressed to her, but she didn't recognise the flowery handwriting. She gave the boy sixpence and took it into the kitchen, a deep frown creased her brow. She gasped when she opened it and read: *Please call on me tomorrow. It's concerning Joseph's future. Regards, Deborah Staverly.* The address was the Thackery townhouse.

She sank into a chair, the breath knocked out of her. Deborah Staverly was Sir Montague's granddaughter, Edmund's sister, and Joey's aunt. She'd never met her, never wanted to. Nor Sir Montague, come to that. All their dealings had been through his solicitor. Better for everyone that way. Now it felt as though she'd been summonsed. How dare she, she thought. *Call on me tomorrow*? Who does she think she is?

She shoved the note into her pocket, thinking she'd ignore it, then she thought about Joey. The note said it concerned his future. From what Martha had told her he was in trouble and, while she and Sam could do nothing, Sir Montague was in a position to help. That irritated her more than it should have. Damn the man, she thought. Perhaps she should go and see the woman, if she had it in her power to influence him.

She sighed and took the note out, reading it again. She'd talk to Sam about it. He'd know what to do.

It was late when Sam eventually returned. "You look tired," Tilly said, putting a saucepan of milk on the stove to make cocoa. "Is there anything I can do?"

"No. We've had a good day, thanks to the fine weather and a favourable tide. I have enough to pay some of the bills and I hope to persuade the yard to work on *Maggie May*. I'll go to the bank first thing. It'll be something I can sort out, a mix up of some kind." His smile was unconvincing. "Don't worry, love."

Why is that when someone says, don't worry, you worry all the more, Tilly thought. She made the cocoa. "Here," she said, handing it to him. "If there is anything, you will tell me?"

"You'll be the first to know," he said, the warmth in his eyes the only thanks she needed.

They drank their cocoa in silence, then Tilly told him about Martha and Theo in the park. He nodded and made the appropriate noises, but she knew his mind was elsewhere. The note from Joey's aunt burned in her pocket. It's about Joey, she thought. Perhaps it's best if I sort it out myself, no point in burdening Sam further. He has enough on his plate.

Monday morning after seeing the children off to school, Tilly changed into her best navy blue suit and tidied her hair. She wanted Mrs Staverly to see that she was the wife of a successful businessman, not the naive young girl she used to be. She reminded herself that she was the mother of five children and a woman of the world. Whatever this Mrs Staverly was after, Tilly would be sure to stand her ground and not let herself be intimidated.

She took a cab to the house. She aimed to arrive mid-morning, not so early as to seem anxious, but not too late to appear uninterested. When she arrived she stood staring at the Georgian facade of the Thackery's townhouse. A lump rose to her throat. She recalled the last time she'd visited such a house. It wasn't a pleasant memory.

She took a breath, mounted the steps and knocked on the door. A tail-coated butler with a yellow waistcoat opened it. "Mrs Crowe to see Mrs Staverly," Tilly said. "I believe I am expected."

The butler allowed her to enter and showed her into to a small room overlooking the road. "I'll let Mrs Staverly know you're here," he said.

Tilly glanced around the room while she waited. It was just as she'd expect, comfortably furnished, but not ostentatious. A vase of fresh flowers stood on the hearth, another on a side table. The pictures on the wall were of flowers or landscapes. Nothing out of place or over-elaborate.

She didn't have long to wait. The butler returned to show her up the stairs to Mrs Staverly's sitting room. Tilly glanced at the pictures adorning the walls, all portraits of military men in uniform. Thackery predecessors, she guessed.

Deborah Staverly sat at a rosewood desk by the window, writing in an open book in front of her. Her mustard-coloured suit, edged with black lace, with leg of mutton sleeves and a narrow waist, gave her an air of business-like sophistication. She stood to greet Tilly as the butler announced her. "Please come in, Mrs Crowe, or may I call you Matilda? You are most welcome." She indicated several over-stuffed armchairs set around a large marble fireplace that dominated the room. "Can I offer you tea, or coffee?"

"Tea would be fine," Tilly said, taking a seat in front of the fireplace where a vase of hydrangeas screened the grate, "and it's Tilly." It was a pleasant room, the morning light bright through the tall, curtained windows. Ornate green and pink floral wallpaper gave the room an outside, fresh feel and a large mirror opposite the window made it look bigger than it was.

"You must call me Deborah, after all we are almost family." The emphasis was on the 'almost'.

Deborah Staverly was not what Tilly had expected. She'd seen her at the passing out parade from a distance, and thought her quite matronly, but now, close-to she saw a surprising intensity of purpose. She'd thought her quite plain too, but she had an energy about her, which gave her an attractive vivacity. Her blonde hair and blue eyes were Edmund's and Tilly's stomach tilted at a sudden memory. A shiver ran through her.

"I hope the traffic wasn't too bad," Deborah said, smiling.

"Not at all," Tilly said, then they went on to talk about the exceptionally fine weather in what Tilly suspected was an attempt to make her feel at home and drop her guard. Once tea was served, she'd find out the real reason Deborah Staverly summonsed her.

The butler brought the tea which Deborah poured and handed to Tilly. Tilly sipped it and gazed over the rim of the cup, waiting for Mrs Staverly to speak. She wasn't going to rush her, she quite enjoyed speculating and waited to see what was so urgent she had to call.

"There is some good news," Deborah said. "You'll be aware of Joseph's pending court martial?"

Tilly nodded. "I had heard of the possibility."

"Well, you'll be pleased to hear that Sir Montague has influence and has been able to intervene on Joseph's behalf." Her tone was light and just short of warm. "They will allow him to resign rather than being court martialled. It means he will avoid a dishonourable discharge."

Tilly paused. She put her cup and saucer back on the table. "So, he'll be out of the Navy?"

"Yes. But without a stain on his character."

"Well, that is good news," Tilly said, as the vision of Joey coming home filled her mind. "Please thank Sir Montague. I'm sure Jo-Joseph appreciates all he's done for him."

"Hmm. Sir Montague wishes to do more." She waited for Tilly's reaction.

"More? That's kind of him, but I'm sure we can manage. Sam will be able to find work for him. He has three boats now on the river and is always short-handed."

"No, you don't understand. Sir Montague is concerned about his legacy. He's unwell and the prospect of imminent death haunts him. On his passing the estate will be left to my mother for her lifetime and then to me for mine. After that there are no heirs apparent. As you know Joseph is his only male blood relative. Sir Montague is anxious to ensure that the estate and his title continue through his bloodline."

Puzzlement creased Tilly's brow. "You mean leave him the estate?" It was unbelievable.

"It's not as simple as that." Deborah stared at Tilly. "Joseph is illegitimate and, as such, cannot inherit."

Tilly swallowed and wondered why she'd been brought here. Was it just to be insulted?

"However," Deborah continued, picking up her cup and saucer. "If there was a way his birth could be legitimised..." She sipped her tea, eyebrows raised in Tilly's direction.

"Is there such a way?" Tilly voice rose with incredulity.

Deborah took a breath. "If you honestly believed that you and his father were married the Court could legitimise his birth."

"But we weren't."

Deborah looked at Tilly "No, but..."

Tilly got the inference. "You want me to swear in Court to something that isn't true. I have never lied and I'm not about to start now." She stood ready to go. "If that's what you've brought me here for..."

"No. Wait. There is another way, but I doubt you'd like it any better."

Tilly sat.

"If Sir Montague were to become Joseph's legal guardian and Joseph his ward, then Sir Montague could recognise him as his legitimate heir and name him as beneficiary in his will. He wouldn't then inherit the title, but could inherit the estate. Of course there would have to be grounds for the guardianship. If Joseph were an orphan," she placed her tea on the side table, "or the son of an unfit mother…"

Tilly had heard enough. Anger flared inside her at this stupid woman's suggestion that she was an unfit mother. She rose to her feet. "I am not an unfit mother, and Sam has been a better father to Joey than anyone ever could. He is not in need of a legal guardian. It's outrageous."

"Don't be too hasty, Tilly. Think about it. As heir in law to a grand estate his life, and the lives of his children, would be very different. He could do whatever he wants, marry whoever he chooses. I believe he has his eye on a young lady, a sister of one of his classmates."

Tilly recalled Martha telling her Joey was besotted, but even so. She struggled to control the fury churning in her stomach. She'd had a lifetime of not being good enough and she wasn't going to let this hoity-toity madam put her down. "Any girl would be lucky to get my son as a husband," she said. "Her loss if she doesn't realise that."

Deborah also rose. "I beg you to reconsider. What can you offer Joseph? A future scraping a living on the river? Don't let your pride deny him his rightful inheritance and the chance of a better life. It's what my brother would have wanted for his son. Do you even know what you're throwing away?"

Tears sprang to Tilly's eyes at the mention of Deborah's brother, his face fleeting in her mind. "I know that my son is part of MY family. He is loved and wanted. Nothing can change that." She gathered her skirts, strode to the door and opened it.

Deborah smiled, without warmth. "Perhaps we should ask him. He is a Thackery too, after all."

The words followed her as she stepped through the door and dashed down the stairs as fast as her legs could carry her. The butler sprang forward from nowhere and opened the front door. All she could think about as she ran out of that hateful house, was that she might be losing her son.

A cauldron of rage bubbled up inside her. It couldn't be true. They couldn't change the past. Joey would be twenty-one next year, old enough to make up his own mind. He'd never choose the Thackerys over her and Sam. They had a good life together, as a family. Families stick together, she knew that. But part of her, the devil on her shoulders, said, *and what would you do if you were twenty years old, had just lost your job and were offered unlimited wealth and everything you could ever wish for?*

Chapter Twelve

That night Deborah Staverly's comments ran round and round in Tilly's mind disturbing her sleep. Joey as Lord of the Manor? It was ridiculous, but her heart told her it was what his birth father would have wanted. Still, he had no right or expectation. Joey's birth out of wedlock made any inheritance impossible. Edmund didn't even know of his existence, Even if he had, he'd never have been allowed to marry her. Sam was the only father Joey had known, and she saw no reason for that to change. She tossed and turned as her thoughts ranged from thinking it insane to the possibility that Deborah may have the power to do the impossible.

Sam was late coming in and she hadn't wanted to add to his obvious worries, so hadn't shared her concerns. Her worries were not for Joey, but for her other children. What would they think? If Deborah Staverly persisted, her past would be paraded before the courts and no doubt turned to show her in the worst possible light. She knew how the law worked, how money and status can twist the simplest story into a tale of scorn and derision. Then she thought of Sam. Would he be able to bear it all again?

The sound of the fire bells in the distance, hardly ruffled her sleep as she buried her head in her pillow, trying to stop the thoughts racing like demented hares through her brain.

Martha had a spring in her step as she walked to work, the memory of the day in the park fresh in her mind. Morning sunlight reflected off nearby buildings, bathing the river in its golden glow. A light breeze rustled the leaves on the trees. The sound of boats hooting as they made their way to the docks filled the air. She'd wanted to get out of the house. The atmosphere at breakfast had been leaden, with Sam and Harry gone out early and Ma in such a state of distraction that she'd taken the clean plates to the kitchen to be washed and left the used ones on the table. She'd also poured her teacup so full the tea cascaded into the saucer for several seconds before she realised and uprighted the pot. She'd been very short with George too when he dawdled over his boiled egg, and Mrs Conway, when she brought in coffee instead of tea. That wasn't like her.

Martha thought she'd cleared the air after telling her about Theo Delahaye's conversation, well part of it, but apparently not, so she skipped the tea and toast, saying she wanted to run an errand before work.

As she walked, she thought about Joey and what Theo had said. What would they do to him? What would he do if he had to leave the Navy? He could sign up on a merchant ship. With his training in the Navy they'd be delighted to have him. Then she thought of his ill-advised pursuit of Ellen Delahaye. How would that affect what he did next?

She sighed. She hoped he'd be happy, whatever happened to him.

She slowed when she reached the river. Walking by the river, watching the ferries and boats going to and from the docks always fascinated her. Where had they come from? Where were they going? What were they carrying? It was too soon for one of her father's boats to be out.

She'd arrived early so bought herself a coffee from a stall set in a small courtyard near the office. Two men she recognised as being senior clerks were already at one of the tables. She took a seat in front of them enjoying the morning sunshine. She wasn't listening to their conversation, but it was hard to ignore it, especially when she caught the words, 'insurance job' and 'done a runner'. Her interest was piqued. She didn't spread gossip but that didn't stop her being entertained by it.

As the men stood to leave, they passed her table. "Never trust a gambler," one of them said. "They all lose in the end."

"Pity Landridge didn't understand that," the other one said.

Marsha jumped up. "Excuse me," she said. "Is that Victor Landridge, you're talking about?"

The men exchanged glances, then looked her up and down. Eventually one said, "Know him, do you?"

"He's my father's partner."

The man's eyebrows shot up. "Really. Well, I pity him, then."

They walked away, chuckling, and Martha's heart sank into her boots. The memory of the last time she'd seen Victor at the restaurant and the row he'd had with Mr Bartholomew spun through her brain. A lump rose to her throat. Something was going on with Victor and she wanted to know what it was. She swallowed the last of her coffee and walked out of the courtyard. A newspaper boy on the corner caught her eye. The poster on the newsstand read: *Fire at Old's Yard. Boats destroyed.* Old's Yard was where her father took his boats to be repaired. She bought a paper and gasped when saw a picture of the burnt-out hull of a boat. Underneath it the caption read: *Charred remains of pleasure steamer Maggie May.*

"Can you tell Miss Todd that I'm sick today," she said to the doorman, as she rushed past the office building.

"You don't look sick."

"I assure you I am," she said and hurried away. She rushed home with her heart in her mouth. Did Ma know what was going on?

Chapter Thirteen

Tilly was just leaving the house as Martha arrived home, breathless from rushing. "Goodness," she said. "Why aren't you at work?"

"Have you seen this?" Martha shoved the newspaper into Tilly's hands.

Tilly stared at it, unable to take anything in, her mind still processing the fact that Martha should be at work. She stared at the picture, struggling to make sense of it. The words *Maggie May* in the caption jumped out at her. Breath punched out of her lungs as realisation sunk in. She grabbed Martha's arm. "Let's get a cab," she said.

They were lucky to find a cab at the end of the road. Tilly read the article as the cab thundered through the streets, her heart pounding like thoroughbreds' hooves. According to the article in the paper a fire at the yard in the middle of the night had destroyed the *Maggie May* and damaged several other boats.

When they arrived at the yard she asked the cabbie to wait. She wasn't sure Sam would be there or if she'd need to fetch him. Stepping out of the cab her hand flew to her mouth. She couldn't believe what she was seeing. She gasped as she gazed around, shocked and deeply disturbed. The acrid smell of smoke and burnt timber permeated the air. Particles of debris floated in the smoking remains of what used to be a vibrant, busy boatyard. A group of men stood around, sullenly staring and kicking the ground around them. One or two attempted to clear up the mess of charred remains. She saw the yard's owner, Amos Old, his face twisted with anguish, his business in ruins. Her heart went out to him.

"Amos," she said. "What can I say? What happened?"

Amos shrugged his shoulders, shaking his head. Tears shone in his eyes, his face grim. "I don't know, lass. A fire in the night, they said. They think it was deliberate."

Tilly's jaw dropped. "Deliberate?" Her voice echoed her horror. "Who would do such a thing? It's unbelievable." She glanced around, helplessness engulfed her. It was no use going any further. The ground was still awash from the fire hoses, rivulets of black, soot filled water ran into the gutters. "Is Sam here?"

"He was. The police came. They've taken him to the station."

Tilly's horror multiplied as sudden fear stabbed her chest. "They've taken Sam? Why?" Incredulity heightened her voice. "Surely they don't think he had anything to do with this?"

Amos shrugged. "Deliberate they said." His tone changed to one of fierce fury. "If I find out who's done this, they'll be sorry."

Tilly didn't doubt his words for one second. Boatmen had a way of dealing with bad apples that had nothing to do with the law of the land. "I'm sorry this has happened to you, Amos," she said, her tone and resolve hardening as her fear for Sam turned to fury. "We'll get to the bottom of it, I promise you, and it won't be anything to do with Sam." She turned to Martha, standing next to her, her face pale with alarm. "Come on."

She strode back to the waiting cab, called out the address of the nearest police station and climbed in. Martha followed.

When they arrived at the police station Tilly paid the cab and ran in first. A uniformed officer stood behind a long wooden counter making notes in a large ledger. In his early forties, with greying hair and a superior manner, he glanced up, but carried on writing. Tilly stood for several minutes before he spoke. "Can I help you?" he said, in a voice that sounded as though that was the last thing he wanted to do.

"I've come to see my husband, Sam Crowe. I believe he's been brought here."

The police sergeant grinned. "Sorry. Visitors aren't allowed to see the prisoners."

"He's not a prisoner, he's here helping with inquiries." Tilly hoped that was true.

"Still can't see 'im," the sergeant said. "No visitors allowed."

"How long will he be?"

The sergeant shrugged. "As long as it takes."

"We'll wait." Tilly turned and sat on one of the chairs set out against the wall.

An ashen-faced Martha sat next to her. "They don't think he did it, do they?" she whispered. "He wouldn't."

"Of course he wouldn't."

Just then two burly policemen came in with a scruffy looking lad in handcuffs, stumbling between them. His face was bruised, his clothes torn and blood dripped from a cut on his lip. Tilly shuddered. Did they put Sam in handcuffs, she wondered? In front of the men at the yard? That would have been a humiliation too shocking to endure. Would they have thought him responsible? Not if they knew him, she rationalised. Still fear and anxiety churned in her stomach.

"Been a naughty boy again, Shaun?" the desk sergeant said, eyeing up the boy. "You'll be in for a long stretch this time." From the grin on his face, the thought appeared to give him a great deal of pleasure.

Tilly sighed.

"It was Victor wasn't it," Martha whispered, twisting a damp handkerchief in her hands. "I heard two men talking. They said something about gambling and insurance. I can't remember exactly, but..." She sniffed and drew a breath.

Tilly patted her hand. "We don't know what happened yet. It could have been an accident. I'm sure..." She wanted to say it would be all right, but couldn't. She knew it wouldn't be.

They sat for half an hour. Tilly was about to go and ask the desk sergeant if he could find out how long they'd be holding Sam, when Ben Crowe, Sam's solicitor brother came in.

"Ben!" Tilly jumped up to greet him. A wave of warmth, hope and optimism filled her at the sight of this tall, sandy haired man with his intelligent face and blue grey eyes. "What are you doing here?"

He grinned. "Sam sent a lad from the yard to fetch me. Don't worry, we'll soon have him out of here." He smiled reassurance and went up to the counter. Tilly watched as the disgruntled desk sergeant let him through. Ten minutes later he came out with a dishevelled Sam. Sam's face and hair were streaked with ash and soot, his clothes blackened and crumpled. The smell of smoke clung like cobwebs, but Tilly couldn't have been happier to see him. She rushed up to him, wanting to hug him, but he held out grime blackened hands. "Let's get out of here," he said, an edge to his voice and steel in his usually warm brown eyes.

Ben had a cab waiting so they all followed him out. It was only when they drove away from the police station that Sam relaxed and told them what he knew.

When they got home Ben paid off the cab and they went indoors, the smell of burning accompanied them. Sam looked as though he hadn't slept for a week. He went into the lounge and poured himself a brandy, lifting the bottle to Ben to see if he wanted one.

"Too early for me," Ben said, "but you go ahead. You look as though you need it."

Sam grunted and swallowed the drink in one swig. "The *Maggie May*'s gone," he said. "Burnt to a cinder. Who would do such a thing?" He poured himself another drink and swigged it back in one go. Tilly's heart crunched. The *Maggie May* was Sam's first boat and she knew it had a place in his heart. Destroying it would be like destroying everything he'd worked for.

"Do you think it was Victor?" Martha asked. "For the insurance?"

Sam shook his head. "They won't pay out if it's arson. Victor knows that. It would be madness."

"Or desperation," Ben said. "You'd be surprised how stupid people can be when they are desperate."

"It could be aimed at Amos," Tilly said, the words drowning man and straw flashing through her head. "He must have made some enemies over the years. Perhaps it wasn't meant for us at all."

Sam brightened. "Do you really think so?"

"It's possible," she said more out of hope than conviction.

"I have to go to the bank." Sam glanced down at himself. "Can't go like this."

"I'll heat some water. You can have a bath."

"No time for that. I'll just have a wash and change."

"I'll make some inquiries about the insurance, and Victor," Ben said. "I'll ask around about Amos too. Someone must know something."

"Can I help?" Martha stood still wringing her handkerchief in her hands.

"Yes," Ben said. "You can come with me. You'll know about the boats and the people on the river. They'll be more likely to talk to us than the police."

Martha looked more cheerful, having something to do and Tilly sent a silent thank you to Ben.

"Is there anything I can do?" Tilly said. "I feel so helpless staying here and doing nothing."

"You can go to the pier and find Harry," Sam said. "He'll either be on the *Matilda May* or in the office. He'll only have heard the rumours. You need to reassure him."

"Of course." It would be a while before they knew the full extent of the damage to Sam's business, but meanwhile Tilly would do all she could to help.

Sam went to wash up and change his clothes.

Suddenly the vision of Deborah Staverly jumped unbidden into Tilly's head. How she would relish the situation. Sam's business in trouble. Could she turn that to her advantage? Tilly shivered and pushed the thought away.

Martha watched her mother pour a finger of brandy into a glass and swig it back. Her hands were shaking. Martha didn't know if it was shock or anger. She was still trembling herself. She picked up a glass and held it out. Tilly hesitated for a second or two and then poured a sliver of the golden liquid into a glass for her. Martha sipped it. It burned her throat but sent a heartening wave of warmth through her body.

"Thank you for getting him out of there," Tilly said. "I don't know what we'd have done without your help."

Ben smiled. "They had no grounds to hold him. Only a trumped up charge with no substance. Don't worry, Tilly. We'll get to the bottom of it, and it won't be anything to do with Sam."

It wasn't long before Sam returned. Grey ash still streaked his dark curls and not all the soot and grime on his face and neck had gone, but as least his clothes were clean, although the smell of burning still clung. "You'll need the paperwork for the insurance," he said and took Ben into his study.

"Do you think he'll be all right, Ma?" Martha said suddenly anxious about her father. This would be a terrific blow to him and to his business and the horror of it was just sinking in.

"I don't know," Tilly said. "But he's tougher and more resilient than you'll ever know." She had a look of the deepest fondness on her face and the reflection of a distant memory in her eyes. "As long as we stick together, we'll get through this and anything else that life throws at us."

Martha hoped she was right.

They set out together, agreeing to meet up later in the afternoon to share what they find out. They separated at the riverbank, each going a different way. Martha walked with Ben who explained the business arrangement he'd helped Sam set up with Victor Landridge.

"Sam was to be in charge of the day to day running of the boats and Victor the finance," he said. "All the assets are in joint names. Sam had the *Maggie May* but needed finance for the upfront running costs. Victor provided it. It's not cheap to put a pleasure steamer on the Thames. The other two boats, *Matilda May* and *Martha May* were bought with loans from the bank which Sam has been working all the hours God sends to repay. If you ask me Victor got a good deal when he signed up with Sam. Sam took on extra responsibilities and worked longer and harder for no extra pay. I reckon Victor's original investment has paid off handsomely."

Martha got the impression that Ben wasn't Victor Landridge's greatest fan.

Their first port of call was to the insurance agent, situated in offices above a bakery in the high street. The smell of baking bread followed them up the narrow stairs. Martha noticed the peeling, stained wallpaper. She hoped the office would be more impressive. It wasn't. The name of the company, emblazoned in gold on a half glass door, looked more promising, but the windowless reception area less so. An elderly woman sat at a desk behind an elderly typewriter. Ben introduced himself and Martha, calling her his associate, which sent a thrill of pleasure through her. They were asked to wait.

"It's a matter of the utmost urgency," Ben said, his tone authoritative and insistent. He presented his card. "It's imperative that I see the manager without delay." His manner and bearing had the desired effect and they were quickly shown through to the manager's office.

Martha gazed around, taking in the filing cabinets piled high with files and the framed certificates on the walls. Grimy windows let in the midday sun but did little to light the room. Martha listened intently as Ben spoke to the manager, a pallid faced man with greasy hair and an equally greasy grey suit. It soon became clear that, while the insured boats were in joint names, the single beneficiary of the policies had been changed to Victor Landridge.

"When was this amendment made?" Ben asked.

"Several months ago," the manager said, showing Ben a typewritten sheet of paper with several signatures on the bottom. One of them appeared to be Sam's. Ben took the original policy documents out of his briefcase. He turned to the signatures to compare them. "I can assure you that my brother never signed that document," he said.

The manager's face flushed. He stared at the papers Ben held out. The signature on the original document was significantly different from the one on the manager's paper. On the Notice of Amendment the signature was carefully written, hesitant and unsure, whereas on the original policy it was bold and hurried as though the writer wanted to get on with things.

"I guess we can add forgery to Victor Landridge's list of misdemeanours," Ben said.

At the mention of the word 'forgery' the manager's manner changed to one of affronted innocence. "I can assure you that I knew nothing of this. I am completely innocent." He paused in thought, stroking his chin. "Come to think of it, the documents were already signed when they were given to me," he said. "There was no way I could have known of any forgery."

In the end, after much discussion, the manager agreed to reinstate the named beneficiaries as those on the original policy. In the case of any claim being made for the loss of *Maggie May*, there would be no payout in any case if arson was proven.

Ben argued the case that the loss of *Maggie May* was a by-product of an attack on the yard and had nothing to do with the owners of the pleasure steamer.

"In that case, claim again the yard's insurers," the manager said. "Nothing to do with me." He closed the file and made it clear that the meeting was over.

Ben put the papers back in his briefcase and they left the office.

"What now?" Martha asked, feeling that they had at least made a little progress.

"Might as well have some lunch," Ben said. He took her to a public house a few streets away. As they walked in the barman looked up. "The usual, sir?" he said.

Ben nodded. "And a half of shandy for the lady."

Intrigued Martha glanced around. The wood panelling was dark with nicotine stain and the air stuffy. Dark wood, ring-stained tables stood in front of faded, velvet covered bench seating around the walls. Heavy ladder-back chairs occupied the other side of the tables. Several men, their cigarettes adding to the fug, sat hunched over tables laden with glasses of half-drunk beer at the back of the room. The pervading smell was of stale beer and nicotine.

Ben brought the drinks over.

"Do you come here often?" Martha asked.

He grinned. "Not the most salubrious place I've visited," he said. "But they serve a good pint and the food's not bad. I've ordered us both a meat and potato pie. I hope that's all right."

"Fine." Martha sipped her shandy and grimaced at the taste.

A few minutes later a girl about Martha's age brought the food over with the cutlery, setting it down in front of them. A spiral of steam rose from the pile of what looked like mush covered in pastry on the plate. Martha wrinkled her nose. Ben smiled his thanks.

Martha took a tentative bite of her pie. It tasted surprisingly good. She took another bite.

Over lunch Ben asked her about Victor. "How much do you know about him?"

Martha shrugged. "Not much. Pa knew him before I was born. I know they are partners. He came to the house once or twice, that's how I recognised him at the office and the restaurant. I got the impression that Pa wanted to impress him." She sipped her shandy and grimaced again. "He was the money man."

"Hmm," Ben said, tucking into his pie. "I only met him when I drew up the partnership papers. Thought he was a bit of a chancer, but he had the money and Sam needed it. Eighteen years is a long time. I suppose things change."

They ate in silence for a while, then Ben said, "You said your boss – Mr Bartholomew, is it?"

She nodded.

"He knows Landridge. Is he a client?"

"Erm. No. I don't think so. I haven't seen anything to suggest he is. I think they go to the same club, or something."

"That's interesting. Any idea which club?"

"No. Sorry. As far as I know it's just a passing acquaintance. Victor Landridge recommended me for the job when I finished secretarial college. I thought he was doing Pa a favour."

Having finished his meal Ben placed his cutlery on the empty plate and pushed it to the other side of the table. He wiped his mouth on the napkin the cutlery had been wrapped in before crumpling it and putting it top of the plate. Martha's pie was still only half eaten but she didn't think she could face any more.

"Landridge's office is our next port of call," Ben said. "I don't expect to find him there, but we may be able to find out more about his business."

Chapter Fourteen

Tilly found Harry down by the wharf. The *Matilda May* was tied up alongside the pier and Harry was in the small cabin that served as an office.

"How's Pa?" he asked as soon as he saw her. "We heard about the fire. They say it's the *Maggie May*. Is he all right?"

Tilly's heart turned over. "The *Maggie May* is gone," she said.

The blood drained from Harry's face. "It's true then?"

She saw him fighting back tears, his face twisted with pain. She wanted to hug him but, in front of his workmates, knew better than to do so. "Pa's gone to the bank to see why the bills haven't been paid," she said. Trying to be as matter of fact and unemotional as she could. "He asked me to come and get you."

Harry shook his head. "I can't believe it. Not the *Maggie May*."

Tilly glanced around. The crew from the boat were trying to look busy, tidying up, and cleaning the deck for the next lot of passengers, while they waited for the same news Harry had dreaded. She was about to speak to them when a portly man in a blue suit approached, a piece of paper in his hand. "This the *Matilda May*?" he asked.

"Yes. Why?" Tilly stared at him, unable to register why he'd be asking.

"You're too early," Harry said. "Next sailing's not for an hour and a half."

He smiled. "I've not come for a trip. I've come to take possession."

99

Tilly gasped. "Take possession? What are you talking about?"

"I've bought it," he said.

"You've what?"

"Well, paid the deposit. Here, look." He shoved the paper he was carrying into her hands. She stared at it, eyes wide with disbelief. It didn't make sense. As she scanned it she registered the words *Bill of Sale* and two signatures at the bottom, one of which was supposed to be Sam's.

Raging fear and fury threatened to explode inside her. This couldn't be happening. She filled her lungs, expanded her chest and tore the paper into tiny pieces, throwing it back at the man. "It's a fake. You've been swindled," she said. "My husband would never sell the boat. Never."

The man's face flushed red, his eyes bulged, two men who'd come with him stepped forward as he raised his arm, as though to hit her.

Harry stepped in front of her as a dozen boatmen materialised around her, several of them holding boat hooks. Tilly recognised the leader, a large, broad shouldered man with a grey beard and a tartan cap. No one knew his real name, everyone called him Jock. He'd worked for Sam for as long as Tilly could remember. The portly man and his mates stepped back.

"I suggest you go back to whoever gave you that bunkum hogwash and get your money back. The boat's not for sale. Not at any price." The fire in Tilly's voice matched the blaze in her eyes.

The man glanced around, saw the men standing ready to defend her, turned on his heel and retreated.

"This is not the end of it," he called over his shoulder as he slunk away.

Relieved, Tilly turned to thank the men who come to help. Most of them were watermen who worked for Sam.

"It's all right," Jock said. "We all know Sam would'na sell the boat from under us."

Sam arrived as he spoke. "What's going on?" he asked, a look of puzzlement on his face.

Tilly fell into his arms, relief flooding over her.

"Some bampot thinks he's bought your boat," Jock said. "An' if I know swindlers, he mayn't be the only one."

"What!"

"You'd better come in the cabin and sit down," Tilly said. "You'll never believe what Victor Landridge has done now."

Sam had given Ben the address of Landridge's office the other side of the river. "Do you know it?" Ben asked Martha as they caught a ferry.

"No. Sorry, I've never been there," she said.

The ferryman gave them directions to a shabby row of shops along a street about half a mile from the pier. The one at the address Sam had given Ben was boarded up with *To Let* written in red paint across the boards. Underneath it said *Enquiries* then gave an address which Ben copied down.

"I don't suppose you know where that is, either?" he said.

"No, sorry again," Martha said, "I'm not familiar with this side of the river."

The office was next to a Greek greengrocer, who hardly spoke English. It took several attempts before he understood what Ben was asking and was able to direct them to the landlord's workshop, a ten minute walk away.

The landlord, a fleshy faced man in his early sixties, stopped what he was doing when Ben approached him. His disagreeable demeanour disappeared when Ben produced his card and asked about the property to let.

Fifteen minutes later they were back at the office. The landlord took them round the back and unlocked the door, giving it a mighty shove to open it. A musty smell of damp greeted them as they walked in. The front office was dark, but Martha could see filing cabinets around the walls and two desks, with padded chairs behind them, set out facing the boarded up windows. Several chairs were placed around the walls. Posters depicting ships hung above them.

"Does the rent include the furnishings?" Ben asked.

The landlord hesitated, stroking his chin in thought. "Tenant owed me three months' rent," he said. "So if you want to make an offer."

"Are there any facilities?" Martha asked.

"Yes. I'll show you."

Ben smiled and nodded as she followed him out to the back of the shop, leaving him alone in the office. The small back kitchen had a sink and a small cooker. The walls were yellow with grease. A water heater over the sink caught her interest. "How does this work?" she said.

The man turned it on and it burst into life. He turned it off.

"And the cooker?"

"That's gas an' all," he said.

Martha nodded and feigned interest in the cupboards. "What's through here?" She opened a door which proved to be a large cupboard.

"Plenty of storage space," the landlord said.

"Any other facilities?"

"The privy's in the yard." He led her out to the small back yard, they'd passed on the way in. Someone had had a go at growing vegetables alongside the path.

"How many people share it?"

"Just the office and the families upstairs," he said.

"How many families?"

"Just the two."

Martha nodded and opened the privy door, standing back as the smell hit her nostrils. She shut it quickly. "Hmm," she said. "What was the last tenant like?"

The landlord looked bemused, but Martha's charm disarmed him. "Waste of space if you ask me," he said. "Left owing me three months' rent."

"What was his business?"

He shrugged. "Import and Export I think. Never got to know much about him. Shady character if you ask me."

Martha smiled.

They went back inside. "Have you seen enough?" the landlord asked.

"I think it's a bit small, for our purpose," Ben said. "But I'll definitely bear it in mind. Thank you for showing us around."

The landlord followed them out. "You know where I am if you change your mind," he said.

"Thank you." Ben smiled. He had a satisfied look on his face and a briefcase that bulged more than it had when they arrived.

"Did you find anything?" Martha asked as they walked away.

He grinned. "Enough to know that Victor Landridge is in serious trouble," he said.

Sam's face crumpled when Tilly told him what had happened. "Jock's right," she said. "Victor could have sold the boat several times over, although you'd have to be simple to buy it sight unseen."

"Or naive," Sam said. "Some city gent unaware of the river trade. One thing we do know about Victor is that he has a glib tongue and no scruples. He's cleared out the bank account."

"No!" Tilly gasped, her hand flew to her mouth. She shouldn't have been surprised, but even so. "What will you do?"

Sam shrugged. "We can run two boats, shorter trips, more frequent. The *Maggie May* crew can do evening and night cruises. I don't want to lay men off, if I can help it. They rely on their pay to feed their families. The docking fees are paid to the end of the year. Over the summer months we'll have enough to pay the crews and keep the boats running, but if we have a bad winter..." His face told her more than his words.

"Supposing..."

"I'll go to the River Authority. I doubt Victor would meddle with the registration or licensing documents. You have to present those in person. But I'll check. Have the boats re-registered in my name if I can."

"What about Victor's family?" Tilly asked. "Do you know anything about them?"

Sam shook his head. "He rents a couple of rooms in Rotherhithe. I've been there, they haven't seen him for weeks. As for his family, they live out in the country, I think. I met his wife once, but that's all. I only dealt with Victor. I thought he was my friend."

Chapter Fifteen

When they left the pier, Harry wanted to stay but Tilly feared there could be more trouble if the man returned with reinforcements.

"I'll look out for 'im," Jock said. "Me and the lads'll make sure nowt 'appens to the wee lad."

Reassured, Tilly thanked him and went with Sam, who looked as though he had the weight of the world on his shoulders. They walked in silence for a while, neither wanting to disturb the other's thoughts. The hot August sun had turned the day sultry as they meandered along the riverbank. Several boats were moored, bobbing in the waves, the slurp of the water slapping their bows and the squawk of ducks were the only sounds. Tilly was glad of the shade of the trees they passed.

Eventually Sam stopped and ran his fingers through his hair, dislodging several flakes of grey ash. The grey matched his face, creased with worry. He rubbed his neck, his fingers black from the grime still there. He glanced around. "Can't go to the Registry like this," he said and peeled off his jacket, shirt and shoes dropping them onto the ground. Then he jumped, barefoot, onto the prow of the first boat, danced across the boat next to it and dived into the water. Tilly stood rooted to the spot. It was several seconds before he surfaced, laughing and tossing his head to flick the water out of his hair. He swam with powerful strokes upstream, stopping to spin around a few yards out.

"Come on in, it's lovely," he called to a bemused Tilly.

"You're mad," she called back, but the water did look inviting. She glanced around to make sure there was no one about. She'd dressed for town in her second-best summer suit, but she stripped off the jacket and blouse and stepped out of her skirt and shoes. I must be mad too, she thought as she sprang, in her chemise and petticoats, across the prows of the moored boats and dived in. The cold water shocked her, taking her breath, but it rejuvenated her. She felt like a young girl again, it was years since she'd felt so alive. This is what we did on the boats, she thought, whenever we needed a wash. I guess it's no different now. She swam to where Sam was treading water. He pulled her into his arms.

"This is why I married you," he said, a huge grin on his face. "I don't care if I lose everything, as long as I don't lose you and the family." He pushed some strands of hair that had come loose from the bun on her head off her face. "You mean the world to me." He kissed her and she felt herself going under. She spluttered up laughing.

"You'd better behave then," she said.

He laughed and swam a few yards further on. She swam after him. When he turned, he said, "I suppose we'd better go back."

She sniffed and glanced around. "Race you," she said and sprinted away from him. He quickly caught up with her and they swam downstream together until they saw a gap between the moored boats. Sam climbed out first, then pulled her out.

Tilly's wet petticoats clung to her legs as she walked back to where their discarded clothes lay in a pile on the floor. By the time she climbed back into her skirt the hot afternoon sun had almost dried her petticoats, almost.

Martha and Ben made their way to the house. Excitement bubbled inside Martha at what they had found. As she opened the front door she heard noises coming from the kitchen. Expecting it to be her mother she hurried in. To her surprise and delight she saw Joey making tea. "When did you get here?" she gasped, running into his arms. "We thought you'd been locked up for conduct unbecoming or something."

"Good to see you too," Joey said, laughing. "And good to know at least one person's glad to see me." She gave him a welcoming hug.

He glanced up and saw Ben following her in. "Uncle Ben. I hope this isn't a business call." He put out his hand and Ben shook it.

"Actually, it is, but we can talk about that later. What about you? What have you been up to?"

"Yes, Joey. What's happened?" A shadow scudded across Martha's face.

"I resigned. Left the Navy. I'm a free spirit."

Martha gulped, her hand to her throat. "Oh dear. I'm not sure what Ma and Pa will say about that."

He shrugged. "Not much they can say. I do have a life of my own. Anyway,. I have plans."

A shroud of doubt fell over Martha. Joey's plans were usually wishful thinking in disguise, more fantasy than possibility.

Just then the front door opened and Tilly walked in. Her jaw dropped and her eyes widened when she saw them all standing around the kitchen table. "Joey! Thank God." She rushed over to hug him, her face lit with joy. Martha guessed that wouldn't last long.

"Well, this is quite a day," Tilly said. "One I won't forget in a hurry."

Martha couldn't wait to hear what Joey had to say, and to tell Ma her and Ben's news. She noticed her mother's hair was wet, her skirt appeared damp and her jacket crumpled.

"Why don't you all go through to the drawing room," Tilly said. "I just need to change then I'll bring us some tea. I'm sure we could use it."

In the drawing room the afternoon sun streamed in through the tall windows. Ben opened the French doors and a blast of cool air from the river blew in. Joey stepped out into the garden and stood gazing at the view of the river far below. "It's good to be home," he said. Martha guessed there was more to his return than he'd cared to admit.

Several minutes later Tilly brought in the tray and set it down on the small table in front of the settee. She'd changed into a light blue cotton day dress, decorated with lace and tidied her hair. She looked refreshed. Sam arrived home just as she was pouring the tea. She fetched another cup and a cake Mrs Conway had left for them. Over tea and cake they chatted about Joey's life in the Navy and what he hoped to do next, although Martha was bursting to tell them about her and Ben's morning.

"I've invited Rob over this evening," Joey said. "I hope that's all right. I'll tell you more about our plans then."

Sam nodded. Martha's heart skipped a beat at the thought of Rob coming, but guessed her father had enough on his mind without adding Joey's worries.

After they'd finished the tea and cake Tilly related the tale of the man at the pier and Sam told them about his visit to the bank and the Water Authority Offices. Victor hadn't changed the boats' registrations, and Sam managed to have a note added that they shouldn't be changed without his authority given in person.

Ben got the papers he'd taken from Victor's office out of his briefcase and showed them to Sam. "I must commend Martha," he said. "She did a sterling job distracting the landlord so I could get them."

Martha blushed with pleasure.

Sam sighed as he read them. "It's just as I thought. Victor has made some bad investments and got into debt. Then it appears that he's been at the gaming tables to try to recover. Never a good solution. He owes money all over town. I'm not the only one he's taken advantage of." He managed a wan smile. "At least I've still got two boats and willing crews. I'm better off than some he's swindled."

The atmosphere over dinner was one of resolute optimism. Tilly tried to look on the bright side, for her children's sake, but there was not much to be glad about. Ben stayed for dinner which helped. Katy and George chatted about their plans for the following week, when they'd be on holiday.

"You're lucky to have a holiday," Harry said. "Make the most of it, we don't all get one."

Martha was quiet over dinner but looked somewhat pleased with herself.

Tilly watched Joey more intently than she intended, the meeting with Deborah Staverly played on her mind. Had she approached Joey? Did Sir Montague's legacy feature in his plans? Is that what he needed his friend here to tell them? That he was joining the well-to-do and no longer had any use for them?

"Are you all right, Ma?" Joey asked, when she slammed the salt pot down in front of him when he'd asked her to pass it.

"Sorry," she said. "Things on my mind."

Sam looked at her, concern in his eyes. He reached out and took her hand. "We'll get through this," he said. "Like we always do."

She immediately felt sorry and smiled at him. "Sorry," she mouthed again.

After dinner they retired to the drawing room for coffee. Katy and George went to their rooms to play, Sam and Ben went into the garden to smoke and enjoy the evening sun. The river below was bathed in sunlight, the only sound the occasional hoot of a horn from boats as they moved up and down stream. From a distance it looked a picture of calm tranquillity, although Tilly knew it would be a maelstrom of movement, haste and scurry as the boatmen vied for position trying to meet impossible deadlines. Their livelihoods depended on it.

Joey hadn't said much, his demeanour one of pensive thought. He's a dreamer, Tilly thought. She recalled his father had been a dreamer too, only he dreamed of growing crops and rearing cows in the sunny countryside. Part of her was glad, at least he had plans to make something of himself, but another part feared for him. He'd always be half in and half out of any lifestyle he chose, never quite accepted, always on the outside. She'd lived half her life on the outside and knew how debilitating that could be.

When Rob arrived, Joey welcomed him warmly. His demeanour changed to one of hopeful enthusiasm.

"It's good to see you all," Rob said, as he shook hands with Sam and nodded to Tilly. Sam introduced Ben and Harry. Rob shook their hands. Harry eyed him suspiciously and Tilly wondered what was going through his mind.

"Good to see you looking so well," he said to Martha. "I hope you're fully recovered after the ball."

Martha blushed furiously and smiled. "I'm fine, thank you."

Sam brought out the brandy and poured them each a glass. "Well," he said. "Joey here says you have plans. We're all dying to hear what they are."

Tilly wondered what Sam's expectations were. Had he hoped Joey would now be free to help on the boats?

Rob glanced at Joey. "Go on," Joey said. "You tell them. You're better at it than I am."

Rob swallowed. "Well," he said, "You know we mentioned our interest in building oil-fired engines for boats." He hesitated as though uncertain how to continue.

"Yes."

"Well, since Joey resigned his commission, we've been thinking, and – well – erm – we want to work on that together, only not in the Navy, but designing and building small river craft for commercial and pleasure boating."

His words were met with silence, while they sunk in. It was several minutes before anyone spoke. "You mean put oil-fired engines in small boats?" Sam's voice betrayed his confusion.

"Yes. Small engines, compact, like automobile engines, in boats especially built to make the most of the advantages they offer."

"You see, Pa. They'd be more efficient than coal fired, and, if the boats were made to accommodate them, they'd drive propellers under water instead of the paddles you use now. The Navy is trialling them on large ships, but why can't it be done on a smaller scale for riverboats?"

His excitement and passion warmed Tilly heart, but was it misplaced? She knew nothing about engines, only that they made a lot of smoke and soot, and she wasn't sure Joey did either. It was obvious that Rob was the engineer. What would Joey's role be? "What about your post in the Navy, Rob? Surely now Joey's left..."

"I've resigned, Mrs Crowe. I want to work on developing the engine as soon as possible and the Navy isn't the best at getting things done without a ton of paperwork, everyone having their say and moving at a snail's pace. At least the two of us will be able to work much more efficiently."

"Sounds like a crazy idea," Harry, who'd sat quietly listening, said. "But it'd be something if it worked."

"What does your grandfather say about it?" Sam asked.

Rob grinned. "It took a bit of persuading, but he sees the potential. If we manage it and get in early, the sky's the limit."

Sam, shaking his head, went on to talk about the many difficulties they would face. "Apart from the technical difficulties," he said, "there would be resistance and a lot of tradition to overcome. Men whose jobs depend on the status quo."

Tilly smiled. "I remember when coal boilers replaced horses on the canals," she said. "There was a lot of resistance then too. But they didn't have to be fed and stabled and they could pull heavier loads for longer."

"Hardly the same." Sam looked peeved.

"But think of the advantages," Joey said. "You won't have to haul coal and pay a stoker, plus you'll have an engine that you can turn on and off at will. Less dirt, smoke and soot too."

Sam still shook his head. "Starting a business, you have to be in it for the long haul," he said. "Years, not months, that's if you can even do it. Then there's no guarantee you'll make any profit."

"We know," Joey said. "But it's what we want to do. Please say you're behind us, Pa. You know the river better than anyone. If you don't think we can do it…" Tilly heard the sudden doubt in his voice. Her heart pumped a little faster.

Sam sighed. "It's a brave idea and I'm not against progress, I only hope you know what you're taking on."

"We do," Joey's eyes shone with optimism. "Of course it'll need financing."

Tilly's heart sank. There was no way she and Sam could finance them, but she knew Sir Montague could. His patronage would come with a cost.

The clock on the mantelpiece struck eleven and Rob said he had to leave. "I'm going back with my grandfather to Oldham in the morning, to look for premises we can turn into workshops and to sound out possible suppliers, so we can formulate a business plan to put before investors."

Ben stood to leave too. "I wish you well," he said. "If you need any advice or help with contracts and the like, you know where I am."

"Thanks, Uncle Ben," Joey said. "I'll hold you to that." He showed Rob out.

Once Rob had gone, Tilly walked Ben to the door. "What do you really think?" she asked as they stood on the doorstep.

"I think that lad, Rob, has got a good head on his shoulders. Joey knows about boats and the river. They're young enough and, if they're passionate enough they'll make a go of it. We all have to start somewhere."

Tilly wished she felt as sure as Ben.

Once the visitors had left Martha helped Tilly clear away before going up to bed. "What do you think, Ma? Will Joey be all right?"

Tilly shrugged but managed a smile. "Let's hope so," she said.

Later, Tilly and Sam were getting ready for bed when a loud knocking came from the front door.

"Who could that be at this time of night?" Tilly said, annoyed at the disturbance.

"I'll go," Sam said. "Probably got the wrong address."

He returned a few minutes later holding a buff envelope. "Telegram for Joey," he said. "I'll take it to him."

Tilly, unable to quell her curiosity, followed him to Joey's room.

Joey's face dropped when he opened the envelope. "It's Sir Montague," he said, his voice filled with confusion and concern. "He's dead."

Chapter Sixteen

That night sleep eluded Tilly as memories of the past haunted her. For so many years Sir Montague Thackery had bedevilled her life, or rather his presence in her son's life had. She'd tried to forget the past with all its ghosts. She had a different life now, with Sam. A respectable life, one she was proud of. She hadn't mentioned her visit to Deborah Staverly to him, not wanting to add her worries to his own, now it could all come back. What would Sir Montague's death mean to her, to Joey and most of all to her family?

The next morning, as dawn crept over the rooftops, Joey left to catch the first train to Warwickshire. He'd wanted to go immediately, but Tilly persuaded him to wait. "You'll never get a train this late," she said, so he'd packed a bag ready to leave at first light. When he left, Tilly's heart went with him.

"I'll write as soon as I get there," he said. "And don't worry, Ma. Everything will turn out for the best. You'll see." The smile he forced to his lips didn't reach his eyes. Tilly saw the anguish there. What would his future hold without Sir Montague's support? Only time would tell.

Thoughts buzzed through Martha's brain as she walked to work the next morning. A light drizzle dampened the pavements, the sky overcast with pewter clouds, the sombreness reflecting her mood. Sir Montague's death was a shock. She'd never met him and knew nothing about him, only that he was Joey's sponsor. She wondered how his death would affect Joey's plans. Then there was her father's business. Pa was making the best of it and not one to show his real feelings. He'd be more upset than he showed. Victor's betrayal would have wounded him deeply. She wished she could do more to help. Sadness clouded her heart when she arrived to find Miss Todd waiting for her.

"A word, please, Miss Crowe," she said, showing her into a small side office. Martha's heart sank even further.

"I understand you were sick yesterday." Miss Todd glared at Martha.

"Er. Yes, Miss Todd. I felt unwell."

"Too ill to come to work?"

"Yes. I did tell the doorman."

"Hmm. He gave us your message. Can you explain why, if you were too ill to come to work, you were seen in a ferry, with a man, crossing the river at about midday yesterday?" Her piercing gaze never left Martha's face.

Martha felt hot blood rise up her neck. "Oh." Her mind raced. "He was my uncle. He thought a little fresh air would do me good."

Miss Todd's eyebrows rose. "And was there no fresh air to be had this side of the river?"

"Well – I—"

"You weren't sick at all, were you?"

"I was. One of my father's boats had been set on fire. It was in the paper. I was suffering from shock."

Miss Todd shook her head. "You lied. You told the doorman you were unwell when there was nothing wrong with you. I'm afraid your behaviour leaves me with no option but to think very carefully about your position here."

Martha panicked. Losing her job was the last thing her family needed. "I'm sorry, Miss Todd. I'll make up the time. It won't happen again."

She huffed. "You'll make up the time and lose two days' pay. Be careful, Miss Crowe. Be assured that I won't be so lenient next time."

Martha hung her head. "Thank you," she managed to whisper, although inside she was seething. Two days' pay! It was brutal! Miserable cow.

Back at her desk Martha worked the rest of the day, fuming. It was her own fault, she knew that. She had lied, but she'd had no option, and she didn't regret it. She'd been helping her father, surely that counted for something.

By the time she left she'd almost come to terms with her punishment. Chrissie, one of the other girls, caught up with her as she walked. "I hear you got Toddied," she said. "Pulled a sickie and got caught."

Martha shrugged.

"It was Reggie Rat dobbed you in. Someone ought to shove his post-cart right up his you know what."

Martha chuckled. Reggie worked in the post room and spread more gossip than fleas spread disease. "Mean cow's stopping me two days' pay," Martha said. "At least I still have a job."

"For what it's worth. Look, me and some of the others are going to the Dog & Duck tonight. They have a pianist and a right old sing-song. Why don't you come and cheer yourself up?"

That sounded just what Martha needed. "Great," she said. "What time?"

"About eight?"

"I'll see you there."

Chrissie smiled and waved goodbye. Martha suddenly felt a lot better.

After dinner Martha walked to the Dog & Duck, a pub in the market which was well known for rowdy nights and a lot of good natured revelry. The earlier rain had cleared, although a light chill cooled the air. She'd told Ma she was meeting friends, and Tilly, having been distracted all evening, simply said, 'Have a good time.' instead of making further inquiries.

When she arrived at the pub, she glanced around. It looked busy, with people sitting at tables, the hum of conversation filling the air. She saw Chrissie and Maisie, another girl she knew from work, standing near the bar with three of the senior clerks. They all greeted her with warm handshakes and comments about being glad to see her. A chap called Tony bought the drinks. The men were drinking beer and the girls each had a half of shandy. They found a table near the piano. Tony sat next to her.

"Chrissie says you need cheering up," he said. "Bad day?"

"You could say that."

"Want to talk about it?"

Martha shook her head. Chrissie said something Martha didn't quite catch, but ended with, "That's right, isn't it, Martha?"

"What?"

Everyone laughed and soon the light-hearted conversation stretched around the table. Then the pianist began to play and customers sang along. They had to raise their voices to be heard so the conversation petered out. The men took turns to get the drinks in and before long they were all singing along with the songs.

At about ten o'clock the pianist took a break and the customers were invited to take a turn at the piano.

"Go on, Martha," Chrissie said, egging her on. "You've got a lovely voice. Go and give us a song."

"No." Martha shook her head. She'd been playing the piano since she was five and was now teaching Katy, but she wasn't one to show off.

"Oh, go on," Tony said, his voice insistent. "I'd love to hear you sing."

A feeling of warmth and bravado fell over Martha, probably due to the drinks that kept coming, so she smiled. "All right then." She went and sat at the piano and played a few notes. "What do you want to hear?"

"Daisy, Daisy," someone shouted, so Martha started to play and sing with everyone joining in. After that she played and sung several more music hall favourites and got a round of applause every time. Several customers sent over a drink for her, more than she could possibly drink, so she passed it on to the others.

After half an hour the pianist returned. "Well done, lass. I hope you're not after my job," he said.

Martha laughed. She'd had a thoroughly good evening, all her worries about work had ebbed away.

"If you ever want to come back and play again," the landlord said, "just come along. You'll always be welcome. No pay but drinks all nights and tips."

"Thank you," Martha said, a balloon of warmth blossoming inside her.

Outside they gathered around saying goodnight. "Can I walk you home?" Tony asked, as the others wandered off in the opposite direction to Martha's.

"Thank you, but it's not far. I'll be fine."

"No gentleman would allow a young lady to walk home alone at this time of night," he said, offering his arm.

"Oh. If you insist."

"I do."

Martha took his arm. As they walked he asked her about herself, her family and what she liked to do. He was easy to talk to and Martha found herself telling him about her family, life on the river, her day with Ben, the trouble with her father's business partner and Miss Todd's punishment.

"I'm sorry," he said. "I wish there was something I could do to help."

"What about you?" Martha asked. "What do you like to do?"

He chuckled. "Walk young ladies home."

Martha laughed. "Apart from that?"

He shrugged. They were approaching her front door.

"This is it," she said. "Thank you for walking me home."

"It's a pleasure. Nice place." He glanced around. "Does your boyfriend live around here too?"

"Boyfriend? I don't have a boyfriend."

He grinned. "Just checking. I don't want my nose broken for walking you home."

Martha laughed. "There's no chance of that."

"So there's no one special?"

Thoughts of Rob and Theo came to mind. She pushed them away. "No," she said. "No one special."

"Good, only I'd like to see you again, if I may."

She suddenly warmed to this unassuming young man, with his fresh face, sandy hair and warm hazel eyes. "I'd like that," she said.

He smiled and lifted her hand to his lips. A feeling of recklessness washed over her. He was nice and he'd been kind to her when she needed someone to be kind. She leaned forward and brushed her lips against his. "Thank you," she whispered before opening the door and going in. She watched through a side window as he slowly walked away, a pang of regret in her heart.

It was after midnight when she crept up the stairs to her room, thankful that Ma hadn't waited up for her. She fell asleep as soon as her head hit the pillow and dreamed of playing piano to a noisy, appreciative crowd at the Alhambra Music Hall, with Tony standing in the wings applauding.

Chapter Seventeen

The next morning Martha woke early, none the worse for her late night. She'd enjoyed the previous evening, the singing and the walk home, especially the walk home. The memory of it put a smile on her face. She took extra care when she got dressed and brushed her hair to an ebony shine. She wanted to look her best.

When she went down to breakfast Sam and Harry had already gone, and Katy and George were yet to appear.

"You were late last night," Tilly said. "Did you have a good time?"

"Hmm, yes. Wonderful, thank you." She didn't want to say any more, so finished her breakfast as fast as she could. She made herself a sandwich for lunch as she'd have to work through to make up for taking the day off. She hadn't told Ma about it as she didn't want her to feel bad about her losing pay. She'd have to make up the money from her savings. "Must dash," she said as she put the sandwich in her bag. "Don't want to be late." The truth was she hoped to run into Tony and thank him again for walking her home last night.

She arrived at the office early but there was no sign of Tony, only the other clerks having coffee before they started the day. She worked through lunch so had no opportunity to join the other girls, but Chrissie kept her up to date with the gossip.

"Tony asked after you," Chrissie said when she managed to see Martha alone in the filing room. "I think he's sweet on you."

Martha blushed. "He walked me home, that's all. It was kind of him, but it doesn't mean anything."

"Really?" Chrissie's eyebrows shot up and her eyes widened.

Martha laughed. "Well, perhaps he is a bit, but I like him."

"Good choice," Chrissie said. "He's a senior clerk and tipped for management. You could do worse."

"It's nothing like that. We're just friends, that's all."

"Of course you are," Chrissie said with a grin.

The warm feeling that enveloped Martha lasted all day. She got through more work than any of the other girls, even Miss Todd was impressed. "I hope this is the beginning of a new start, Martha," she said. "A great improvement in your work. Keep it up."

"Yes, Miss Todd." Martha sighed. It was even worth working late if she could see Tony again.

Tilly spent the days after Joey's departure in a swelter of anxiety. Joey's position in the Thackery family bothered her. She didn't want him given hopes of something that could never be. He was her son, the son of a girl from the boats who'd had a brief encounter with a Thackery. Surely that didn't entitle her son to any expectations. She wasn't acquainted with the law surrounding inheritance, never having ever had anything to inherit, but she was certain it didn't entitle Joey to anything, despite what Deborah Staverly had said.

Her heart lifted a little when she got his letter saying he'd be staying until after the funeral and he didn't want her to worry. He'd be home after that.

She guessed it would be a long time before the estate would be sorted out and she was glad about that. The longer it took the better as far as she was concerned. Let Joey get on with his life. Her priority now was to help Sam. Tilly hardly saw him as the days passed. He was busy at the pier, re-arranging the schedules to make the most of the two boats he still had. August was traditionally his busiest time with the harvest holidays and people coming to town to see the sights. A trip on the river was often the highlight of their visit and he did his best to make it memorable. When he returned home each day, he'd spend hours going over the books, the creases on his forehead getting deeper.

"How bad is it?" she asked one day when he looked particularly worried.

"I'll have enough with the daily takings to pay the crews and some of the suppliers," he said. "But it means cutting down all round I'm afraid."

Tilly wanted to help. There'd be fewer outings for the children over the summer and she and Martha would forgo any new clothes. She could increase the number of petticoats and chemises she was able to make for her friend to sell in the market. She could even remodel some of her own clothes and take them to the chap on the second-hand clothing stall together with outfits the children had outgrown.

"These are quality," the man said last time she took some of George's things. "I'll give you a fair price for anymore you bring."

It was only a few shillings, but Tilly always felt better for being able to contribute.

Every day Tilly saw the deep anxiety on Sam's face and worried more and more about him. Every day he'd go to the boatyard to try to salvage what he could from the burnt-out remains of the *Maggie May*. Every day he'd come home with the smell of charred timber clinging to his clothes and ash colouring his face and hair.

"Most of the brass and iron fittings are reuseable," he said, "and I've found other bits and pieces, buried in the embers. If we can't use them, I can sell them." The sorrow on his face wrenched her heart.

Things improved one day when Harry came home, buzzing with excitement. Sam had come home to wash and change before he went out again.

"You'll never believe it, Pa," Harry said, his voice high with glee. "Someone's booked the whole boat for an entire evening. What do you think about that?"

Sam frowned. "The whole boat?"

"Yes. A chap came to the cabin. Wanted to know how much it could cost to hire the boat for a private party. Said it was his client's sister's birthday, and he wanted to, wait for it, push the boat out." Harry guffawed at his own joke. "Jock told him a hundred at least and he took it. Can you believe it, Pa? A hundred pounds for the evening. And he paid upfront." He pulled out a bundle of five pound notes. "In cash," he said, grinning widely.

Tilly did a quick calculation in her head. The most they'd take per trip if the boat was full would be £40, less if it wasn't full. Someone was paying more than double that. She couldn't help but wonder why.

Sam took the notes, staring at them as though he could hardly believe what he was seeing. He counted them out. "Well, done, lad," he said. "Pity there aren't more like him, eh?" He paused. "Who was it by the way? No one we know I don't suppose."

"Oh, he gave me a card." Harry fished in his pocket again and brought out a business card and a piece of folded paper. "Some of the details." He handed Sam the card and paper.

"Frederick H Bolton, Bolton and Barnaby, Agents," Sam read out. He shrugged. "Agents for what, I wonder." He unfolded the paper and stroked his chin. "It says up to one hundred guests. They want a bar, supper and music, extra costs to be paid on the night. Well, we can arrange that."

Harry nodded. "Perhaps that's the way to go, Pa. Hire the boats out at night for private parties."

Sam shook his head. "I doubt many people could afford to pay even half that. Still, it's an idea."

The *Martha May* had been booked for the party the first weekend in September, giving Sam time to prepare. He bought extra lamps for the inside salons and to string along the upper outside deck. All the brass and floors were polished and the windows cleaned. Some of the seats in the main salon were removed to make room for dancing, and a small platform put up for the music ensemble.

A few days before the party, the summer heat still lingered but the nights were beginning to draw in. Soon the weather would mellow into autumn. Tilly was at the pier helping out when the agent from Burton and Barnaby arrived to check the arrangements. He boarded the boat and walked around it, making suggestions and nodding approval to Sam's initiatives.

"We'll be providing the drinks, food for supper and the music," he said. "They'll arrive by four in the afternoon. I trust that's acceptable."

Sam nodded.

Tilly had decided that all the family should be involved. "It'll be fun," she said. "And a riverboat party is an experience you'll never forget."

"I'll pilot the boat myself," Sam said, "with Harry and Jock as crew. We'll be serving supper in the downstairs salon. Perhaps you and Martha can serve?"

Tilly nodded and made a note.

Martha and Katy were happy to pitch in. George shrugged. "What do I have to do?" he asked.

"Just be your adorable self," Tilly said. "You can stand at the gangplank and greet the guests."

"What can I do?" Katy asked.

"How about you take their coats? Pa will empty one of the storerooms to make a cloakroom."

Katy smiled and nodded. "So, I get to see all the guests?"

"Me too," George said.

"You'll all need to help with the loading of the food and everything," Tilly said. "It'll be hard work and on your best behaviour all day, but it will be worth it, especially if they enjoy it."

"Do you really thing we can hire the boats out for parties, Pa? With music and dancing?" Harry asked.

Sam looked at Tilly. "Just like the old days," he said.

Chapter Eighteen

Working through lunch and late every day for a week to make up for her unauthorised day off, Martha hadn't seen the others and Tony had made no attempt to see her or ask her out. Perhaps he's changed his mind, she thought, or even didn't mean it, just being polite. She tried to tell herself she wasn't disappointed, but she was. When Chrissie said they were going to the Dog & Duck again on Wednesday, Martha was happy to join them. She told herself it was for the music and the fun, but her heart knew it wasn't.

When they arrived at the pub Tony kissed her cheek. "Good to see you again," he said. The look in his eyes confirmed his pleasure.

"Wouldn't have missed it for the world," she said. He put his arm around her as they walked into the bar and guided her to a seat next to him. Perhaps he is interested after all, she thought.

Jimmy, one of the other clerks, bought the first round of drinks and they sat chatting about what they'd done at the weekend. Chrissie talked about a show she'd been to see, and Maisie said she'd been dancing. "With my brother and some friends," she added.

Jimmy said he'd had to work in his father's chandlery. "No peace for the wicked," he said.

"What about you, Tony?" Chrissie asked. "What have you been up to?"

"I spent the weekend with my parents. A family thing." He shrugged and glanced at Martha as he said it, as though apologising.

She sipped her drink trying to appear uninterested.

Once the piano player began, they were soon engrossed in the music and songs and the evening sped by. Martha was aware of Tony's presence next to her. A comfortable feeling of belonging warmed her. She urged Chrissie to play the piano in the break and they all joined in with her songs. At closing time Tony offered to walk her home.

He offered his arm, she took it, breathing in the citrus smell of his aftershave lingering in the fading warmth of the day. As they walked beneath the sky dark with stars, they talked about the evening, some of the outstanding things they remembered and had laughed about, the shared experience seemed to bring them closer. They were nearing her home when he said, "I meant what I said about seeing you again." He appeared suddenly serious. "I can get tickets for a show on Saturday, if you like, or we could go dancing if you prefer."

Martha was just about to say how much she'd love that, when she remembered the boat party. She'd be serving drinks on Saturday. "Oh dear," she said. "I'm sorry. I can't see you on Saturday. Perhaps another day?"

Disappointment filled his face. "Oh. Don't worry, as you say, perhaps another time." He glanced around. They were at her front door.

"Thank you for walking me home," she said.

He smiled, leaned over and kissed her cheek. "You're welcome," he said, before turning and walking away.

Martha wanted to grab hold of him and haul him back. "I meant it," she called. "Another day."

He raised his arm, but didn't turn back. Martha's heart sank.

Saturday morning, the day of the boat party, Tilly woke early, thoughts of the day ahead filling her mind. She glanced out of the window afraid that the fine weather they'd enjoyed all week might have come to an end. She saw the sun rising on the horizon and breathed a sigh of relief. "Please God, may it all go well," she whispered. She rose and dressed. They wouldn't need to go to the pier until mid-afternoon at the earliest, but she wanted everything to be ready.

After breakfast she packed a hamper of food for the family and crew. Sam and Harry had gone out early for the morning trips. Then she helped Katy and George practise their roles. Martha nipped out to the market saying she needed some new stockings. Tilly thought it an excuse to be out of the house while everyone was getting so excited and fussing around. She couldn't blame her.

Sam had checked the tides. If they sailed at about eight o'clock, they could catch the last hours of the outgoing tide for their journey down river and turn back to catch the incoming tide for the return. Tilly had made uniform jackets with brass buttons for Sam, Harry and Jock and pinafores for herself, Martha and Katy with a sailor suit for George, all embroidered with the *Crowe's Cruises* motif. The rest of the crew would wear navy jumpers also embroidered with the motif.

"Why can't I have a uniform, like the others?" George protested.

"Because the sailor suit's sweeter," Martha volunteered, which earned her a wrinkled nose face pull from George.

When they arrived at the pier people were disembarking from the *Martha May* having just returned from Gravesend. Tilly was pleased to see the boat had been almost full for the trip, people making the most of the good weather.

"Good trip?" she asked Harry as he helped the last customer ashore.

"Not bad. We made good time." As he spoke a carriage drew up and a man got out. Harry rushed forward. "Mr Bolton, good to see you again. Please come aboard."

Mr Bolton turned and waved to two other men who'd dismounted the coach. "Bring it," he called. The men unloaded several hampers of food which they took aboard the boat. A few minutes later another carriage drew up and three musicians got out, two of them carrying their instruments.

"I take it the piano arrived earlier," Mr Bolton said.

"Yes," Harry replied. "It arrived this morning. It's all set up in the upper salon."

"Good." Mr Bolton tipped his hat to Tilly and went aboard. Harry, Tilly and the rest of the family followed him. Apprehension tingled Tilly's chest as they walked around the boat, Mr Bolton, nodding and touching the tables, glancing around the salons and gazing at the decorations around the upper deck. She was still intrigued as to who his client might be.

Once Mr Bolton was satisfied, Tilly, Martha, Katy and George spent the next two hours setting everything up for the evening party trip. By six o'clock it was ready. "I can't believe it's the same boat," Martha said. "I've never seen it looking go luxurious."

Tilly grinned. She too was amazed at the transformation. Lights glowed and sparkled, decorations glittered all around the salon, tables were set with clothes and flowers that scented the air. Every deck had been polished and every fitting shone.

Thankfully the day was fine and the breeze light. The river rippled, its waters churned by the passing boats. The *Martha May* rocked gently against its moorings. Tilly hoped it would stay that way. The last thing they needed was a storm to blow up and the trip to be cancelled.

She breathed a sigh of relief and hoped the guests would appreciate their hard work. "Do you know who Mr Bolton is working for?" she asked Sam when they were taking a welcome break, enjoying the early evening sunshine with a cup of tea on the top deck.

"Oh yes," Sam said. "I asked who he was and how he'd heard about the boat trips. Apparently, he knows Joey, a college friend, he said. His name's…er…" Sam took out a notebook and glanced at it. "Theodore Delahaye."

The guests began arriving in a procession of carriages at around seven-thirty. Harry guided them up the gangplank onto the boat where Sam greeted them. George showed them to the cloakroom where Katy could take their coats, if they had any. Then he took them to the foot of the steps, at either end of the gangway, that led to the upper salon. Martha and a lad called Arthur, who usually worked on the *Maggie May* but had been pressed into service for the evening, held trays of glasses filled with champagne, one at the top of each set of steps.

Martha watched the guests arrive. She hadn't known what to think when Ma told her that the boat had been hired by Theo Delahaye. Part of her wanted to laugh out loud at the idea of him and his toff friends spending the evening on the river in one of her father's boats. It sounded so ridiculous. But another part cringed at the idea of seeing him again. She hadn't forgotten the last time and wasn't sure how she felt about it.

Theo and his party were the first to arrive. He looked dashing in his uniform, moving with easy charm, grace and confidence. He was accompanied by Ellen, resplendent in a lemon and cream gown, voluminous with lace and frills, followed by her friend Constance Beaumont, also elaborately dressed in silk and lace. Tubs and his cousin Abigail Abbot and another man Martha didn't recognise came next. All the ladies were dressed in extravagant silk gowns, Ellen's full skirted creation being the most ostentatious. Martha stifled a giggle as they attempted to navigate the narrow walkway which ran around the boat and then climb the tapering steps to the upper salon, as the boat rocked. The men fared better.

Theo stopped in front of Martha and took a glass from her tray. "Martha, how delightful to see you again," he said, a glint in in eye. His gaze lingered.

Martha forced a smile. "Welcome aboard, sir," she said, her stomach churning.

He was about to say more but his sister arrived at the top of the stairs, clutching her skirts and complaining loudly at the climb. "I swear I shall never get down again," she gasped dramatically, ignoring Martha and taking a glass of champagne. "You should have warned me, Theo, I'd have worn something more suitable."

Constance merely tutted when she arrived. She glanced at Martha, tight lipped and moved on. Abigail smiled. "Well, that was fun," she said.

Tubs and the man she didn't recognise brought up the rear, Tubs being red in the face and quite out of breath. He grinned sheepishly at Martha, nodded and raised the glass he took before moving on.

The narrowness of the stairs meant that people arrived slowly but the room soon filled with the chatter of guests mingling with the clink of glasses. She recognised some faces from the ball. Of course, she thought, they would be Theo's college friends.

"What a novel idea," Martha heard one guest say. "A party on a boat."

Another complained about the constant movement and wasn't sure how he felt about that. She heard mummers from some of the ladies about the difficulty of getting on the boat, but she was sure that, as soon as they were underway, everything would be fine.

Once they guests were all aboard the gangplank was pulled up and the gate fastened. Harry cast off while Jock started the engine and the boat moved out onto the river.

Sam stepped up onto a small dais in the salon to welcome everyone. "Good evening, ladies and gentlemen," he said. "Welcome aboard. My name is Sam Crowe, I am the Captain of the *Martha May* and will pilot the boat for this evening's trip. It's a fine night and the river should be fairly calm. If you require any assistance or have any questions about the *Martha May*, please don't hesitate to ask a member of the crew. We are at your service. Now I'll hand you over to your host for the evening, Mr Theodore Delahaye." He stepped down and Theo took his place.

"Good evening, everyone," he said, his voice smooth as honey. "First I'd like to thank you all for joining me to celebrate my sister Ellen's birthday." He held out his hand and Ellen stepped up beside him. "I hope you all have a pleasant evening."

The ensemble began to play. Theo stepped onto the small dance floor with Ellen and several people joined them as the boat moved out for its journey along the river.

Martha relaxed and went down to the lower galley to refill her tray of glasses, the music swirling above her. Most of the guests were happy to stay in the upper salon and dance or listen to the music, but some of the more adventurous went up to the upper deck to enjoy the evening sun, the passing scenery and the cool fresh air.

Chapter Nineteen

Martha spent most of her time weaving through the cluster of guests, serving drinks until the band took a break at ten and supper was served in the lower salon. Not many of the ladies ventured downstairs, most sent their partners to fetch the buffet food which Tilly and Martha served. She'd managed to avoid Theo, who spent most of his time chatting or dancing with his guests. Halfway through the supper interval she returned to the upper salon to top-up people's drinks. She arrived just as Theo stepped onto the dais and called the party to order.

"Firstly, I want to thank you all again for making this such an unforgettable evening. Special thanks too to the ladies who have been so charming and elegant. Thank you, ladies." He raised his glass in salute.

Martha froze as his gaze caught hers. Hot blood warmed her cheeks. She bowed her head, her pulse racing. Was the glint in his eye mischief or malevolence? She wasn't sure.

"And, of course," Theo continued, turning his attention to the room at large, "my gratitude to the Captain and crew for accommodating us so splendidly." A muttering of approval, or possibly something else, ran through the room. Martha's blush deepened. "Ellen would like to say a few words too," he said.

He stepped down and Ellen took his place, smiling at him. "Thank you, Theo. I just wanted to thank you all, and Theo especially, for giving me such a lovely surprise. It's certainly a birthday I won't forget in a hurry." Everyone laughed. "And to thank you all for coming, it's wonderful to see so many friends." She raised her glass before stepping down, her gaze briefly meeting

Martha's. There was no doubt about the glint in her eyes. Malevolence, definitely.

Theo jumped up again and raised his glass. "A toast. To my beautiful sister. Many happy returns of the day." Everyone raised their glass and toasted the birthday girl. Martha turned away. The ensemble reassembled and the music and dancing resumed.

Some of the guests drifted off, either to the lower salon or the upper deck. Martha went up to collect glasses. A cool breeze caressed her cheeks, a welcome change from the heat of the crowded salon below, lamps all around cast a warm glow as they swung with the movement of the boat, the light dancing on the deck.

The chugging of the engine and the rhythmic slap of the paddles in the water filled the night air. Martha took a breath and leaned on the railings watching the reflection of the moon and stars sparkling on the water and the light from the lamps shimmering in the wake of the boat.

"Beautiful, isn't it?" The voice came from behind her. She spun round, her heart jolting. "I think you've been avoiding me," Theo said. He stood with his hands casually in his pockets, his smile disarming.

"You flatter yourself," Martha replied cooly. "I've been too busy to even notice you."

Theo laughed, the sound rich and low. "So, what do you think? Me hiring the boat? I wanted to see you again."

A tingle of delight tinged with disbelief ran down Martha's spine. He'd hired the boat so he could see her again. She wasn't going to let him see how impressed she was. "And now you have," she said. "Sorry. I must get on." She took several steps to get away from him, just as a steel-hulled dredger, going in the opposite direction, sailed past. The *Martha May*, caught in its wake, rolled and listed in the turbulence. Glasses and plates tumbled from tables, crashing to the floor, and guests standing on the open deck, caught off-balance, grabbed onto railings with startled cries. Martha staggered as the deck tilted. She gasped and lurched helplessly forward, flung into Theo's arms as the boat pitched and tossed.

"Easy there," he murmured, his voice infuriatingly calm. She was aware of his breath on her cheek, the heat of his body and the clean, crisp smell of him. A wave of warmth washed over her. His grip was firm and comforting. He held her close until the boat righted.

"I'm so sorry," she said, easing herself out of his arms.

"Don't be," he said. "I'm glad to help." He looked a bit too self-satisfied for her liking, but the warmth and humour in his eyes sent a tingle of pleasure down her spine. She had to admit she'd quite enjoyed the experience.

Tilly spent most of her time in the lower salon, serving drinks at the bar that had been set up there, but she couldn't resist going up to look at the man who'd paid to hire the boat and turned her daughter's head with diamonds. Most of the male guests were naval cadets in uniform, with their slicked down hair and shiny faces. They were all so young and eager, with all their lives ahead of them. They reminded her of Joey, also young and foolishly confident. She hoped they fared better in their careers.

When she saw Theo Delahaye she immediately forgave Joey for punching him, assured that he would have deserved it. She wasn't surprised at his good looks, fashionably styled dark hair, immaculate clothing, expertly cut to flatter, or the self-belief that comes with wealth. His bearing was that of a man who needed no one's approval and cared little for anyone's opinion. What did surprise her was the easy charm he could turn on when he chose to. She could see why the ladies were so drawn to him.

Then she watched Theo's sister, Ellen. From Martha's description she'd expected her to be a shy, retiring beauty, why else would Joey be interested? But, far from being the blushing violet she'd expected she saw a girl well practised in the art of seduction, able to flatter and tease the men she spoke to and yet appear naive and vulnerable into the bargain: a skill Tilly had seen many times during her work for Miss Sylvia De Vine. Together they made a formidable team. The rest of the guests showed due deference when speaking to them.

These are Joey's friends and colleagues, she thought. Would Joey have been invited to the party, were he not away due to Sir Montague's demise? She guessed not. In fact, had Joey been around there probably wouldn't have been a party at all. To her mind the whole exercise was a way to humiliate them, to get them serving Theo and his friends, a reminder that they belonged to the lower orders. Joey would never have stood for that, or would he? No. He may have worn the same uniform, but he was never one of them. That's what this party was all about.

Perhaps his resignation was for the best. The part of him that took after her side of the family would never be happy serving their turn among the well-to-do. They'd want and need to be their own people, independent of the favour of others. As she collected the empty glasses she was glad Joey was away. The booking had been a godsend for Sam, she had to admit the money would come in useful. But it wasn't something she'd want to do on a regular basis, not for the sort of people who could afford to pay a hundred pounds to hire the boat for a night. Would she have felt different if they hadn't been Joey's friends? She wasn't sure, but in her experience associations with people who considered themselves superior had never ended well.

When the supper interval was announced Tilly and Martha put out the dishes of cold meat, cheese, salads and savouries, pies, pickles and pastries. There was fresh fruit, cakes and a selection of desserts. Mr Bolton had provided quite a spread and the supper table took the whole length of the salon.

Most of the guests coming for food were men in naval uniform.

After the supper interval the dancing resumed and Tilly and Martha cleared away. There was quite a lot of food left over.

"What are we going to do with that?" Katy asked. "Can we keep it?"

Tilly shuddered at the thought. "No. We'll be handing it back to Mr Bolton, but I might suggest he send it to the nearest workhouse. Shame for it to go to waste."

"I'm hungry," Katy said. "Surely they won't miss a bit of it?"

Tilly sighed. It did seem stupid not to take some for themselves, but on the other hand… "Just a ham sandwich then, nothing else. I don't want to be accused of taking what isn't ours."

Katy and George both dug into the cold meat with pickles and rolls. Tilly sighed again.

"I think it went well," Martha, who was helping clear up, said. "Judging by the amount of drink they managed to put away."

Tilly nodded, "I'm glad we're not paying for it," she said.

"Most of them seemed all right," Martha said, "although there were some who complained about the boat rocking. Imagine that. A boat rocking in the waves."

Tilly chucked. "It was mostly the women complaining, but from my experience that's what they enjoy doing most. They'd be upset if there was nothing to moan about."

It was well after midnight when the boat pulled into the dock. Relief washed over Tilly as it bumped against the quay. Sam had announced their imminent arrival five minutes earlier, thanked them for coming and said he hoped they'd had a pleasant trip. "Should we go up and watch them disembark?" Tilly said. "Show our faces and thank them for coming."

Martha put down the cloth she was holding and together with Katy and George they went up to stand with Harry and some of the crew as they helped the guests onto the gangplank. Some of them stopped to thank them and said what a good time they'd had, while some of the ladies grabbed Harry and insisted he walk them to the shore.

Theo and Ellen were the last to leave. Theo shook hands with all the crew, thanking them. When it came to Martha he paused, lifted her hand to his lips and gazed into her eyes. A smile lit his face as he whispered something Tilly couldn't quite hear before he moved on.

When he stood in front of Tilly, her stomach turned over. This was the man who'd called her a whore, ruined the ball for Martha and possibly her son's life. The intensity in his eyes burned into her.

He bowed his head. "Mrs Crowe," he said, "a pleasure to meet you."

"Likewise." She stared at him. She wasn't going to let him think she even registered who he was. She wouldn't give him the satisfaction of showing her anger.

He nodded and moved on.

Once everyone had left the boat the work of getting it ready for the Sunday day trippers began. Everywhere had to be cleaned, lamps removed, seating put back, galley cleaned and the boat restocked. They worked until dawn, then made their way home just as sunlight crept over the rooftops bathing the city in a golden glow.

Sam looked as pleased as any man could be. "I think it went well," he said, "and I couldn't be prouder of my family. You all did a great job. I must be the luckiest man alive."

Tilly melted into his arms. "No," she said. "I'm the lucky one."

Chapter Twenty

Sunday morning Tilly let the children sleep in. Sam and Harry were up despite the late night as they had to take the boat out again for the day trippers. Tilly cooked them breakfast and, once they'd left, she settled down in her sitting room with a cup of coffee to write some letters she'd been putting off for a while.

Receiving letters and hearing other people's news always lifted her spirits, but replying often became a bit of a chore. She struggled to make her letters as chatty or her life sound as busy and interesting as theirs. Mostly she wrote about the children and how they were growing up so fast. She wouldn't tell them about her worries, especially now with the fire at the boatyard and her worries about Joey's future. She wasn't one to share her concerns or burden her friends with her problems, preferring to deal with them herself. This morning, she had no excuse to put off letter writing any longer.

About eleven o'clock she was in the kitchen getting herself another cup of coffee and thinking about waking the rest of the house, when she heard the front door open and close. Puzzled she hurried to the hall in time to see Joey making his way upstairs.

"Joey, how lovely to see you," she said, then remembered the bereavement he'd been to in Warwickshire. "How are things? How is Lady Thackery?"

Joey stopped and stared at her. "Sorry," he said. "I can't stop. I just came to collect a few things. The funeral's next week." She sensed his reluctance to see her or anyone.

"Surely you can stay long enough for a cup of tea? I was just making one."

"Erm…well, I suppose. A quick one." He smiled but Tilly wasn't sure he meant it.

A swell of anxiety churned her stomach. She didn't know what to think. It was as though she'd missed a step and wasn't sure what it was. Had he hoped to get in and out without seeing her or Sam? The memory of her visit to Deborah Staverly filled her mind. Had she said anything to Joey? Had she told him that he would be heir to a fortune if only his mother would cooperate? She shuddered. No. She was being silly. This was Joey, her son. He was just in a hurry. She took a breath and went back into the kitchen to make the tea. She made the tea and started to pour it when she heard footsteps coming down the stairs. She smiled at the thought of seeing him, even if only for a while, picked up the freshly poured tea and turned to hand it to him when, to her surprise Martha, still in her night clothes, came into the room.

"I saw Joey. Is he home for good?" she asked.

Tilly handed her the tea she'd just poured. "No, he's not staying. Just came to collect a few things."

"Oh." Martha took the tea and sat by the table. "What a shame. I expect he's upset, what with the funeral an' all."

"Ask him yourself," Tilly said as more footsteps pounded down the stairs. She took another cup and saucer from the cupboard and poured Joey some tea. He looked flushed and out of breath when he appeared in the kitchen with his bag which he put on a chair. Tilly handed him the tea, forcing a smile. "How is Lady Thackery?" she asked. "It must be a dreadful time for her."

Joey nodded and took the offered cup and saucer. "She's in deep mourning, as you'd expect." He glanced at

Martha and smiled. "Good to see you're up and about. I understand you had quite a late night last night."

So, he's heard about the party, Tilly thought. Is that what's bothering him? There was certainly something.

"Early morning more like," Martha said. "It was work not pleasure."

"Really? You must tell me all about it." He raised the cup to his lips.

Martha sniffed. "Not much to tell. What about you? How are things in Warwickshire? Has Sir Montague been buried yet?" She glanced over her the rim of her cup as she spoke in what Tilly thought was a somewhat provocative manner.

Joey pressed his lips together until they formed a thin line. "Not yet," he said. "Funeral's next week."

Martha nodded. "Well, if you're going back to the station I'll walk with you. I said I'd meet Chrissie near the market." She put her teacup on the table and stood. "Won't take a minute to get dressed." She smiled at Tilly as she dashed out.

Joey bowed his head as he drank his tea. Tilly got the idea he was trying to avoid any further questioning about Warwickshire. There was no point pressing him. She wasn't even sure she wanted to know anyway. If Mrs Staverly had spoken to him it was something he'd have to decide for himself. "Pa will be sorry to have missed you," she said.

A smile spread across his face and his features relaxed. "I'm sorry I've missed him too," he said. "And Katy and George. How are they?"

"They're well. Glad to be off school, of course. You know what holidays are like."

He nodded and continued drinking his tea. When Martha's steps sounded on the stairs he looked up and swallowed the rest of his tea. "I'll be in touch," he said, putting the cup and saucer on the table and picking up his bag. Tilly saw them to the door.

"Safe journey," she said. "Please give the family my condolences."

He nodded and together with Martha walked away. Tilly watched them until they turned a corner out of sight.

Outside, Martha breathed in the fresh air. She'd hurriedly thrown on a summer dress and picked up a light coat and hat. Now she felt a chill as the sky was grey and overcast, yesterday's sun having given way to banks of cloud. She hadn't eaten either and her stomach rumbled. A sharp breeze blew up from the river, sending the leaves on the trees fluttering to the ground. She pulled her coat closer around her. She'd made up the story about meeting Chrissie because she wanted to speak to Joey. It was the first time since the ball there'd been a chance to see him alone, now she was beginning to regret it. "So," she said. "How are things really? I mean, how are you?"

Joey slowed his pace. "I'm sorry about what happened at the ball," he said. "I ruined your evening. I regret that."

Martha shrugged. "What's done is done. It wasn't your fault, you were drunk and Theo provoked you." She grinned. "In your place I'd probably have done the same."

"That's kind of you to say so, but it was stupid of me. I thought the drink might give me confidence and I wanted to impress Ellen."

"Well, I guess she was impressed," Martha said. "But not how you'd hoped."

He gave a wry smile. "How was she on the boat? Did she enjoy the party?"

Martha hesitated. The question hung in the air. She sensed it was important to him and didn't want to burst his bubble of hope, didn't want to tell him that Ellen spent the whole evening flirting with everything in uniform, including some of the crew. How she acted like a spoiled child determined to do whatever she wanted. How she didn't care about anyone except herself and her puffed up friends. Martha wanted to say: *I don't think she missed you as much as you missed her,* but instead she merely shrugged and said, "How should I know? I was serving drinks, not talking to guests."

"Sorry. I shouldn't have asked."

"How about you in Warwickshire. What is Lady Thackery like?"

"Hmm. She's all right, I suppose. I don't know her that well. I'm not sure what she thinks of me. I often see her staring at me, as though looking for something in me. A family likeness, or something, or perhaps wishing I was someone else. It's creepy. I don't really fit in. I feel like an intruder, although Aunt Deborah assures me Sir Montague would have wanted me there. I know he was fond of me. He wanted me to have a military career. I'm afraid I may have disappointed him."

"Surely not? Wouldn't he be proud you were defending a lady's honour?"

Joey shook his head. "I'm not sure he ever saw Ma as a lady."

"What do you mean?"

"I mean – she is of no consequence to him. It's difficult to express, but it's the Thackery blood that interests him." He sighed. "Aunt Deborah does her best to make me feel at home, but you can see it's all put on for my sake and I wish they wouldn't." He hung his head, put his hands in his pockets and kicked a stone out of his path.

"Will you go back there, you know, after the funeral? Keep in touch?"

He shrugged. "I don't know. Sir Montague was very generous and kind to me, but I'm not sure that applies to the rest of the family. Difficult to judge when Lady Thackery is so deeply distressed. She is, you know. Deeply distressed."

"I suppose that's natural."

"The atmosphere there is oppressive, the whole house draped in black. Rooms that were normally buzzing with life are silent, everyone talking in whispers, lest they disturb the spirit of the dead. I had to get out."

"Why don't you stay with Ma?"

He shrugged again and kicked another stone into the gutter. "I don't know. It didn't feel right."

"What will happen to the estate now, do you know?"

"They have a competent estate manager. He'll keep it running on Lady Thackery's behalf. There's a distant cousin who inherits the title. I'm not sure about the estate after Lady Thackery and Aunt Deborah pass. I suppose he'll get that too."

"Perhaps Sir Montague has left it to you, given he was so fond of you," Martha teased.

Joey laughed. "I'm a summer visitor, like the swallows and have no more right to it than they do. I have no expectations."

"Be nice though, wouldn't it?"

"I don't know. There's a lot of responsibility that goes with it. It's not all dressing up and servants. Anyway, I'm not cut out to be a farmer." He put his hands in his pockets and kicked another stone. He couldn't have looked more uninterested if he'd tried.

"It'd impress Ellen though, wouldn't it?"

Joey grinned. "I would hope she'd want me for myself, not the land and status I could provide."

Some hope, Martha thought. They walked on in silence for a while, then Martha said, "How's Rob? Have you heard from him? Will you still be working on boat engines?"

Joey perked up, and Martha saw a flash of passion in his eyes. "That's the plan. Losing my sponsor won't stop me. I'm not sure if the Thackerys will back me now, but I'm sure someone will. We just need investors. It's an exciting project. It shouldn't be hard to find people interested in it. The rewards will be significant if we succeed."

They came to the turn off for the bus to the station. "This is me," Joey said.

Martha nodded. She wished they could talk for longer. "Take care of yourself and please write. I want to hear all the gory details of the grand funeral."

He half-smiled. "I wish I didn't have to go. I wish I could stay here with you and spend the rest of the summer messing about on the river."

"Except that I have to work and we're not children anymore." Martha's smile warmed her face. "You just take care of yourself and don't forget to write," she said.

He kissed her cheek. "Take care of Ma and Pa. I promise I'll write."

Martha sighed as she watched him go. If he had his heart set on Ellen Delahaye it was bound to be broken.

Chapter Twenty-One

By the end of September the nights were drawing in, the days shortening. The trade on the river was slowing and Tilly knew Sam was worried about their future. There was still no sign of Victor.

A week went by and Tilly heard nothing from Joey. She knew the funeral had taken place. She'd read about it in the newspaper, Sir Montague's obituary took up more than half a page in *The Times*. She'd scanned it for any mention of an heir or the extended family. It mentioned Lady Thackery, Mrs Staverly, and a cousin who inherited the title, but nothing about the estate. She read it so often she knew it by heart.

Where did it leave Joey? She supposed his position would be clearer when the will was read, but it had been more than three days and still she'd heard nothing. She'd expected at least a letter telling her about the funeral. Had Mrs Staverly spoken to Joey as she'd threatened to do? If so, that might explain his long silence. Her head burned with the thoughts whirling through it. She paced the floor. Perhaps Joey needed time and space to come to terms with what he'd learned. She was sure the talk at the funeral would have centred on the inheritance, it always did. Had Deborah Staverly mentioned the possibility of a windfall to Joey? Had she laid out the facts of his birth so he could decide his future? Was that why he was keeping so quiet? She had to find out.

She thought about it for days. The family would be in mourning. Perhaps it was time to pay her respects. Sir Montague had played a big part in her life, although not through her choice, but she felt a connection to the family. In the past their loss had been her loss too.

She shook her head at the memories that assailed her. The past is best left in the past, she thought, but not at the expense of the future. She decided it would be a matter of good manners, under the circumstances, to send a note of condolence to Mrs Staverly. In it she mentioned that she would be in the area visiting a friend the following week and wished to call to pay her respects in person.

The reply came by return of post. Mrs Staverly would be at home on Monday and would be pleased to receive her. She must think I've been swayed by the possibility of future wealth and changed my mind, Tilly thought. She huffed. Well, she could keep her money, all Tilly wanted was her son back.

Monday morning Tilly told Sam she was going to the country to visit an old friend. Sam hardly took any notice, merely kissing her cheek. "Have a good time," he said.

Tilly could see he was still worried about the investigation at the boatyard. He'd told her that the police had been round again asking questions. It was obviously playing on his mind.

She caught the first train to Warwickshire to arrive mid-morning. She'd brought a packed lunch as she didn't want to be beholden to anyone at the house. Walking along the road that had once been so familiar brought a kaleidoscope of memories. Names and faces of people she knew cascaded through her head in a carousel of emotion. The people she'd lived with, some kind and some not so kind, the ones who'd helped and the ones who'd liked nothing better than seeing her in trouble. What would they think of her now? The thought brought a smile to her lips.

She wandered past the canal, the Anchor pub where her father would spend his time and money, she passed the remains of the Imperial Hotel, razed to the ground and never rebuilt. Boats chugged past, the smoke and smell from their engines filling the air. On the opposite bank two laughing children threw bread into the water watching the ducks scurry after it, squawking loudly. They reminded her of when she was a young girl living on the canal. She paused for a moment to stop, reflect and remember the good times when she was young and the sun always shone. She sighed for those long-ago days. It's strange, she thought, you never know what direction your life will take. The scene was one of serene tranquillity, but still her heart hammered. Was she doing the right thing? Would her presence make things worse for Joey?

Mrs Staverly lived in the estate's Dower House. Tilly swallowed when she saw it. She'd forgotten how grand and imposing the buildings were. She took a breath and walked up to the front door. It was opened by a footman in blue and gold livery. Tilly forced a smile. "Mrs Staverly's expecting me," she said.

The footman showed her into the front parlour to wait. The room, decorated in pale green with a high ceiling, struck Tilly as what she would expect from a grand house like this. Heavy brocade curtains hung at the window, an extravagant vase of summer flowers on the highly polished table scented the air. The pictures on the walls were of hunting scenes, fields and landscapes. Probably part of the estate, Tilly guessed.

She didn't have to wait long. The footman returned and showed her into a room overlooking the garden. Mrs Staverly sat at a desk near the window. She rose when

Tilly entered, and showed her to the well-padded, armchairs set in front of a large marble fireplace. "Tea or coffee?" she asked.

"Tea please," Tilly said. It had been a long journey and a cup of tea would be most welcome. The footman nodded and left. Tilly walked over to the window, refusing to be intimidated by this woman who'd caused her so much consternation. "What a lovely view," she said.

"Yes. I like it," Mrs Staverly said. "Please won't you take a seat I'm sure we have much to discuss."

Tilly forced a smile and went to sit on one of the seats by the fire. Coals were laid in the grate but hadn't been lit. "I came to give my condolences," she said. "I'm sorry for your loss. Lady Thackery must be taking it hard."

"Of course," Deborah said. "We all feel the loss, but I'm sure you haven't come all this way to commiserate." The footman came in with the tea on a tray which he placed on a low table in front of Mrs Staverly. She nodded and poured them each a cup, handing one to Tilly.

"No. I wanted to know where Joey stands," Tilly said. "Is he here? I expected to see him."

"No. He's gone to visit a friend. Someone in Oldham, I believe. He said something about a project." She smirked. "A project which I imagine will need some financial backing."

Tilly's heart turned over. Of course. Joey would be expecting Sir Montague, or his family, to support his latest venture. She guessed that support would depend on the result of this conversation. "Sir Montague has been most generous, but I don't expect that generosity to continue, given that I haven't changed my mind following our last conversation. I wanted to make that clear."

Mrs Staverly waved her hand in a dismissive manner. "Oh, don't worry about that. My grandfather's will has been read." She grinned in a self-satisfied way. "It's academic. You see, he's added a clause stipulating that the Executor, Sir Joshua Fanshaw, should pursue inquiries as to the possibility of an heir in his direct bloodline. It's not unusual for Executors to make such inquiries."

"But we both know Joey is in his direct bloodline."

"Yes. Quite. So, you see, Sir Joshua will discover Joseph's birth certificate and produce it – poof – like a rabbit out of a hat. A direct descendant."

"But illegitimate, as you so kindly pointed out."

Deborah Staverly grinned. "Sir Joshua assures us that, with the letter Edmund wrote to you, he will have no trouble persuading the Court that he intended to marry you on his return from South Africa."

Edmund's letter! She'd forgotten about that. She sat stunned, trying to recall the words he'd put on paper all those years ago. She could only recall snatches: *the most wonderful night of my life; I wish we could be together forever; I promise to return*. She supposed, with the right emphasis and interpretation, it could be construed as a wish to marry her. How foolish of Edmund to put his sentiments in writing. "But he wrote that to me! It's mine. You can't use that."

"It's part of his effects."

A cauldron of rage burned inside Tilly. How dare they! But Deborah was right. She'd given the letter to Sir Montague. She'd wanted nothing to do with them, she just wanted to put the whole episode behind her. Now they would be bringing it up again to parade before the Court, to make her past the subject of idle gossip and tittle-tattle all over again. She couldn't do that to Sam. And what about her other children...?

"There will be opposition, of course," Mrs Staverly continued. "Cousin Jasper has already petitioned the Court regarding my grandfather's state of mind. He wants him declared *non compos mentis* and implied that he has been subjected to undue influence." She glanced at Tilly. "Then he'll dispute that Joseph is Edmund's child. Much will be made of your lifestyle and how you made your living. You may have to swear to Joseph's parenthood and explain the circumstances of his conception, but I feel sure we will win in the end."

"And what does Joey...Joseph...think about all this?"

Mrs Staverly shrugged. She glanced at Tilly. "Surely it's not too much to ask for Edmund's child?"

The volcano of rage inside Tilly threatened to explode. "Edmund's child!" she shrieked, anger and disbelief heightening her tone several octaves. "A child no one would have wanted or acknowledged had Edmund lived. We both know he would never have been allowed to marry me."

"Ah yes. That's as maybe, but he didn't live, did he? The child has his blood and my grandfather was most anxious that his bloodline continue through his great-grandson. It would be very remiss of me to thwart his wishes."

Tilly's worse fears were coming true. Ever since that fateful day Joey's parentage was discovered she'd dreaded Sir Montague, with his vast wealth, taking her son from her. He didn't in life, but it seemed that now, in death, he would. She loved Joey with every fibre of her being, but she wasn't going to sacrifice everything she held dear so he could inherit an estate to which he had no legal right.

"It's preposterous. I won't do it. I won't put Sam and my family through what would follow." She jumped up and , gathered her belongings ready to leave. "Joey is my son, and Sam has been a father to him, treating him as one of his own. All the fancy lawyers in the world won't change that. If Joey wants me to betray Sam and all he's done for him, he'll have to ask me himself."

With that she stormed out, her mind in turmoil. She hadn't even touched her tea.

Fury burned inside her as she walked back to the village. She had hoped that Sir Montague's death would be the end of it, but clearly it wasn't. The picture Deborah Staverly painted horrified her. Did Joey know what was in the will?

She found a bench by the canal to sit and think. Still seething she watched the boats going by, not so many now, thanks to the railways, but still families scraping a living taking goods to markets. She sat for a while, eating the sandwiches she'd packed for lunch. Her mind turned the problem over and over in her head. She wasn't going to speak to Joey about it. She'd wait and see what happened. Joey would have to make up his own mind where his loyalties lay. Memories filled her mind. Life on the water was very different from the life she now had on land. She'd been lucky to get away from the poverty and hardship of the canals.

The chugging of the boats and lapping of the water filled the air. A breeze ruffled the trees, sending showers of gold, red and yellow leaves to float gracefully to the ground. Shafts of light shone through branches dappling on the water. The sun warmed her face. The quiet serenity calmed her but did nothing to lessen her resolve. She wouldn't stand in Joey's way if he wanted to pursue the possibility of the inheritance, but she wouldn't be part of it. He'd enjoyed privileges and opportunities denied to her other children. He'd been shown a lifestyle beyond his reach and she wasn't sure that had done him any favours. He'd never belong in their circle. She knew that and guessed he did too.

Sighing, she packed up her bags and rose to walk to the village. She walked along country lanes edged by fields golden in the sun. It was many years since she'd passed this way and when she reached the village she noticed the changes. The cobbler on the corner had gone, replaced by a tobacconist selling sweets and confectionery, the ironmonger and grocery were still there, but the old stable yard had gone. She noticed the tea shop had fresh lace curtains at the window and a sign outside offering tea and fresh strawberries with cream. Smiling, she went in.

She didn't recognise the rosy cheeked woman behind the counter. She greeted Tilly with a wide smile on her chubby cherub face. Curls of blonde hair hung haphazardly from the white linen mop cap on her head while her white baker's overall strained at the buttons to contain her ample figure. "Morning," she said. "What can I get you, me dear?"

"Tea please, and one your delicious looking scones with jam and cream."

The woman nodded. "Up from Luddon, are you?" Tilly must have looked surprised as she added, "We don't get many strangers around 'ere." Tilly smiled. She'd forgotten what it was like living in the country, everyone knowing everyone else's business.

"Yes, just a day trip."

"I 'speck you got business up at the big 'ouse," the woman said. "What with 'im recently gone. Shame that, 'im going." She nodded as she spoke while placing a large metal pot under the flow of boiling water pouring from a large urn. Tilly guessed the whole village had known her business from the moment she arrived.

"Er, yes," she said.

"Well known around 'ere 'e was." The woman turned and smiled at Tilly. "Bit of Devil though. Know what I mean?" She winked as she said it. "All the ladies round 'ere knew 'im…" She stopped suddenly as though realising she may have spoken out of turn. "No offence if 'e were a friend…"

Tilly stifled a chuckle. "No. I didn't know him, not personally."

Relief flooded the woman's face. "Ah, well, as I say, takes all sorts. You take a seat, me dear. I'll bring tea over."

"Thank you." Tilly went and sat at a table by the window. So, Sir Montague was a well known philanderer. Hmm, I wonder what Lady Thackery thinks about that.

Chapter Twenty-Two

Martha had been disappointed not to see Tony the week after the boat party. He wasn't at the Dog & Duck the following week either. She didn't ask about him as she didn't want to appear forward, or even worse, desperate, but he had said he'd like to see her again. She'd liked him too. He'd listened to what she said, even seemed interested and, unlike so many of the other boys she'd been out with, didn't talk about himself all the time.

When he wasn't there again the third week her curiosity got the better of her and she asked one of the other lads if they'd seen him.

"Missing him, are you? I could walk you home if you like," he said.

"No. It's not that. I just wondered why he hadn't come back. He seemed to enjoy the evening."

"He's not been in the office either. May have been temporarily posted to another office, either that or he's gone. Law unto himself is Tony. I'm afraid I don't know much about him. I could ask if you like?"

Martha shrugged. "No. It's all right. I just wondered, that's all." She didn't want to make a big thing of it, but she was curious. Even Chrissie didn't know where he might be, and Chrissie knew everything.

That Wednesday it had been a busy day at the office, with Miss Todd in an even worse mood than usual. Martha was looking forward to the evening at the singsong. She made a point of getting there early as she knew Chrissie was always the first to arrive. To her surprise, when she arrived Tony was waiting outside. Martha tried not to look too pleased to see him.

"Hello, stranger," Chrissie said. "Remembered who your friends are at last?"

Tony grimaced. "Sorry, I've been away. Family stuff. But I'm here now. Come on in. First round's on me."

They went in and minutes later they were all back in the swing of singing along to the music, drinking, chatting and having a good time. At the end of the evening Tony fell into step with Martha as she walked home.

"Sorry," he said. "I've been away. I hope you missed me."

Martha shrugged. She didn't want to appear too keen, but on the other hand she didn't want to discourage him. "I suppose," she said eventually. They walked in silence until Martha said, "I'm sorry I couldn't go out with you before. I had to work on my father's boat." Then she told him about the party, omitting that she knew the man who'd arranged it.

He smiled. "That sounds like fun."

"No. It was work. Hard work too. We didn't finish until the early hours."

"I see. I remember you told me about some problem with your father's business. His partner – Vincent – Victor – something like that?"

"Oh yes," Martha said surprised that he'd remembered. She could hardly recall that evening, only that she'd drunk more than she was used to. "No further forward I'm afraid." She shivered in the chill of the evening and pulled her coat closer around her.

"Well, I wondered, if you're free next weekend, if you'd like to come to a show with me. A group my sister belongs to is mad on Gilbert and Sullivan. They're attempting a performance of the *Pirates of Penzance*. All amateurs, and it's only a small theatre but there's supper afterwards. I can't promise much but you might enjoy the music at least."

A thrill of delight ran through Martha, her spirits lifted. He'd forgiven her for turning him down and was offering to include her in something he'd be attending, probably with his family, if his sister was involved. "I'd love to," she said, a beaming smile on her face and a rush of warmth in her heart.

It had been over a week since Tilly's visit to Warwickshire and she'd heard nothing from Joey. She couldn't help worrying what Mrs Staverly might have said to him. He must have been present at the reading of the will. What did he think of it? Had Deborah Staverly told him he could be a legitimate heir? A swell of relief mixed with trepidation filled her when she received a letter from him. Her hand trembled as she opened it. She scanned the page for any mention of an inheritance. There was none. No mention either of the will or the Thackerys. All he said was that he would be staying with the Mathersons for a few days sorting out a business plan. Tilly didn't know what think.

She sighed and put the letter in her pocket. But it didn't stop her from worrying. She decided to walk down to the pier where Sam's boats were moored. She knew at least one of them would be there getting ready to leave on the next tide. She hoped to see Sam. Seeing him always reassured her. The busyness of the river would put her problems into perspective.

She made some sandwiches to take for Harry and Sam, the activity soothed her mind. The walk to the pier was a pleasant one, she nodded to people she knew as she passed. Although there was a chill in the air, she enjoyed the walk. She was surprised to see Ben when she got there. He was talking to Sam. Both looked deeply dismayed.

Fierce fear gripped her. "Hello, Ben. Is anything wrong?"

Sam nodded. He ran his fingers through his hair. "They've taken Harry in. They say he set the fire. Someone at the yard told the police that Harry was the last one there that night, that he was alone and that he went aboard the *Maggie May*. It's rubbish, I know. They've already made up their minds that he's guilty."

"No!" Tilly's heart crunched. This can't be happening! "Not Harry! They must be mad if they think he'd do anything to one of Sam's boats."

"I know," Ben said. "I'm going to the police station now to see what I can do."

"And I'd like to have a word with Amos at the yard," Sam said. "I can't believe he'd go along with any accusation against Harry."

"I'll come with you," Tilly said, fear twisting her stomach. She was as anxious as Sam to hear what Amos might have to say about her son and his boatyard. Sam nodded. Ben left for the police station and Sam and Tilly walked along to catch a ferry across to the boatyard. "Why would anyone say that about Harry?" Tilly asked, her voice betraying her bewilderment.

Sam sighed. "Well, it seems he did go back to the boat on his own. Jock said he told him he'd left his jacket on board and went to fetch it. Jock waited by the ferry.

The ferryman confirms that Jock waited for Harry, and Harry was wearing a jacket when he turned up, but didn't know where he'd been. I can't believe that's enough evidence to take him in though."

Tilly wasn't so sure. She knew enough about the police to know that just being there would be all the evidence they needed to fit him up for any sort of crime they wanted. "I expect Ben will sort it out." She struggled to keep the doubt out of her voice. She had the distinct feeling that someone was out to cause trouble for Sam and was making the most of the situation to do so.

When they reached the yard the charred remains of the *Maggie May* dominated the scene. The fire had gutted the boat and very little remained. Tilly swallowed. Seeing the timbers blackened and burned, made her heart squeeze. It had been Sam's pride and joy, now it was a burnt-out wreck, fit for nothing but the scrapyard.

"Is Amos about?" Sam asked the foreman as they entered the yard.

The foreman, a surly willow-stick of a man, shrugged. "I s'pose."

"I'd like a word with him."

The foreman nodded and pointed. "In the workshop."

Sam strode toward the workshop with Tilly hurrying behind. She feared for Sam and his temper. She could tell he'd been bottling his anger since they left the pier, she dreaded the explosion that was bound to erupt when he confronted Amos. They found him working on a set of paddles. He looked up.

"What's this about you accusing Harry of setting the fire," Sam said, fists curled, eyes blazing. "You know he'd never do that. The *Maggie May* was my boat, my business, my livelihood. Why'd you do it, Amos?"

Amos stared at Sam, Sam stared at Amos, each man waiting for the other to blink first. Eventually Amos turned away. "'E was 'ere. It was late, there was no one else in the yard. I told the police the truth, that's all."

"Truth? You say my boy's an arsonist and call that the truth? How dare you!" Sam stepped forward; Amos stepped back.

"Wait!" Tilly said. "What time was that?"

"About seven o'clock," Amos said. "I was shutting up for the night. The gates were locked after him. No one else could have got in."

"What time did the fire start?" Tilly knew it was in the middle of the night.

Amos looked shamefaced. "'Bout midnight," he mumbled.

"Midnight!" Tilly almost shouted. "Harry left the yard at seven. How could he start a fire at midnight?"

Amos shook his head and glanced up at the roof of the workshop. He shrugged "Must 'ave set up some sort of delaying device."

Tilly huffed. "Harry is a fifteen-year-old boy. He'd no more know how to set up a delaying device than fly to the moon. You know that, Amos."

"The gates were locked There was no one else 'ere."

"Someone could have broken in. Were the gates locked when the firemen arrived?"

A heavy silence fell over the workshop while Amos thought about it. "I don't know," he said. "You'll have to ask them. Now, if you don't mind, I have work to do."

"Work to do!" Sam said. "Lucky you. That's more than I'll have thanks to the fire."

"Come on," Tilly said, anxious lest Sam should lose his temper. "We're wasting our time here. Anyone could have broken in and set the fire, or it could have been someone at the yard. Someone Amos has upset wanting to get their own back."

Amos perked up at that. He shook his fist, which still held a ten-inch wood chisel. "None of my men would do that. I'll vouch for all of them."

"And I'll vouch for my son," Tilly said. "We both know he didn't do it."

With that she turned to sweep out. Sam glowered at Amos, then turned and followed Tilly. They walked in silence to the ferry to catch the boat back.

When they got back to the pier Tilly saw Harry with Ben. She rushed up and threw her arms around him, hugging him. "Are you all right? What did they say to you? We know you didn't do anything. Oh, I'm so pleased to see you."

"Aw, Ma," Harry said, wriggling free.

Sam slapped him on the back. "Good to see you, son," he said.

A broad grin stretched across Harry's fresh, boyish face. "Good to be back," he said.

"How did it go at the station?" Tilly asked Ben, who'd stood watching them. "What did they say about the fire?"

"Well, I managed to persuade them that young Harry had nothing to do with it, but I got the distinct feeling that someone at that yard's got it in for you. Have you upset anyone recently, Sam?"

"Upset someone? Me?" Sam pouted and shook his head. "Not that I recall. 'Course I've had to pull one of two of the lads up for some stupid mistakes, but I can't think of anyone who'd bear the sort of grudge that'd make 'em set fire to the *Maggie May*." He stroked his chin, deep in thought. "I can't believe Amos would do owt to hurt me. I've known him since we were in short trousers, kids together, growing up by the river. No, I can't believe he's behind it."

"Perhaps it's Victor they've got a grudge against," Tilly said. "Or perhaps it was even Victor who set fire to the boat hoping to claim on the insurance."

Ben and Sam both nodded. "Still no sign of him," Sam said. "He's disappeared like smoke in the wind."

"I've been looking into his finances," Ben said. "Going through some of those papers I took from his office. It seems one of his companies collapsed leaving a number of investors out of pocket, plus he owed money to some very nasty people. Gambling debts. They'd be the sort to set the fire to give him a warning about what might happen if he doesn't pay up. I've passed the papers to the police."

"Good," Tilly said. "Let's hope they have more luck finding him than we've had."

Chapter Twenty-Three

By Saturday evening Martha was in a tither of indecision. She spent the day going through her wardrobe wondering what to wear. Tony had said it was quite informal, but all the same she wanted to look her best. In the end she decided on a mulberry cotton dress with a fitted bodice, puff sleeves and a square neckline edged with lace. Swirls of lace adorned the skirt which fell to a ruffled hem. She swept her black as jet hair up into curls, caught at the back of her head to fall in ringlets to her shoulders. A mulberry satin bow kept them in place. She thought about wearing Theo's diamonds but decided against it. Tony was a colleague from work and she didn't want to look too fancy. She pinned her cameo brooch to the mulberry satin ribbon and tied it around her neck to rest at her throat. Aware that the evening could be chilly, she thought she could take the velvet evening cape her mother had made for the ball. She hoped it wouldn't look too formal. A plain straw hat decorated with mulberry ribbon, feathers and net completed her outfit.

She was just putting the finishing touches to the hat when she heard the doorbell. Glancing out of the window she saw the waiting cab. She took a breath and one last look in the mirror before going downstairs. Tilly had shown Tony into the parlour to wait.

"You look wonderful," Tilly said. "I hope your friend knows how lucky he is."

"Aw, Ma," Martha said. "He's a friend from work, that's all."

"Hmm. So I see." Tilly's eyes twinkled.

Tony beamed when he saw Martha. He said how lovely she looked and offered his arm. Together they went out to the waiting cab. "I hope you don't mind," Tony said as the cab drew away. "I've offered to pick up a couple of friends. We've got plenty of time."

Martha's heart sank a little as she'd hoped to have him all to herself, but she smiled. Perhaps going in a group would be a better idea, she thought. In case it's awful and she hated it.

They stopped to pick up a couple called Ralf and Leticia, who Tony said were old friends. Ralf wore an evening suit, like Tony and Leticia wore a multi-flounced, red and gold dress that Martha guessed had cost a fortune. Tony introduced Martha as a colleague from work. Her heart sank a little more.

When they arrived at the theatre Tony and Ralf got out first. Tony paid the cabbie and went to see about the tickets while Ralf handed Leticia and Martha down from the vehicle. When Tony returned, he handed Martha and Leticia a programme each.

Martha glanced at the glossy, colourful picture of pirates and a three masted clipper on the front. It looked very professional. Tony pointed out his sister's name in the cast list, which read *Celia Fairchild as Mabel*.

"You must be so proud," Martha said.

Tony shrugged and they went in.

From the outside the theatre looked unprepossessing and inside it was, as Tony had said, quite small. There were several boxes and about five hundred seats. They found their places in the middle of the auditorium, not too near the front, but near enough to get a good view. Martha found she was sitting between Ralf and Tony. Tony squeezed her hand. "I hope you enjoy it," he said.

She squeezed his hand back. "I'm sure I will," she whispered, although she wasn't at all sure.

A buzz of muted conversation hovered in the air as the theatre filled, although Martha noticed that many of the seats remained empty. Leticia said something about another opera she'd seen and hoped this one would be as good.

"They're all the same to me," Ralf said, "but I feel one has to support the cast's efforts."

Martha's stomach churned with apprehension, but as soon as the orchestra, a small band of musicians curtained off in front of the stage, started to play her worries fell away. She quickly became engrossed in the music and the story. She thrilled at the swashbuckling enthusiasm of the players and applauded every scene. To Martha's surprise Tony's sister had a wonderful voice. She also played the part with sincerity, bringing a tear to Martha's eye and earning the loudest round of applause. By the interval Martha was totally enthralled.

"Drinks?" Tony asked.

"Rather," Ralf said, so they made their way to the bar. Martha asked for lemonade.

"My usual," Leticia said, which turned out to be a large glass of white wine.

Tony and Ralf joined the queue to order.

"What do you think of it?" Leticia asked as she stood waiting with Martha.

"It's very good, isn't it?" Martha said with enthusiasm. "I love the costumes and the music."

"Hmm," Leticia murmured, sniffing with disdain. "It's a good effort I suppose. Not a patch on a professional performance, but then one wouldn't expect it to be. You must have noticed one or two hitches. Surely you didn't miss them?"

Martha wondered what she meant. As far as she could see it was all going perfectly well.

"I thought Celia was particularly good though, didn't you?" Leticia continued before Martha had a chance to answer. "Her interpretation of Mabel was different, even unique I'd say, wouldn't you?"

Martha didn't know what to say, but luckily Tony and Ralf returned with the drinks before she could reply.

The lemonade was sharp and refreshing and saved her from making any other conversation. Both men commented on the performance, saying they'd enjoyed it, although Martha guessed they were both too well-mannered and polite to say otherwise. She was about to ask Ralf if he was in shipping too, when the bell for the second half went. They finished their drinks and made their way back to their seats.

The second half proved even more enthralling than the first. The players seemed to have gained confidence from the reception of the first half and it was a band of jolly pirates that took over the stage. Again, Martha was carried away with the music and songs. Afterward they went to the supper room where patrons could mingle with the cast over a light buffet supper. Ralf and Leticia went with them to wait for Celia to join them. They had planned to go on to a nightclub after the performance.

"The night is still young," Leticia said. "I want to dance it away."

Ralf tutted, but grinned. "You shall have your wish, my darling," he said. Martha thought it all a bit pretentious but said nothing.

While they waited Tony and Ralf went to the bar for drinks. Martha and Leticia found a table. "How well do you know Tony?" Leticia asked. "I mean, how long have you known him?"

Martha shrugged. "Not long. We both work at the same shipping office. I've seen him a few times, that's all. Why?"

Leticia raised her shoulders showing indifference. "I just wondered." She smiled. "You just don't seem the type he usually goes for, that's all."

Martha frowned. "I'm not sure what you mean," she said. "What type does he usually go for?"

"Oh, nothing, forget I said anything." She glanced around as though wanting to change the subject.

"Have you known him for long, then?" Martha asked.

Leticia turned back to face her. "No, not really. I know Celia better. We were at school together. I've always thought of Tony as being very protective of her. She's lucky to have such a caring brother." She paused. "Do you have brothers or sisters? Ah, here they come."

Ralf and Tony's arrival with the drinks distracted them so Leticia's question was forgotten. It was only asked as a way to distract her from any more questions about Tony, Martha thought. She couldn't help wondering why.

They chatted about the performance until Celia appeared, rushing up to Leticia her eyes shining. "How was it? What did you think? Wasn't it marvellous?"

Leticia's smile was the most genuine Martha had seen all evening. "If you say so, darling." She greeted Celia with a kiss on each cheek. "You still look fresh as a daisy and the dance floor awaits."

Celia kissed her brother and Ralf on their cheeks. "Thank you for coming," she said. She glanced at Martha, then at Tony.

"This is Martha, a friend from work," Tony said.

A broad smile lit Celia's face. She leaned over to brush her cheek against Martha's. "Don't believe everything he tells you," she whispered in Martha's ear. Then they were gone in a flurry of kisses and waves. Tony suddenly looked a little sad and Martha wondered if he wished he was going with them.

"Now, supper," he said. "What can I get you?"

After the dazzling performance the rest of the evening felt a little flat.

Chapter Twenty-Four

Sunday morning Tilly hummed as she made herself a pot of tea. She'd heard from Joey at last and he was coming home. She'd been to the market yesterday, bought apples and asked Mrs Conway to make his favourite apple turnovers. Now, with Sam and Harry gone to work, Katy and George sent off to Sunday school and Martha still not up, she looked forward to a few hours to herself when she could relax and read the paper. She had some letters to write and some sewing to finish but she could do them later.

As she settled down with her tea she opened the paper to the society pages. She always read them first, nothing else being of much interest. Scanning the pages she spotted something that brought her up short.

She read: *A Memorial Service is to be held at The Royal Naval College, Greenwich, in Honour of Sir Montague Thackery, Bart. a long-time Patron of the College*. Then it gave details. At the bottom it read *All friends welcome*. She sat back her mind whirring. So, that was why Joey was coming home.

The more she thought about it the more disturbed she became. It would mean Lady Thackery and Mrs Staverly would be in town. Joey would be expected to attend. The more time he spent with them the more likely it was that Mrs Staverly would influence him and possibly tell him about her plans for him, if she hadn't already done so. Tilly took a breath. She tried to envisage Joey as Lord of the Manor. Would it be so terrible? What was it that made her so against it? Most people would jump at the chance of their offspring being better off with no effort required. She sighed. It was the Thackerys and their like. He'd be pulled into a world that derided him. Oh, they'd be all charm to his face, then have great joy laughing behind his back because of who his mother was. He'd never live it down. Never be accepted. The incident at the ball had shown her that.

Then there was the effect it would have on her other children. They'd never begrudged him the privileges he enjoyed growing up, but the promise of such wealth would set him apart. They all loved Joey as part of the family. They'd feel betrayed, second best, inadequate. How would Sam feel? The hard work and struggle to get where they were would fade into nothing, Joey's expectations would eclipse them. It wasn't envy, but a deep-seated knowledge that money didn't buy happiness. She'd seen the misery that a shallow meaningless life can bring. Joey was better than that. He was her son, part of her family, and she'd be blowed if she'd let them take him away. She sighed. It was about time she spoke to Joey and found out exactly what his plans were.

A little while later she heard Martha coming down. She went into the kitchen to make herself some breakfast. Tilly gathered up her tea things and took them in to join her. She busied herself making a fresh pot of tea before she asked, "How was the show last night?"

Martha brightened. "It was good," she said. "Wonderful music and spectacular costumes. Well worth going."

"And what about Tony?"

Martha shrugged. "I think he enjoyed it too," she said. "Is this the last of the bread, only I wanted toast."

Tilly went to the larder and brought out a fresh loaf. She guessed Martha didn't want to talk about it. She hoped that was a good sign.

Martha cut herself some bread and put it under the grill to toast. "I thought I'd go down to the pier and help Pa on the boats today," she said. "While it's still nice."

Tilly glanced out of the window. The sun was shining and the sky azure blue. "Good idea," she said. "I'll make you up a picnic. You can take Katy and George too. Make the most of the warm weather while it lasts."

Martha nodded and, when she'd finished her tea and toast, helped make up the picnic.

Katy and George were happy to be going with Martha. George took a book of boats he'd borrowed from the library and Katy took her skipping rope.

Tilly wondered what was on Martha's mind when she kissed her goodbye. She was sure there was something bothering her. Probably nothing a walk in the fresh air wouldn't solve, she thought.

Joey arrived just before lunch, walking into the hallway and dropping his bag as his mother rushed to greet him. "Hello, Ma," he said. "It's good to be home."

"Come on in. I was just going to make some lunch. Won't you join me?"

"Yes, please. I haven't eaten since early." He glanced around. "It's very quiet. Where is everybody?"

"They've gone down to the pier to watch the boats." She smiled. "Making the most of the autumn sunshine."

"Good idea. I'd like to go down there later and see Pa. How is he? It must be near the end of the season. Soon be winter. I expect he's worried, what with losing the *Maggie May* and everything."

"I won't say it wasn't a blow, but we'll manage. We always do." Tilly went to the larder and brought out bread, butter, ham and cheese She made them both sandwiches and slices of sultana cake Mrs Conway had baked the day before.

Over lunch Tilly asked him about his work with Rob. Joey spoke enthusiastically about the project. He mentioned Mr Matherson's support several times and Rob's expertise with engines. "I really think we've got something going for us." His eyes shone with excitement. "But we do need more investment."

Tilly thought that a good time to broach the subject of Sir Montague's will. "Have you heard what's in it?" she asked.

Joey shook his head, a look of surprise on his face. "No. Why should I have heard? Nothing to do with me. It'll be for the family. No doubt he's left everything to Lady Thackery, or at least made provision for her to be looked after. That's what most people expect." His brow creased in a frown. "I did hear there's a cousin who could inherit. Why?"

Tilly shrugged. "I just wondered. You are a Thackery after all."

Joey guffawed. "A Thackery? Me? I may have a bit of Thackery blood, but I'm a Crowe. Or at least I hope I am." He looked at Tilly.

A broad smile spread across her face. "Of course you are," she said and suddenly her heart felt lighter. "But you'll be going to the memorial service?" Tilly pointed to the paper still open at that page on the table.

Joey glanced at the paper. He took a breath. "Yes. All this year's passing out cadets will be there. I've had an invitation."

"From the college?"

"From Lady Thackery."

"Oh."

After he'd had his tea Joey got ready to leave to go to the pier. "Why don't you come, Ma? I'm sure Pa would be glad to see you."

Tilly was tempted, but she still had some sewing she wanted to finish and dinner to prepare. "No. You go on. I know he'll be chuffed to see you. Here, I'll make up a flask and some more sandwiches. They'll appreciate that. They don't get enough to eat when they're working."

Once he'd gone Tilly thought more about what he'd said. So, Mrs Staverly hadn't talked to him yet. The devious hussy was trying to go behind Tilly's back, she felt sure of it. She'd never forgiven her for spending Edmund's last night in England in his bed. Turning Joey against her would be her revenge. She wondered if Lady Thackery felt the same. She had invited Joey to the memorial service. Did that mean she saw him as a possible heir? Only one way to find out, she thought. Lady Thackery would be in London for the service. Tilly determined to find a way to go and ask her. Then she'd know for sure, one way or the other.

Monday morning Harry left early to go to the pier. Sam had some paperwork to do so stayed to have breakfast with the family. Tilly had promised to take Katy and George to the Science Museum in South Kensington as a treat before they went back to school. George talked excitedly about the proposed visit.

"They have real engines that work and buttons you can press to make things happen," he said. "Jimmy Tyler told me about it. He went with his ma last week."

"I'd rather see the pictures in the Art collections," Katy said. "We will, won't we, Ma?"

"I'm sure we'll see everything we want to see," Tilly said, grateful that at least her children were enthusiastic about the visit. She hoped the day out would take her mind off things and put her worries into perspective. She was lucky to have such a loving family. She should never forget that.

They'd hardly finished breakfast, Sam was about to go to his office, and Tilly began to clear away the plates when Harry came rushing in carrying a newspaper. "You have to see this," he said, waving it in the air. "Look, Pa, it's Victor."

"Victor? What do you mean, it's Victor?" Sam took the paper and spread it out on the table so everyone could see.

Tilly wasn't sure which bit they should be looking at. "What is it? What does it say?"

"It says that a body's been dragged out of the Thames. It's Victor Landridge." Harry pointed to a headline which read: *Missing businessman's body found*.

Sam gasped and sank into a chair. Everyone gathered round to stare at the newspaper.

"What does it mean, Ma?" A deep frown creased George's face.

"It means, my love, that Pa's partner, Victor Landridge, is dead."

Martha paled. "You don't think he was...?" Her hand flew to her mouth in horror. "I mean he couldn't have been... you know..."

"It'll have been an accident," Sam said, finding his voice at last. "A terrible accident."

The frivolity of the morning evaporated and a dark cloud hung over the room while the enormity of what had happened sank in. Tilly leaned over to read the rest of the article, but the words floated before her eyes, not making any sense. "I think we should all get on with our day as usual," she said. "This is nothing to do with us."

"But the police..." Harry said. "They're bound to come here asking questions."

The words were hardly out of his mouth before Tilly heard someone knocking at the front door. She gulped as, her heart in her mouth, she went to open it. Sure enough two uniformed police officers stood in front of her.

"Can I help you?" she asked

"We've come to see Mr Samuel Crowe," one of them said.

Sam stepped out from behind her. "I'm Sam Crowe. Won't you come in?"

The two men followed him into the breakfast room where the rest of the family were waiting. One of the men shuffled his feet, looking most uncomfortable. "We've to take you to the station, sir," he said. "You have to come with us."

"Am I under arrest?"

The two officers looked at each other. "We was just told to bring you to the station," one of them said.

Sam nodded. "Very well." He turned to Tilly and smiled. "Tell Ben and don't worry. It'll be routine I expect." He glanced at the men. "I'll get my coat."

Tilly watched as they left. She took a breath. As Sam climbed into the police van her heart faltered. This couldn't be happening, she thought. Not again.

Chapter Twenty-Five

Martha stood gazing in shock at the door her pa and the police had just gone out of. She couldn't believe what had just happened.

"It's all right," Harry said. "Pa's right. It'll be routine. They'll want to speak to everyone who knew Victor, all his business partners. Only natural."

Martha picked up the paper. "It says here that the police are asking anyone with any information to come forward. What do you think that means?"

Harry took the paper. "It means they haven't got a clue what they're doing."

Tilly came back into the room.

"Should I go for Uncle Ben?" Martha said, hoping to be included in whatever happened the rest of the day.

"No. Certainly not." Tilly's voice sounded sharper than Martha had ever heard it. "The last thing we need is you losing your job. You'd better get to work, or you'll be late."

"But, Ma..."

"Please, Martha." Tilly turned to the table and collected the plates together, crashing them loudly on top of each other as she did so. The tension in the room stretched tighter than violin strings.

"I think you'd better go," George whispered, his eyes wide with anxiety.

Seeing the fear in his little face Martha immediately felt sorry. She swallowed. "Of course," she said. "I'll be off then."

George's wan smile did nothing to reassure her.

"I'll go for Uncle Ben," Harry said.

Tilly nodded. "Thank you. I'll meet you at the police station."

"What about us?" Katy asked. "What should we do?" Martha could see she wanted to help too.

Tilly took a breath. "You look after George. Special treat when I get back."

George frowned. "I don't need looking after," he said.

Tilly kissed his head. "You look after Katy then. There's a good boy."

"Right then," Martha said and went to get her coat and hat. Tilly followed her out.

"Thank you," she said a look of gratitude on her face. "At least I won't have to worry about you today."

Martha nodded. "I'll find out what I can at work. You never know, they may have more news."

"Good girl." Tilly saw her out.

Outside, Martha paused to breathe in the cool fresh air. To her surprise nothing had changed, the world was still spinning on its axis. The fact that her father had been taken in by the police investigating the death of his partner had changed nothing outside of their family. She let her breath go, then hurried to catch her bus. At least she'd have something to talk about when she got to work.

When Martha arrived at the office everyone was talking about the body found in the early hours of the morning. "He was your father's partner, wasn't he?" Chrissie asked. "The story going around is that he owed some disreputable people a lot of money. What do you think? I mean, they'll never get their money now, will they?" Chrissie looked at Martha as though she actually expected a sensible answer.

"Don't believe everything you hear," Martha said. "I expect it was an accident. Probably drunk and fell in. It happens."

"Oh. You're probably right," Chrissie said, although her tone told Martha she didn't want to believe anything so mundane.

"Come along you two, stop gossiping." Miss Todd's shrill call stopped any further speculation. And so it was for the rest of the morning. Under the gaze of Miss Todd's steely eyes there was no chance of any of the girls even raising their heads or stopping their fingers clacking the keys of their typewriters. It didn't stop Martha thinking about Pa at the police station. Surely they didn't think he had anything to do with Victor's death? She felt so useless sitting here typing stupid manifests. She wished she could be there with Ben working to help him. Were they questioning everyone who knew Victor? She wondered whether Mr Batholomew knew anything more than she did. She'd see what she could find out at lunchtime when they had a break.

At lunchtime she discovered that Mr Bartholomew hadn't turned up for work that morning. She heard some of the senior clerks complaining about his absence. She saw Tony with a group of them. Her heart lifted a little as he came over to her.

"Hello," he said. "I heard that the body in the river was that chap you were talking about, Victor something wasn't it? Any idea what happened to him?"

Martha was taken aback and more than a little upset that Tony hadn't asked how she was and if she enjoyed the opera on Saturday. He appeared more interested in Victor Landridge than her. She wasn't about to tell him that her father was at the police station being questioned. She didn't want to discuss her father's business with him, not now, not with what had happened to Victor. "It was him but I'm afraid I know nothing more than what I've read in the paper," she said.

"What about your father? He must know something?"

"My father? Why would he know anything?"

"Sorry. I thought you said they were partners."

Martha shrugged. "I don't suppose it makes any difference now he's dead," she said. She gave him her most engaging smile. "I enjoyed the show on Saturday. I thought your sister was very good."

"Saturday? Oh, yes, the show. Excellent. Must do it again some time." He looked over to where several other clerks were having lunch. "Better go," he said. "See you sometime."

Martha's heart dropped. What does that mean? See you sometime? She frowned. He did seem preoccupied, so she supposed she ought to forgive him. She sighed. This romance business isn't as easy as it looks, she thought.

The afternoon wasn't any better. Miss Todd's vigorous vigilance ensured that there was no chance of any chatting or exchange of views with Chrissie or any of the other girls. As the day lengthened Martha's worries grew. She couldn't wait to get home and find out what had happened at the station. As soon as the whistle blew, she grabbed her coat and hat and hurried out before anyone could stop and interrogate her.

When she arrived home all the family were there. She rushed into Sam's arms, thrilled to see him. "They let you go. Thank goodness."

Sam laughed. "Of course they let me go. They just wanted to ask me about Victor and what I knew of him. I've given them all the information I can. There's nothing more we can do."

"What about his family?" Martha asked. "It must be dreadful for them?"

Sam nodded. "His wife and her father were at the station." His voice softened. "I said I'd do what I could to help, but unfortunately Victor kept so much of his business to himself. I'm afraid I wasn't much help."

"I'm sure they appreciated your offer," Tilly said.

"Do they think it was an accident?" Martha's voice rose with her anxiety.

"They're looking at all possibilities," Sam said. "Ruling nothing out." He paused, a look of deep distress on his face. "They are looking again at the fire at the yard. Victor had an interest in the *Maggie May*. They're wondering if there's a connection."

"It's possible," Ben said. "I've been looking at the list of investors who lost money when his firm collapsed. A lot of them were locals, Victor's friends. There are some interesting names on there."

"Interesting? Who?" Martha asked.

"Well, your Mr Bartholomew, for one, then the foreman who works at the yard, Lenny Hayes. He lost quite a bit. Look."

Ben passed Martha the list, another name jumped out at her. Mr Augustus Fairchild? The sum next to his name was substantial. Her heart fluttered. "How long ago did the firm collapse?" she asked.

"A couple of months, why?" Ben said.

Martha nodded. No wonder Tony Fairchild was so keen to ask her about her father's business and his partner. Of course, it could be a coincidence, and Augustus Fairchild could have nothing to do with Tony, but… The day she met him at the Dog & Duck and him walking her home replayed in her mind. She'd told him everything about Victor and how they'd been trying to find him. Suddenly the possibility that his interest in her was not as she'd hoped, became clear and her heart fluttered even more.

Chapter Twenty-Six

Victor Landridge's untimely death caused a great deal of work and worry for Sam. Ben came daily to help with the paperwork which, to Tilly, seemed never-ending. A week passed during which they'd heard nothing from the police. Tilly did everything she could to support Sam who worked night and day trying to sort things out. It was a worrying time for all of them, but still the prospect of the memorial service was never far from Tilly's mind. She read in the paper about Lady Thackery's arrival in London with her granddaughter.

The more she thought about it, the more determined she was to see her and speak to her. She'd built up a decent life with Sam and had a family she loved beyond measure. She had to let Lady Thackery know that she wasn't prepared to have her past paraded through the courts in an effort to secure an inheritance for her son at the cost of her and her family's future happiness. She knew the damage that gossipmongers and tittle-tattlers would do. They'd never be able to show their faces again in decent society. She'd be called names and her children ridiculed. She wasn't going to have it.

Then she thought about Edmund. During their brief but intense time together she'd found him to be kind, caring and compassionate. He'd talked of families and values. He wouldn't want her name dragged through the mud any more than she wanted it, no matter what Lady Thackery said. She had to make that clear.

She pictured Lady Thackery in her mind. She recalled her grief at Edmund's death and the look of hate filling her eyes when she realised Tilly's relationship, not only with her son, but also her grandson and the part she'd played in both their lives, if not both their deaths. Did she still feel the same? Would she take pleasure in destroying what life Tilly had built for herself as some sort of vile revenge?

It had been nearly twenty years. Had the years mellowed her? She'd seen Edmund's son grow up, spending time at their home in Warwickshire. Seen the blossoming relationship between him and her husband. Had it softened her sentiments? It had been Sir Montague who wanted to get to know the child and have him as part of their lives. Joey would never take the place of those she'd lost, Tilly knew that, but did his presence go some way to make up for it? Would the bonds of blood be strong enough for her to bury the past and look to the future or did her hate for Tilly override all other passions? There was only one way to find out.

Once everyone was out of the house, Tilly dressed in her best blue suit and picked an impressive, but not flamboyant hat to pin on top of her dark as night curls. She wrote a note, enclosing her cameo brooch to remind Lady Thackery of Edmund's affection for her and the happiness she'd brought to his final hours in England, which, from the note he left, couldn't be denied. Surely that counted for something.

It was mid-morning when she arrived at the house. She took a breath, squared her shoulders and rang the bell. She wasn't sure she be received and cursed herself for not writing first. It was answered by a footman in blue and gold livery. She presented her card and the note. "Please ask Lady Thackery if she will see me," she said. "I wish to give my condolences on her recent loss and speak to her about her great-grandson's future."

The footman showed her into the front parlour where she glanced around, pacing the floor her mind in a whirl. She remembered the last time she'd been here. That hadn't gone well. Suddenly she regretted her impulsive action. She wasn't sure what she was doing there even supposing she did get to see Lady Thackery. She had no idea how she would be received and suddenly began to regret coming.

She was about to make her escape and say she'd changed her mind when the footman returned to say Lady Thackery would see her now. She swallowed and followed the footman up the stairs to the same room in which she'd met with Deborah Staverly. The footman announced her and withdrew.

Lady Thackery sat on the long settee in front of the fire, its flickering flames sending shadows dancing on the hearth. Tilly stood staring at her, not sure what to say. She looked older and more frail than she remembered. She'd only seen her at a distance at the passing out parade. Now close up she saw the pain etched on her face and the damage the years had done. Her once deep chestnut hair had turned to grey as had her complexion, her eyes dull with no spark at all.

Lady Thackery glared at her. Time stood still, the silence stretched to the fill the room. Tilly shuddered. It felt like eternity before Lady Thackery spoke, although it was probably only half a minute or so. "I remember you," she said. "You've got a nerve coming here, I'll give you that."

"I'm sorry for your loss," Tilly said.

Lady Thackery took a deep breath and motioned for her to sit on one of the chairs next to the hearth.

Tilly edged onto a chair and sat, her hands held in front of her. "I didn't know your husband," she admitted, "but he was very generous to my son, Joseph. I'll always be grateful for that."

Lady Thackery's eyebrows rose. She stared into the fire for several seconds. "He wasn't an easy man," she said. "But I loved him, and I miss him every minute of every day."

"Of course. I'm sorry."

She glared at Tilly again, her gaze lingering far longer than was comfortable. "I recall that day, you know. It's etched in marble on my memory. How I hated you. You'd spent his last night in England with Edmund. I couldn't forgive you that." Her eyes narrowed. "You were young, so young." It was as though she was replaying that day over in her mind. "I knew about his women, you know. But it didn't matter. Not then, not now." She stood and walked to the window to stare out as though lost in grief.

"Charles and Edmund." She spun round to face Tilly. "At least you kept it in the family." She turned back to gaze out of the window. "Both of them gone – and all your fault – or so I always thought." She shrugged and walked back to her seat. "What does it matter now? What does anything matter?"

A maid came in with a tray of tea which she set down on the table in front of Lady Thackery, bobbing a curtsy before she backed out of the room. Tilly's note and her brooch lay on the table next to the tea tray. Lady Thackery picked up the silver teapot and poured tea into two Royal Worcester, bone china teacups. "Milk?" she said. The silver milk jug hovered over one of the cups.

"Please."

Lady Thackery let a few drops of milk splash into the tea, put the jug down and handed Tilly one of the teacups balanced on a Royal Worcester saucer. She put her hand on the note with the brooch and silently pushed it towards Tilly. Tilly picked it up. "Thank you," she whispered. Lady Thackery sniffed and sipped her tea. "I've come about Joseph. Your great-grandson," Tilly said.

"Of course you have. Why else would you be here? He's hardly been gone a month and already the vultures are circling." Her voice echoed her contempt.

Tilly pushed her tongue to the roof of her mouth to stop the response that sprang to her mind. She didn't want to upset the old lady. Why would she?

Lady Thackery's face turned to granite, her voice hardened. "I know Deborah has some ridiculous idea about Joseph and the estate. Complete nonsense of course." She glanced at Tilly. "No offence, my dear, but you are hardly the sort of person I would choose to be the mother of the next Baronet." She sniffed and shook her head. "And as for Joseph – well – I know he's Edmund's son, but he too has his faults. I've never been a great admirer of today's passion for exalted notions and decaying morality." She sipped her tea and smirked at Tilly. "I'm sorry, my dear, he's just not up to snuff."

Tilly's motherly heart leapt to Joey's defence. Decaying morality, she thought. Whatever can she mean? "I assure you that Joey..."

Lady Thackery held up her hand to silence Tilly. "Monty was obsessed with the continuity of his bloodline, whereas I have no such obsession. If you harbour any hopes in that direction, I'm afraid you will be sadly disappointed."

Tilly relaxed. So, Lady Thackery wasn't as keen as Deborah Staverly to have Joey inherit the estate. You arrogant, conceited, stuck-up snob, she thought but said, "You've no idea how pleased I am to hear you say that."

A dither of dilemma assailed Tilly on the day of the memorial service. Half of her wanted to go along and see who was there and hear what was said, the other half wished to have nothing to do with it. She wanted the day to be as normal as possible, but of course it couldn't be. Victor Landridge's death and the fact that Joey was home at Lady Thackery's behest, to celebrate his benefactor's life, cast a shadow that hung over the breakfast table. While she was delighted to see her eldest son, the reason for his presence still tarnished her pleasure.

When he came down to breakfast in his morning suit Tilly's pulse raced. His blond hair was smoothed back, his black tie perfectly tied, his shoes polished, gold links gleamed at his cuffs. With his fresh face and long limbed frame he looked every inch the gentleman he'd grown up to be.

"Will I do, Ma?" he said.

Deep pride filled her heart. She brushed her hand over his shoulder as if to remove a spot of dust. "You'll do them proud," she said. Lady Thackery's words ran through her head. Not up to snuff? What a hypocrite. Still, at least she no longer feared Deborah Staverly. She'd have a fight on her hands, and the clause in the will couldn't be ignored, but Tilly felt sure Lady Thackery would prevail. He'll make his own way in the world without their help, she thought, looking at him as he took his seat at the table. Edmund would be proud of him too.

Sam's pride was clear. "Big day today, son. Memorial service, isn't it?" he said.

Joey nodded and gave a wry smile. "All the lads will be there, and their friends and families. It'll be good to see them again."

"Does that mean Theo Delahaye and his sister will be there?" Martha asked, eyes wide with innocence.

"I expect so."

"Hope so you mean," Martha chuckled. "How is Ellen? Have you heard from her since you resigned your commission?"

"None of your business," Joey said. "What about you and whatshisname? Tony, wasn't it?"

Martha coloured. "None of yours." She turned to Tilly. "Is there any more tea in that pot? I'm gasping."

"He seemed a nice lad," Tilly said, hoping to draw the conversation away from Joey and his friends as she poured the tea.

"Good luck. I hope it goes well for you," Sam said. "I know you'll do us proud, son."

"Thanks, Pa." Joey's face lit with affection.

Tilly made a point of asking Martha, Sam and Harry about their plans for the day and talked to Katy and George about how they were getting on now they were back at school until Sam rose to leave.

Harry grabbed the last piece of toast, biting into it as he also rose to leave.

"Let me know if you hear anything about...you know..." Tilly said.

Sam smiled. "I doubt we'll hear owt else." He kissed her goodbye and promised not to be late. "Enjoy your day," he said to Katy and George before he went out with Harry close behind him.

Tilly started to pack up the dishes.

"So, what are you doing today, Ma?" Martha asked. "Not tempted to go and see Joey and his friends at the service? I expect it'll be quite a spectacle."

Tilly was tempted but wasn't going to admit it. "I'm sure I've plenty more things to think about," she said, more sharply than she intended.

Once everyone had gone Tilly thought about the service. Perhaps she should go, just to have a look. She wouldn't go inside of course, but she could pay her respects by going along just to see. The Thackerys had played a huge part in her life before she married Sam. Meeting Captain Thackery had changed the course of her life and Edmund was the father of her first child. Sir Montague had been a presence for as long as she could remember, not in her every day, but a constant reminder, hovering in the background, never quite forgotten. His passing felt like the end of an era. The end of a chapter in her life. A chapter she could put behind her for good. An ending and, hopefully, a new beginning free from the shadow of the past.

She sighed as she brushed her hair to put up under her black hat. Her coat too was black. She wore her best boots and pinned her cameo brooch, the Captain's gift, to her lapel. It felt fitting.

She took a cab to Greenwich and walked to the college drawing breath again at the size and timeless elegance of the multi-columned facade of the Baroque building. A small crowd had gathered to watch the carriages arrive and Tilly joined them. They stood in reverent silence as they passed. She recognised Lady Thackery's coach and caught her breath as she saw Joey, head bowed sitting beside her. She wondered what was going through his mind.

When the last of the coaches had gone through the gate she heard the bell toll for the beginning of the service. She bowed her head. "Rest in Peace, Sir Montague," she whispered. The vision of his face floated through her mind, followed by the faces of his son and grandson. She felt their presence, then they drifted away like morning mist. She suddenly felt free. She'd paid her dues, kept her word to Sir Montague, she owed him nothing more. The past is best left in the past, she thought. She smiled, drew a deep breath into her lungs that expanded her chest, then let it out slowly and walked on into the rest of her life.

Chapter Twenty-Seven

Martha didn't see Tony when she went to work the day after seeing the list of investors in Victor's failed business. She didn't see him for several days, nor did he come to the Dog & Duck on Wednesday. Martha was on the warpath. Every day when she got to work, she looked for him. She needed to know if Augustas Fairchild was any relation, although her heart told her she'd be better off not knowing. For several days she waited for him at lunchtime, until, eventually, she saw him with two of the other senior clerks.

"Hello," she said. "Have you been avoiding me?"

"Er." A look of sheer panic crossed his face. "No. I mean...No, but..."

"Don't tell me you've been too busy."

"Er. Yes. Actually, I've been..."

She took the list she'd copied out of her bag and showed it to him. "Would this be of any interest?" she asked. He glanced at it. His face flushed. He coughed and led her away to a corner for some privacy.

"When did you find out about my father being Victor Landridge's partner?"

"I'm sorry," he said. "I overheard you tell one of the other clerks."

"So, you decided to befriend me to find out what I knew about him?"

"When I got the chance to walk you home, I couldn't resist."

"So, you were just using me?"

"At first. But I like you, Martha, I like you a lot. You must believe me. I didn't mean any harm by it. I'm truly sorry. I hope we can be friends."

"Friends don't lie to each other."

"I never lied."

"You didn't tell me the truth."

"My father lost a lot of money when Landridge's business failed and he was convinced it was a swindle. What could I say? 'Hello, Martha. Please can you tell me everything you know about Victor Landridge because I think he's swindled my father?' For all I knew your father could have been—"

"What? Part of it you mean?" Martha's jaw dropped at the admission. "But he's not. He's lost as much as anyone. He might lose his entire business..." Martha's eyes widened as his words sunk in. "You thought my father was a swindler?"

"He was Victor's partner. You must see—"

Martha's temper flared. She lifted her arm to slap his face.

He grabbed it. "Please don't," he said. "I know I deserve it, but perhaps I can make amends."

Martha calmed but her temper hadn't melted away. "How?"

He smiled. "Have dinner with me and I'll tell you."

"Tell me now."

He gave a sigh of resignation. "Well, my father is very rich. He owns a shipping company. I hear your brother is looking for investment in boat building."

Martha gasped. "How did you know that?"

"It's a very small world, shipping and boat building. Word gets around. Have dinner with me and I may be able to persuade my father to look at your brother's business."

Martha's stomach churned. She bit her lip. Could she trust him, after the way he'd treated her? He said he liked her, and she had liked him, until...then, if he could help Joey... "Purely business," she said.

"As friends. No strings."

"I'll think about it."

All afternoon the conversation played through Martha's brain, along with every other conversation they'd ever had. She could see now how easily she'd given the information away, pleased to have been able to entertain him. Had she been too hard on him? He was only trying to get information for his father, albeit in an underhand way. Wouldn't she do the same if she had a chance? She had offered the information freely to keep him amused. He'd never put any pressure on her. Now Victor was dead it would be up to the police to look into his affairs. There was nothing more she could tell him, so if she did go out with him...

When the whistle went for the end of the day, she grabbed her coat and hat and hurried out. Tony was waiting outside. He smiled. "Well?"

She stared at him, her mind racing. She found herself doubting her feelings. She couldn't get over the fact that, while he hadn't lied, he hadn't told her the truth. Then she thought of Joey, if he could really help. "Perhaps we could go for a drink," she said, "then I'll think about it."

He nodded and held out his arm. She ignored it to show her displeasure and strode off in the direction of the Dog & Duck.

It was early evening when they went in, the pub still empty save a few men sitting at a table playing cribbage. She found a seat near the back while Tony bought the drinks. He brought them over to the table and slid into the seat next to her. A stone of apprehension had settled in her stomach.

"Cheers," he said, lifting his pint of ale.

"Cheers." She lifted her glass of lemonade and sipped it. The drink was cool and refreshing.

"I'm sorry about mistaking your father for a swindler," he said. "I see now how wrong I was."

She took a breath but didn't speak, taking another sip of lemonade.

"You never know who to trust."

That's an understatement, she thought, a smile twitching her lips. She managed to turn it into a smirk. "Tell me about it," she said.

He looked shamefaced. "Okay, I get it. The thing is, you see, my father knew Landridge as they both belonged to the same club." He glanced at Martha. "Mr Bartholomew is a member. That's how I got the job, learning the business. He thought he could trust him and it seems he was wrong. I believe several club members lost money so when I heard that you knew something...I can only apologise. I was wrong to lead you on or let you have any expectations..."

Had she had any expectations? Then she remembered the way she'd kissed him and her face flamed. She shook her head. "Water under the bridge," she said. "What do you know about my brother and his business? How did you find out something like that?"

He shrugged. "Word gets around. I've heard he's looking for finance that's all."

"But you looked into his business, looked into my family and our business."

He exhaled heavily and sat back. "I looked, yes. It's all in your personnel file."

She gasped. He'd taken the trouble to look at her file! She couldn't have been more shocked, if she'd found him riffling through her underwear drawer. The intrusion felt as deep. "How did you...?"

"I told you. Mr Bartholomew is a member of the same club as my father."

"What did you find?"

"Nothing. I found nothing, only confirmation that Landridge had business dealings with your father. That's all."

"And my brother?"

"Heard something in the docks. He's been looking for a small yard. Word gets around."

Martha still wasn't sure she could trust him. She certainly didn't want to depend on him for anything. The revelation of his investigation was devastating. She swallowed a gulp of lemonade and put the glass back on the table.

"Thanks for the drink," she said, and stood up.

He stared at her, a look of shock on his face. "Martha, please..."

"See you sometime," she said as she hurried out. Outside she stopped and took a breath to calm herself. How stupid am I, she thought. Thinking he liked me. She shook her head and walked slowly home.

Chapter Twenty-Eight

The inquest into Victor Landridge's death, overseen by Coroner Livingston Bailey, was held in the back room of The Hope & Anchor public house, there being no suitable public building available. Tilly went with Sam and Ben to the well-attended hearing. Nerves knotted Tilly's stomach as they made their way to their seats in the second row, behind the grieving widow and her brother. Tilly had never met Mrs Lenora Landridge, but Sam had. He leaned forward as they took their seats and put his hand on her shoulder. "I'm sorry for your loss," he said. "If there's anything I can do."

She nodded and touched his hand. "Thank you," she breathed.

"I wonder how many of Victor's investors are here today," Ben said as the room filled.

Tilly wasn't surprised at the interest of the crowd shuffling in. The newspapers had published ongoing details of the investigation, appealing for witnesses, none of whom had come forward. There was much speculation in local pubs and hostelries.

The room itself was bare, the sound of chairs scraping the floorboards as people took their seats, and muffled conversation the only sounds. The only light came through dusty windows set high along the far wall. A long, polished wood table served as the bench and a boxed-in raised platform as the witness box. Several members of the press sat with their notebooks open, pencils poised. Tilly sat entranced; her fists curled as memories of other court hearings ran through her mind. Sam sat silent beside her. She reached across and squeezed his hand. He smiled.

As the clock chimed eleven, Coroner Livingston Bailey entered, accompanied by his clerk, a stenographer and the court reporter, all carrying folders of paper. They took their seats at the bench and the hearing was opened.

The first witness to be sworn in was the boatman who found the body. He couldn't tell the court much, except that it was a particularly busy stretch of the river and he thought the deceased may have fallen from one of the boats. "I was fair mithered when I found 'im," he said. "'E was in a right two an' eight. I thought 'e'd bin two sheets and fallen in, poor soul." He shook his head, his face creased in sadness.

The coroner frowned and glanced at his clerk. "Two sheets?"

The clerk coughed. "Er. Two sheets to the wind, sir. Intoxicated."

"Ah."

Coroner Livingston Bailey thanked him and called the medical examiner to the witness box. Tilly held her breath. This will be the worst part, she thought.

The medical examiner, Doctor Peabody, a florid paunchy man in his fifties, with wiry ginger hair, a full beard, and a surprisingly high-pitched voice, said that the body was that of a dark-haired, well-muscled man, five foot ten inches tall, in his late fifties. It was fully dressed with the exception of boots and had been in the water for several days. "Upon examination," he said, "the body was not much decayed, the cold water acting as a preservative, although discolouration and some disfigurement had occurred. The lungs were full of river water. There were no major injuries. Cuts and bruises were present, as one would expect on a body nibbled by

203

fish and left to the vagaries of the tide over time. His personal effects consisted of two gold rings, one wallet, empty of content, and a card case containing business cards and memberships cards from various gentlemen's clubs." Shock and grief surged through Tilly as she listened to the evidence. It was worse than she'd ever imagined.

"Thank you, Doctor Peabody. Was there any evidence of alcohol consumption prior to his decease?"

There'd hardly be any after, Tilly thought, putting her hand to her mouth.

"No, sir. The stomach contents were too decayed to identify, due to the time since decease, but there was nothing to suggest intoxication."

"Thank you, Doctor. You may step down."

The next witness was Inspector Rolleston, the investigating officer, who had been called to the scene when the body was found. A tall man, his composure spoke of discipline and serious application to his post. He had a thin moustache in a pale face and slicked-back black hair, which made him look younger than he probably was. He gave his evidence in measured tones, occasionally referring to his notebook.

He outlined the actions taken at the scene when the body was recovered and steps to identify it. "The body was identified by the deceased's wife, Mrs Leonora Landridge." At that point the said Leonora Landridge gave a sob and held her handkerchief to her nose. Every head in the room turned towards her. Her brother put his arm around her. The inspector paused, swallowed and continued, "And her brother, Mr Matthew Harcourt. Our investigation found that the deceased was a well-respected gentleman with interest in various businesses, who had, of late, fallen into some financial difficulties. He had in fact amassed a considerable amount of debt..."

Leonora Landridge wailed loudly at that and Tilly shuddered.

The inspector went on to detail the debts they had uncovered, the businesses he was involved in and the clubs he belonged to. The sum owed was unimaginable. Tilly and Sam exchanged horrified glances. His whole life laid out for public scrutiny and derision, she thought. What a grim end.

Inspector Rolleston continued, "There is no suggestion, however, that any of his creditors were in any way involved in his demise. No witnesses have come forward, but Mr Landridge's boots were recovered from a...er...gentleman of the road, commonly known as..." he consulted his notebook, "Mitch the Snitch." He paused to take a sip of water from a glass that had been provided on the ledge of the box. "The gentleman in question was seen wearing the boots which were of good quality and barely worn. He later admitted to having found them, but couldn't recall where, given that he was..." again he consulted his notebook, "well and truly bladdered. We later checked his movements and found that his route home from the hostelry where he spends most afternoons and evenings takes him over London Bridge. We can only surmise that he may have found the boots there. A search of his lodgings revealed a gold watch engraved with the inscription..." he checked his book again, "To Victor with love from your adoring wife, Leonora."

Leonora Landridge gave another loud sob. Tilly's heart went out to her. She hadn't asked for any of this. What on earth was Victor thinking? She saw the anguish on Sam's face and her heart flipped. She tried to imagine the scene – Victor calmly removing his boots and watch as he prepared to end his life. It was beyond comprehension.

"So, what is your hypothesis?" the coroner asked.

"Well, sir. It's pretty clear that the deceased removed his boots and watch before entering the water."

"Is there any evidence of that?"

"No, sir."

"No note?"

"No, sir. I did ask if there was such a thing but, regrettably, the gentleman who found the boots cannot rightly remember."

"And is this gentleman," the coroner looked at his pad on the bench, "Mitch the Snitch, likely to appear today?"

"I regret, sir, that we have been unable to locate him despite rigorous attempts to ascertain his whereabouts."

"Thank you, officer."

Inspector Rolleston stepped down and retook his seat in the audience. Tilly squeezed Sam's hand again trying to reassure him. It wasn't his fault and he had nothing to blame himself for, but she knew he'd feel deep grief at what they'd heard today.

Coroner Livingston Bailey consulted his clerk. A whisper of 'suicide' rippled through the assembled crowd. The coroner banged his gavel, silence fell over the room.

"Firstly, I wish to offer my condolences to the widow, Mrs Leonora Landridge. She is not responsible for the actions of her husband, and in no way to blame for the circumstances in which she finds herself today. One can only imagine what may have gone through the mind of the deceased, a well-respected gentleman fallen on hard times. The pressure of financial hardship is not insignificant. In fact, one wonders how one may act in such circumstances, a man of previous good character, well respected by his peers and a credit to society, fallen into the clutches of unscrupulous dealers. Given the evidence before me today I can do nothing other than declare that Victor Landridge, desperate with despair, took his own life. The verdict of this court is – suicide by drowning." He banged his gavel. "Court is dismissed."

A clamour of commotion greeted the verdict as he rose to leave, followed by the clerk of the court. The press reporters scraped back their chairs as they jumped up, eager to file their copy in their various papers. People huddled around murmuring between themselves. Tilly sat, not sure what to think. Suicide! How would Sam feel about that and what effect would it have on his business?

"Drink?" Ben suggested as they filed out of the inquest.

Sam nodded and Tilly followed them into the bar. She found a table at the back while Ben and Sam went up to buy the drinks. There was a wait to be served as quite a few other people had the same idea. Eventually Sam and Ben brought the drinks over.

They sat for a while in sullen silence, each lost in their own thoughts.

"So, suicide," Ben said, shaking his head. "I never saw Victor as the type to take his own life."

"No," Sam said. "He wasn't. I can't see it myself. Why didn't he talk to me?" Tilly squeezed his hand, his anguish was clear.

"You couldn't have helped," Ben said. "Hearing the amount of debt he was in I don't think anyone could have helped."

"I suppose you're right." Sam nodded but didn't look any happier.

"What will happen now?" Tilly asked.

Ben shrugged. "I'll make arrangements to speak to his solicitors about the partnership agreement, but it's quite clear in the document that, if one of the partners dies the assets are left to the other." He sipped his beer. "I don't think Sam's got anything to worry about."

"Doesn't make me feel any better," Sam said. "I can't believe Victor would do such a thing."

"It's his family I feel sorry for," Tilly said. "It won't be easy for them."

"No," Ben said. "The life insurance won't pay out if it's suicide."

Tilly shuddered. "I don't suppose they'll pay out on the *Maggie May* either."

"I could stop the boats running for a day as a mark of respect," Sam said.

Tilly gasped. "Why would you do that? You can't afford to lose a day's work, Sam."

Sam shrugged. "I just want to do something. He was my friend."

"Not a great friend," Ben said. "He left you in the lurch, same as everyone else. I saw several angry investors in the hall. I doubt they'll be thinking of paying their respects."

Tilly put her hand on Sam's arm. "There was nothing you could do, my love. It was Victor's decision. His family will have to pay for it."

Sam looked more bereft than ever. Tilly sighed. The hurt would strike him to the core. He thought the best of Victor and his faith in him had been shaken. What would he do now?

Chapter Twenty-Nine

After Tony's revelations about his father, Martha avoided him, although that wasn't difficult as he didn't appear in the office for several days. Neither did Mr Bartholomew. The rumourmongers had a field day, speculating on his involvement with Victor Landridge's business, but it blew over in a couple of days.

Martha's heart wasn't broken, she just decided that you couldn't trust men, and she was off them anyway. Who needs the aggravation, she thought, although her heart told her how much she missed him.

A week went by, November mists rolled in over the river. Morning frost iced roofs and windows. A winter chill filled the air. Martha had almost finished her breakfast one morning when Tilly brought the post in.

"There's one for you, Martha," she said, handing her a large cream envelope embossed with a crest she didn't recognise. "There's one for Joey too." She placed a similar envelope on the sideboard awaiting Joey's return. He spent most of him time in Oldham working with Rob in the workshop they'd found for their project, only returning to London when they needed supplies or finance.

"I wonder what it could be?" Martha said, puzzled.

"Only one way to find out," Tilly said.

Martha slit the envelope with a knife and pulled out the gold embossed card. Her jaw dropped when she read it. "It's an invitation."

"Yes?" Tilly's eyebrows raised in expectation.

Martha stared at the card eyes wide with disbelief. "It's from Captain and Mrs Delahaye They request the pleasure of my company for an evening of music and dancing to celebrate the coming of age of their son, Theodore Granville Delahaye." She glanced at Tilly. "They're giving a party for Theo's twenty-first birthday." A whirlpool of mixed emotions swirled inside Martha. She'd vowed never to see Theo again, but the chance of attending what was bound to be one of the most talked-about, lavish and glamorous events of the year was irresistible. She gasped. "Please say I can go, Ma."

Tilly hesitated. She glanced at the sideboard where Joey's invitation lay. "I don't know," she said. "After what happened last time, I'm surprised they've even thought to ask you and Joey."

Martha shrugged. "Theo apologised and Joey doesn't seem that bothered about it. He told me he saw Theo at the memorial service, and after the service he went to dinner at Theo's club with some of the other officer cadets. It seems they are all friends again. I know he'll go if he thinks Ellen Delahaye will be there."

"Another reason why neither of you should go. I could write and make your excuses."

"No, Ma. Please." Martha put on her 'I'll never forgive you if you don't let me go' face.

Tilly sighed. "I'll think about it."

Martha smiled again, although Ma's *I'll think about it* often meant she'd find a reason for Martha not to do whatever Martha wanted to do. "Thanks, Ma." She jumped up and kissed her cheek, grabbing Joey's invitation from the sideboard. "I have Joey's address," she said. "I'll send this on to him, shall I?" She rushed out of the door before Tilly could reply.

Upstairs in her room she put her writing case into her bag. Joey wouldn't want to miss the opportunity to spend an evening in the presence of Ellen Delahaye, she was sure. She could write him a note when she got to the office and have it in the post by lunchtime. Suddenly the future looked brighter. I'll wear the diamonds Theo gave me, she thought. That'll show them.

Tilly sat for some time over breakfast. The whole world seemed to have gone mad. First Victor kills himself, then Theo Delahaye, the man who called her a whore, invites her son and daughter to his twenty-first birthday party. She'd been shocked when Martha said it was from Theo's parents. What on earth could they want with Martha? Then she thought about it. Obviously Theo enjoys humiliating people, she thought. The fracas at the ball, the hiring of the boat so they could wait on him and his friends, now it seems he'd invited Joey to dine at his club. Was that a further attempt at humiliation? She decided she didn't like or trust Theo Delahaye, even though she'd only seen him at the boat party and had never actually met him.

She had grave doubts about the invitation, but Joey was nearly twenty-one, an adult who could make his own decisions. Martha on the other hand was too impressionable for Tilly's liking. She knew how easy it was to get carried away with the glamour and excitement of situations you're not used to. Then there was the fallout afterwards, the return to reality.

She shook her head and sighed. Was she being too hard on Martha? Didn't she deserve a little fun, a chance to see how the other half lived? Anyway, there wasn't much she could do to stop her headstrong daughter doing something, once she set her heart on it. She could talk to Sam. If Sam said no, Martha wouldn't go. She'd never disobey her father. But would Sam say no? He wouldn't see the harm in it. He always indulged her. Anyway, Sam had greater problems on his mind.

Tilly picked up the paper. She'd read the full details of the inquest, Victor's life laid out for everyone to see. All his misdemeanours, a full account of his business that had collapsed leaving investors thousands of pounds out of pocket. Sam's business, *Crowe's Cruises* was mentioned. How would that effect his trade? Suppliers were already asking for cash before they'd supply any goods, and he was having a hard time paying the crew.

She put the paper down and gathered up the breakfast plates to take out to Mrs Conway in the kitchen. Mrs Conway was putting the finishing touches to a casserole she'd prepared for their evening meal. A pie sat on the side ready for the oven.

"I'm nearly done, Mrs Crowe," Mrs Conway said. "This just needs two hours in a slow oven. The pie is apple. Put it in half-hour before casserole's finished. Vegetables done too." She glanced at her handiwork. "Should be enough for the whole family," she said.

"Thank you, Mrs C. I'm very grateful."

Mrs Conway nodded, took off her apron and grabbed her coat and hat. "See you tomorrow," she said as she went out.

Tilly closed the door behind her. I wonder how long we'll be able to afford to keep her, she thought. Surely things hadn't got that bad. She washed the dishes and remembered the letter for Sam which also arrived that morning. She didn't recognise the hand. Perhaps she'd take it to him at the pier, along with some sandwiches and a flask. Talking to Sam always made her feel better.

She made sandwiches and tea and put them in her basket, along with the letter. As she walked along by the river her mind returned to Martha's invitation. Victor's death had brought home to her how fleeting life could be. Shouldn't they all make the most of what's on offer? She sighed again. Despite her reservations she wouldn't stop Martha going to the party, she'd just be here for her when it all turned to ashes.

When she got to the pier, she was alarmed to see Sam painting a *For Sale* sign. The *Matilda May* was berthed alongside the pier but there were no passengers or crew around.

"What are you doing?" she said. "Where is everybody?" She glanced at the sign. "Oh, Sam, surely it hasn't come to that?"

Sam sighed. "I have to think about it. There isn't the trade to support two boats over the winter, and I can't afford to berth her past the end of the year. I can barely afford next year's berthing fees for one boat let alone two."

"I hadn't realised it had got that bad."

Sam shrugged. "I didn't want to worry you." He smiled his magical smile that always sent Tilly's heart aflutter. "We've managed with one boat before, Till. We can do it again. I can still work a full day, and, with Harry's help, we can keep going until next season." He threw the wooden sign onto the table in the cabin they used as a booking office.

"What about the men?"

"I'll keep as many as I can, but I'm not running a charity. They know that." He turned and put his hands on Tilly's arms, holding her. "We'll be alright, Till. I promise. I'd never let you down, you know that."

"I know." Bloody Victor, she thought. This is all his fault. "Oh. I've brought you some sandwiches and a flask." She held them out.

"Thank you." He leaned towards her and kissed her cheek.

"Oh, and there was a letter." She handed it to him.

He put the flask and sandwiches on the table and opened the letter. "It's from Leonora Landridge." He frowned as he read it. "She's staying with her father in town and wants us to call on her tomorrow morning." He glanced at Tilly, puzzlement and doubt in his deep brown eyes. "She thanks you for your kindness."

"Kindness? I sent a note of condolence when I heard of Victor's death, that's all. Anyone would have done the same."

"I don't suppose many others did," Sam said. He frowned. "It's a morning meeting. That usually means business, not social. What do you think?"

"I think if she's expecting to get any money out of you, she's going to be sadly disappointed."

Sam laughed.

Chapter Thirty

The next morning Tilly dressed in her most sombre outfit. She was visiting a recent widow. Sam too dressed in his best suit with a black tie. With his dark hair slicked back, Tilly thought him as handsome as the day she married him. The day too was sombre with light rain and mist. A chill blew up from the river and Tilly was glad of her thick coat. They took a cab to the address in Bloomsbury. The five-storey townhouse was in a fashionable square with Georgian facade set back behind iron railings. Three stone steps led to a porticoed entrance. A livered footman opened the door. Sam presented his card and said they were there to see Mrs Landridge. The footman showed them into the morning room, where Leonora, her father and brother were waiting, with another man. A fire blazed in the ornate marble fireplace around which they were seated. Leonora sat on a long settee on one side of the fire, while the men occupied two armchairs in front of it. Another settee stood on the other side of the fireplace. Heavy brocade curtains, in a shade of deep plum, gave the room a cosy feel. A large aspidistra sat in a pot on a table by the window.

Leonora rose to greet them, "I'm so glad you came," she said. "May I offer you some refreshment? Tea or coffee?"

Sam chose coffee, Tilly tea. The footman nodded and backed out.

"This is my father, Earnest Harcourt and you know my brother, Matthew."

Tilly remembered Matthew from the inquest. Sam shook their hands, and Tilly nodded to each of them as Leonora showed her to a seat by the fire.

"Oh, that gentleman there is father's legal representative, Mr Lowestoft."

Sam nodded as Mr Lowestoft took a seat behind Earnest Harcourt. Tilly wondered why they'd need a legal representative.

Sam expressed his condolences again and Leonora thanked him. Tilly studied her. Ash blonde curls framed her delicate, fine featured, pale as parchment face. Dark shadows bruised her limpid blue eyes, red rimmed from crying. She appeared to Tilly to be quite fragile, not at all like her handsome, broad shouldered brother. 'Genteel' was the word that came to mind. Tilly guessed she'd been indulged, the only daughter of a proud man. This must be so hard for her, she thought.

Leonora said something about the inclement weather and asked about their journey to make small talk until the tea and coffee arrived. She poured, then handed everyone a cup of tea or coffee. Once the footman had left, the atmosphere shifted as they got down to business.

Earnest Harcourt, a mutton-whiskered, butterball of a man, almost popping out of his yellow waistcoat, began. "I expect you're wondering why we asked you here," he said.

"Indeed, I am," Sam replied.

"I have a proposition for you," Earnest said. "I know about Victor's involvement in your business, and that he stole from you as well as everyone else."

"Oh, Papa." Leonora's distress was clear in her voice.

"I mean to be blunt," Earnest said. "No point shilly-shallying around. I'm sure Mr Crowe hasn't come here for fine words. Ay, Mr Crowe?"

"Sam," Sam said, putting his coffee on the table in front of him. "If you've a proposition, I'd like to hear it."

Earnest nodded. "I'm willing to replace all Victor stole from you. I've looked into your books." Sam glanced up in shock. Earnest had the grace to look a little uncomfortable. "Well, what Victor had of them, and it seems to me that you had a thriving business before he...er..." He coughed and glanced at Leonora as though aware of her fragility.

She smiled briefly. "Go on, Papa, it's all right."

He nodded. "I'd like to take over the partnership. I'm willing to put money in to set you up again, on the same terms as Victor. But there's something you have to do for us in return."

Tilly's suspicions were immediately raised. "Why would you do that, Mr Harcourt?"

"Please call me Earnest. Because I'm a businessman and recognise a good business opportunity when I see it. Besides, Victor did you wrong and I know Leonora feels responsible for that."

"She's not responsible for the actions of her husband," Tilly said. "The coroner said so."

"Ah yes. The coroner. That's where we come into what you can do for us. If you're willing."

"Which is?" Sam said.

Earnest Harcourt took a breath. He stood and paced the room before returning to say, "As you know the verdict of the coroner's court was suicide." He sniffed in disdain and his whole body shuddered. "Apparently we have no grounds to appeal the verdict, in which case the

Church of England refuses to allow my son-in-law a Christian burial."

Tilly gasped in shock. That was too cruel. As if losing her husband wasn't enough.

Leonora leaned forward. "They won't allow us to bury him in sacred ground," she said. Tears welled up in her eyes. "I don't want him put into the ground with no ceremony, no headstone and nothing to mark his passing, like a common criminal. I couldn't bear it, not for me, nor for my children. It would be too awful."

Tilly's heart went out to her. She could imagine her distress. Even the worst villains she knew had a Christian burial.

"So, what can I do about it?" Sam said.

"You have a boat," Mr Harcourt said. "There is a vicar in town who has agreed to perform a blessing if Victor is buried at sea."

Sam looked horrified. "Is that legal?"

"It's quite in order," Mr Lowestoft said. "There's nothing sacred about the sea."

Sam looked at Tilly. "What do you think?"

Tilly shrugged. "You run trips to the coast. I can't see that going out a bit further is any different."

"I want him to have a respectful ending," Leonora said. "He wasn't always a scoundrel. He was a good husband and father. He got into bad company. You know that, Sam."

Sam nodded. "I know. I've known him a long time. We were friends." He paused in thought, then took a breath. He smiled and his eyes lit with warmth. "If I can give him a decent end, I will. Yes, Mr Harcourt. I'll take Victor's body out to be buried at sea. It's the least I can do."

Earnest Harcourt rushed over to shake Sam's hand. "Good man. Leonora said we could depend on you."

Sam stood to shake his hand. Matthew also shook Sam's hand. Leonora jumped up and planted a kiss on his cheek. "Thank you," she whispered, her voice husky with emotion. Tilly had never felt so proud of him as she did at that moment.

"I'll have the partnership papers drawn up immediately," Earnest said. "Leave your bank details with Mr Lowestoft and the money will be in your account by end of day. I think that calls for a drink. What's your preference?" He went to the sideboard where several decanters and glasses were set out.

"Whisky, please," Sam said.

"And for the lady?"

"Thank you, I'll have a sherry if you have one."

He brought the drinks over and they lifted their glasses and toasted the new partnership. A sliver of hope blossomed in Tilly's chest. "Long may it last," Earnest said.

When Martha got home from work, she was surprised to see Pa, Harry and Jock in the drawing room with Ben, who was going over some papers. Ma was fussing over a cake she'd obviously bought from the bakery. A bottle of champagne stood in an ice bucket on the table and another tipped upside down in the bin. They all had glasses, some half-full. Even Katy and George were giggling away over half-drunk glasses of champagne.

"What's going on?" she asked. "Some sort of celebration?"

Sam beamed. "We're celebrating new beginnings," he said. "A new partnership with Victor Landridge's father-in-law. *Crowe's Cruises* is back in business." He looked so happy a swell of love filled Martha's heart.

"That's wonderful," she said, suddenly realising how strained the atmosphere had been over the last few weeks, now the tension had melted away.

"Here, have a glass." Sam rose, poured some champagne into a fresh glass and handed it to her.

"Here's to new beginnings," she said.

For the next hour they talked about how the partnership would work and Sam's plans to keep both boats running through the winter.

"It's a generous offer," Ben said. "It seems he's happy to be a silent partner, with little oversight. It's a good deal."

"Good, considering the way Victor let everybody them down," Tilly said. "Leonora especially."

"I think it was more Leonora's idea than her father's," Sam admitted. "She felt guilty for what he'd done to people and wanted to make amends."

"Nice to know she has a conscience," Martha said, sipping the champagne.

"Plus, she wanted a favour and can twist her father round her little finger, like most daughters," Tilly said, so quietly Martha hardly heard her.

Sam grinned. "When did you become so cynical?" His eyes shone with deep affection.

Tilly laughed. "One of us has to be."

"So, what was the favour?"

"She wants her husband buried at sea," Sam said. "Wants to avoid the disgrace of a burial outside of consecrated ground, for the sake of their children. I can't say I blame her."

Martha listened while they spoke about the arrangements for Victor's funeral. "I couldn't do it without Jock," Sam said, pouring him another glass. "He's had more experience of the North Sea than I have."

Jock nodded. "Always good to be useful," he joked.

"No. Seriously, Jock. I couldn't run the business without you either, so how about I make you my Chief Operating Officer? There'd be pay rise of course."

They all raised their glasses again to Jock's promotion.

"What about me?" Harry asked. "Do I get a pay rise too?" He chuckled as he said it.

"You, my son, can be chief dogsbody and bottle washer." Sam words were slightly slurred as he'd had several whiskies before starting on the champagne. Tilly invited them all to stay for dinner and Martha guessed they were in for a long night of celebrating.

Over dinner they were all in high spirits chatting about the future. Joey's name came up. "Have you heard from him?" Tilly asked Martha, pointedly. "Only he never mentioned the party in his last letter to me."

"Party? What party?" Sam glanced at Martha.

"Joey and I have been invited to a party to celebrate Theo Delahaye's birthday," she said. "Joey says most of the officer cadets are going. Rob Matherson will be there too. Please say I can go, Pa."

Sam smiled. "I don't see why not, if Joey's going, and Rob. I liked the lad." He turned to Jock. "Rob Matherson is working with Joey putting oil engines in riverboats. What do you think of that?"

Jock pouted. He too had had several drinks before dinner. "It'll never catch on," he said. They both laughed.

"Joey writes very enthusiastically about it," Martha said, sticking up for her brother. "He says they almost have a prototype."

"A prototype, eh? Well good luck to them." Sam took another drink of champagne.

Harry said he'd like to see it, too, and Martha was glad the conversation had moved on from speculation about Theo's party without Ma having the opportunity to veto her going.

Chapter Thirty-One

As the day of the party neared Martha worried about what she would wear. Even she realised how foolish it would be to ask for another ball gown, which she'd only wear once. Tilly assured her that, with a little alteration, the lace swapped for a fur trim, the addition of a deep crimson velvet bolero-style jacket and extra petticoats, the dress she'd worn to the ball would be perfectly suitable. I'll wear the diamonds Theo gave me, she thought, but didn't mention them to her mother.

She asked Joey about a gift, it being a birthday. He said he and Rob were giving him a replica of a sailing ship Rob had made in their workshop. She spent time in her lunch hour looking for an appropriate coming of age gift. In the end she decided on a small silver compass she found in an antique shop. She hand-stitched a case for it which she embroidered with the words: *I hope this helps you find your way*. The embroidery had taken a while, but she was pleased with the finished result.

Saturday morning Martha went to the market. She told Ma she wanted to pick up some last minute ribbons to attach to her gown, but actually she wanted to get out of the house, away from her disapproval. She felt it hanging like a black cloud over the day, but she wasn't going to let it spoil her enjoyment of what she knew would be a wonderful evening. She doubted Theo would even notice her presence, the invitation being extended by his parents as she was Joey's sister and, she guessed, Theo's friends all being officer cadets, they wanted to even up the numbers.

She shivered in the November chill and pulled her gloves on as she walked along roads white with ice.

Some shops and had already put up their Christmas decorations ready for the festive season. Chestnut vendors stood on street corners, their braziers giving a warm glow to the frosty streets. She wandered around the market, many of the stalls displaying their Christmas wares. She bought some ribbon and a large bouquet of flowers for Ma hoping to soften her up.

She dawdled over lunch, not wanting to eat much. All afternoon she watched the clock, its hands seeming to crawl around the dial. Joey and Rob were picking her up at seven-thirty to take her to the Delahayes' London home where the party was being held.

"Most of his friends, live in town," Joey said. "So it was easier than having it at their house in the country."

Butterflies danced in Martha's stomach while she got ready. Ma helped her put her hair up, pinning deep crimson velvet roses into her curls.

"I thought I'd wear these," Martha said, taking the box with the diamonds out of her drawer. She saw Tilly bristle, but she held out her hand, a look of resignation in her eyes.

Once she was dressed, Martha twirled in front of the mirror, pleased with the overall effect. Her pleasure mounted when she saw the admiration in Rob's eyes when they came to collect her. Tilly helped her into her evening cape and wished her a good evening, her voice betraying her doubt.

"Don't worry, Ma," Martha said. "I'm sure we'll be perfectly fine."

When they arrived at the grand entrance of the ornate four storey, mid-terrace Regency townhouse, a footman in red and green livery stepped forward and opened the carriage door. Joey and Rob got out first, Rob turning to hand Martha down. Inside the vast hallway, another footman took Martha's cloak and the gifts they'd brought which would be unwrapped and displayed on a table in the supper room with labels saying who the gifts were from. Martha tried not to be impressed, but seeing the grandeur of the house and the luxurious opulence inside brought home to her how huge the difference was between their world and hers. She handed the footman her gift. He showed them into a large reception room where they joined the queue to be greeted by Theo's parents.

Theo's father, a well-upholstered, upright man in his sixties with a greying beard that covered half his face, shook hands with Joey and Rob, saying how pleased he was to see Theo's friends. "I trust you will all have a good evening," he said.

Joey and Rob mumbled their replies and passed on. A footman standing next to Captain Delahaye whispered Martha's name into his ear. He smiled and said how pleased he was to meet her. He then passed her on to Mrs Delahaye who repeated what he'd said.

Theo stood next in line. A flush warmed Martha's face as she put her hand in his.

"I'm glad you could come," he said. "I've been looking forward to seeing you again." He kept hold of her hand far longer than manners decreed.

"I'm glad to be here," she managed to say as she pulled her hand away. "Happy birthday."

He grinned, playful recklessness in his eyes as she moved on.

"Are you alright?" Rob asked.

"Who me? Yes, thank you, I'm fine." Well, she would be if those butterflies would stop ricocheting against the walls of her stomach.

As they entered the ornate music room Martha was glad to see some faces she recognised. Tubs and his cousin Abigail called them over. The room was set out for a musical recital, which would be followed by a light supper before they danced the rest of the night away. Waiters stood around with glasses of champagne. Rob took two and handed Martha one. Joey took one.

"Don't worry," he said. "I'll be sticking to this tonight. I've learned my lesson."

Martha chatted to Abigail while Rob told Tubs about their work on the engine for the riverboat. She liked Abigail, she was easy to talk to and didn't put on airs, like so many affluent women. She also noticed how she kept looking at Joey and trying to include him in the conversation.

"Theo's landed a job at the Admiralty," Abigail said. "What do you think of that, Joey?"

Joey glanced at her, distractedly. "What?" His brow furrowed.

"Abigail said Theo's landed a job at the Admiralty," Martha repeated for his benefit.

"Oh, has he?" Joey glanced around the room again. "Jolly good. I'll just go and say hello to Ellen. It's ages since I've seen her." He smiled briefly and made his way across the room towards where Ellen, with her friend Connie Beaumont, were deep in conversation with a tall, ginger haired man in Highland dress. Older than her she laughed as they talked. To Martha it looked like an intimate discussion.

Abigail sighed.

"Who's Ellen's talking to?" Martha asked.

"That," Abigail said, "is Angus McTavish, 19th Earl of Rossness. His family own a large estate in Scotland. I believe the Delahayes have high hopes in that direction."

"Really? In that case Joey's going to be bitterly disappointed," Martha said.

Abigail blushed. Martha had the distinct feeling that she'd just put her foot in it. "Oh, I'm sorry," she said. "It's just that...you know..." She shrugged.

"Yes," Abigail said, "I know."

The host and hostess entered and took their seats in the front row, the Earl of Rossness sitting next to Ellen and Connie next to Theo. The Master of Ceremonies walked to the front of the small platform set up at the end of the room. "Please take you seats," he called out. "The performance is about to begin."

They found seats near the back. Abigail took the seat next to Joey with Rob on her other side. Martha sat next to Rob with Tubs beside her. A small ensemble began to play. Martha looked at the programme she'd picked up from the seat. The room filled with wonderful, uplifting music and haunting melodies. She was soon enthralled. She couldn't follow the programme, unaware of the pieces, but Tubs helpfully pointed out each piece as it was played. She noticed Abigail attempting to engage a sullen Joey in conversation. She guessed his approach to Ellen had not gone well. Martha silently wished her the best of luck. Why do men always want what they can't have, she thought, and don't appreciate what's in front of their eyes?

The recital ended in loud applause. Martha joined in, wishing she could cheer and show her appreciation more loudly, but of course she couldn't. After the recital they filed into the dining room, walking past the table where the gifts were displayed. Martha was pleased to see her gift next to a label with her name on it.

Over a light supper of soup followed by roasted quail with vegetables, they all said how much they'd enjoyed the music. Martha, sitting next to Tubs asked about Abigail and how long she'd been living with his family. "It's a long story," Tubs said, "and quite a sad one, but she's the best girl in the world and I'd move mountains for her. I hope she finds real love and happiness." He paused and looked along the table to where Abigail was sitting next to Joey. "I'd probably kill anyone who hurt her."

Martha swallowed. He said it so casually, but she wasn't fooled. He clearly cared about Abigail and would do anything to protect her.

As desserts were served the Master of Ceremonies called them to attention. The chatter and clink of cutlery fell silent. Captain Delahaye stood, glass in hand for the toasts.

"First I'd like to thank you all for coming to join me and my dear wife," he gazed fondly at his wife, "in celebrating the coming of age of our much loved son, Theodore Granville Delahaye. I'm sure my wife would agree that it's been a privilege and a pleasure to be his parents." He grinned. "I'm not saying he's never been any trouble, but..." he shrugged and several of the guests tittered in amusement. The Captain continued, "No parents could wish for a better son. You make us proud." He raised his glass. "To Theodore. Happy twenty-first birthday. Here's hoping for a life filled with health, wealth and happiness, always."

A murmur of, "health, wealth and happiness, always," went around the table. Glasses clinked and they all drank to Theo's good health and happiness.

Theo stood. He thanked his parents, friends and guests for coming, "Especially the ladies," he said, "who I know find these events a bit of a trial." He glanced directly at Martha, who, to her dismay, blushed furiously.

Captain Delahaye stood again. "Thank you, Theo. Now I have another announcement to make." Martha looked at Rob. He shrugged. "I'm delighted to be able to tell you all, good friends, that my beautiful, talented, much beloved daughter, Ellen Felicity Delahaye has today become engaged to be married to a wonderful man who, I'm sure, will make her very happy." A surprised gasp rippled around the room. Martha immediately thought of Joey. "Please raise your glasses." Everyone did so. "To the happy couple, Ellen Felicity Delahaye and Angus McTavish, Earl of Rossness."

Martha raised her glass, glancing down the table to see Joey, but he was too far away. Half of her was relieved that at least Theo had his wish. His sister was marrying an Earl, but another part of her ached for Joey, who'd had such high hopes.

After supper the dancing began. Captain Delahaye led his wife onto the floor. Theo marched across the floor and, to her acute embarrassment, insisted on dancing the first dance with Martha. "Birthday boy's choice," he said as the band struck up. She could hardly refuse. Angus McTavish offered Ellen his arm and they joined them on the floor.

"Congratulations on your sister's engagement," Martha said as Theo took her in his arms.

Theo grinned. "Things are as they should be," he said. He whirled her around the room as the floor began to fill. In his arms she felt the same strong grip she'd felt on the boat. She pushed the memory away. "Thank you for the gift," he said. "I'll treasure it. It's the nicest gift I've ever received."

Martha doubted that. She'd seen the array of expensive watches, clocks, diamond and silver pins, cufflinks, cups, plates, silver and crystal glasses and other items, laid out on the table. There was even a pair of shooting pistols.

"You must have gone to a lot of trouble," he said. "I take it the sentiment and embroidery are yours."

"Of course." Martha was surprised he'd even noticed. She thought he was just being polite and hadn't even seen the gift. It was something you said, wasn't it, thank you for the gift. Quite meaningless. "I hope you find whatever it is you're looking for," she said.

"And, what if I've already found it?"

Her heart fluttered. "Then you're a very lucky man." She glanced around the room. She didn't like the way this conversation was going. She noticed Joey dancing with Abigail, who looked radiant in a forest green silk dress, which complemented her auburn hair. He looked remarkably cheerful, for a man whose hopes had been dashed. "You must have known about the engagement. Is that why you invited us, to have the pleasure of seeing my brother humiliated?"

Theo looked shocked. "That's not why I invited you. I'm sorry you think so little of me." He looked into her eyes. "I invited you because I wanted to see you again." He grinned. "I was right about the necklace, its beauty is definitely enhanced by being around your neck." She turned her head away, acutely conscious of the blush creeping up her cheeks.

"I am glad to see my sister happy, is that so bad?"

"No. Of course not."

"He'll get over it, Jojo. Last I heard he was deeply involved in his project with Rob. I can't see my sister chomping around boatyards and being overcome with a passion for motors. Perhaps it's just as well, eh?"

Martha knew he was right, but that didn't make her want to agree with him. "Like you said before, we come from two different worlds."

"It doesn't have to be like that."

"Oh, I think it does."

He shook his head and pulled her closer to him as they danced on.

She danced the next dance with Joey, anxious to hear what he thought of the engagement. "I hope she'll be very happy," he said as they waltzed around the floor.

"Really?"

His laughter didn't convince Martha. "Yes," he said, "really. I like her, but I don't know her well enough to think of anything more than that. Academic now, anyway. She's made her choice."

Or her family have, Martha thought.

"One day I'll have money," Joey said. "If this thing with Rob turns out, we'll both be rich, then I'll be able to provide for a wife and family. No use thinking about it until then."

Martha wasn't fooled by his bravado, but at least he seemed to understand why Ellen was so attracted to the Earl of Rossness, and it wasn't for his personality.

Halfway through the evening she visited the room put aside as a ladies powder room. She was just about to leave when Connie Beaumont came in. She hadn't taken to her when she met her, but it would be rude to ignore her. "Hello," she said. "Are you enjoying the evening?"

Connie glared at her. "Good heavens, it's Miss Crowe," she said. "I didn't expect to see you here after the debacle at the Celebration Ball. I'm surprised Theo invited you and your brother."

"Not as surprised as I was," Martha said, tweaking her hair as she glanced in the mirror. She'd noticed Constance at the recital and how she kept leaning in and whispering in Theo's ear. When he stood to leave, she'd grabbed his arm even though he hadn't offered it. "But then, Theo is so forgiving, isn't he?" she said with a smile in Connie's direction. She touched her necklace. "And so very generous." The look on Connie's face gave Martha a buzz that lasted the rest of the evening.

By the time the music finished Martha had managed to avoid Theo and danced with Rob and Tubs in turn. She noticed that Theo danced with each of the ladies present, and guessed good manners dictated that he did so. Not that she wanted to dance with him again, heaven forbid. Joey turned his attention to Abigail. Martha hoped he meant it and wasn't using her to show Ellen what she was missing. She liked Abigail and couldn't bear for her to be hurt by Joey's careless regard. She danced a lot with Rob, who was gentlemanly and attentive. That was probably good manners too, she thought.

As they were gathering their coats and waiting for their cabs Tubs said, "We're throwing a party on Christmas Eve. You must all come, I won't take no for an answer. There'll be rum punch, carols, party games, holly and mistletoe. Only the most select invited. What do you think?"

"Count us in," Joey said, helping Martha into her cloak. "It sounds wonderful."

"If it's alright with Ma and Pa," Martha said thinking of their usual Christmas Eve, when the whole family got together for mince pies and carol singing.

"Of course it'll be alright," Joey said, a little too sharply for Martha's liking. "We'll look forward to it."

Chapter Thirty-Two

Tilly gazed at her reflection in the mirror as she put on her best black hat, with the black satin roses around the brim. She recalled the last time she'd worn it. It had been Peggy's funeral. Peggy, the redoubtable landlady of The Lock and Quays pub where Sam and his brothers grew up.

She'd been good to Tilly, taking her in when she was at her lowest ebb, something Tilly would never forget and always be grateful for. Today she'd be going to Victor's funeral. Sam had worried all week about it, checking the barometer for the weather and the forecast in the newspapers. Every day he wandered down to the river, gazing up at the sky. If the weather was bad, even with a reinforced hull, the *Martha May* could be badly battered and hard put to withstand the waves they would encounter in the North Sea.

"Not the best time of year for a funeral," she said to Sam.

"No," Sam said, "but Leonora wants it done before Christmas. I can't say I blame her."

No, Tilly thought. Nor me.

Thankfully the day dawned bright and cold, with little wind. Tilly breathed a sigh of relief. It was going to be all right.

Sam and Harry were waiting for her downstairs. They'd spent the previous day getting the boat ready. Swags of black crepe adorned the railings, the windows too had been draped in black. They would collect the weighted coffin at the pier and transport it to the coast where the mourners would join them, having travelled there more quickly by coach and carriage.

Tilly had arranged for tea, coffee, sandwiches, pastries and cake to be available for the family for the journey which would take several hours. At Leonora's request several cases of champagne, supplied by Earnest Harcourt, were aboard to toast Victor as his coffin slid into the sea.

She sighed and went downstairs. She thought again how handsome Sam looked in his great coat and Captain's cap and how lucky she was to have married him. He'd been her anchor through troubled times, now she'd stand with him in his difficulties.

Together with Harry they made their way to the pier. Tilly went aboard and walked around the boat, making sure everything was in place.

At eleven o'clock the hearse carrying Victor's remains arrived. Earnest and Mark Harcourt accompanied Leonora aboard, while six strong men followed carrying the coffin. They manoeuvred it downstairs. They had suggested putting it on the front deck, but Sam pointed out that, even with a light breeze, it would be bitterly cold. He wouldn't fancy standing out for hours in that weather, so it was decided to put it in the lower salon. Once the coffin was in place the pallbearers stood around it as they would throughout the journey. The family retired to the salon where Tilly served them tea, coffee, pastries and cake.

"Would you like anything stronger?" Sam asked.

Earnest smiled. "Thank you, a brandy if you have it."

Leonora stuck with tea, but the men drank brandy. Once they were settled, Sam went up to the wheelhouse with Jock. Tilly stayed in case they needed anything else, but Leonora merely gazed out of the window lost in her own thoughts throughout the long journey. Tilly soon relaxed with the rhythmic rocking of the boat and the chugging of the engine breaking the silence. They passed many places familiar to her and then, further on stretches of river she'd never travelled along before.

They stopped at the pier at Southend where Reverend Lovel and other mourners joined them. Tilly recognised Mr Bartholomew and some of the people from the inquest. Mr Harcourt, Mark and Leonora greeted them as they came aboard. It took a while for them to board and settle before they set off again, heading for the open sea with Jock at the helm. Gusts of wind hit the boat and waves crashed against the hull as they left the relative calm of the estuary. The boat rocked so fiercely that Tilly had trouble keeping her feet. She hoped they wouldn't go too far out.

They were a fair way out, but still within sight of land, when the boat stopped. Tilly joined the family and other mourners on the top deck for the solemn service. She shivered in the cold, sharp air as the boat rocked at anchor.

Reverend Lovel started the service with a short prayer. They then sang a hymn, their voices lost in the wind and the screeching of the gulls overhead. Ernest Harcourt read the eulogy, praising Victor as a husband and father. Mathew read Christina Rossetti's poem; *Remember Me* which Leonora had asked him to read. The Reverend asked if anyone else wanted to speak, but no one did. He said a few words about forgiveness and everlasting love, and gave a blessing, then the coffin slid into the sea. Leonora stepped forward and threw a wreath and a kiss after it. "Farewell, my love," she said, the look on her face one of the deepest grief.

Sam stepped forward, tossed a bouquet of lilies and watched as they floated away. "Goodbye, old friend," he said. "Rest in peace."

One or two of the other mourners paid their tribute to Victor, each dropping flowers into the water to drift away on the restless tide. Harry handed round glasses of champagne and they all drank a toast to Victor and a life well lived. Even if it did all go wrong at the end, Tilly thought.

Overall, it was a sad ceremony and Tilly was glad when the boat turned around and they headed back to shore.

When they reached Southend, Earnest, Mark and Leonora thanked everyone for coming, shaking their hands as they left to continue their journeys on land. Leonora held Tilly's hand. "Thank you for everything," she said. "I hope to see you again in happier circumstance."

"I hope so too," Tilly said.

"Thank you," Earnest said to Sam. "Keep in touch. You know where I am if you need anything."

"Oh," Leonora said. "I nearly forgot." She handed Sam an envelope with his name on it. "I found this among Victor's things. It was obviously meant for you."

Sam took the envelope. "Thank you," he said.

Leonora smiled and then they were gone, leaving Tilly, Sam, Harry and the crew to take the *Martha May* back to London. Once again Tilly had the sense of an ending and a new beginning.

"What was that?" she said, nodding at the envelope still in Sam's hand.

He shrugged and opened it. Inside the note read: *I'm sorry, Sam. Desperate days call for desperate deeds. I hope in time you can forgive me. You were the best of friends, I'm sorry I let you down. Victor.* He passed the note to Tilly, tears glistening in his eyes. "Why didn't he speak to me?" he said, his voice soft with despair and bewilderment.

"I don't suppose anyone could have helped," she said. "But it was Leonora he let down the most. It's her and her family he's left to pick up the pieces.

The day after Theo's birthday party was the day of Victor's funeral, so Martha didn't mention Tubs' invitation until Monday morning. She was reluctant to mention it to her mother anyway, as Joey was the one who had, to her mind recklessly, accepted the invitation.

"You best tell Ma, then," she'd said on the way home.

"I can't stop," he said. "I have to be back in Oldham with Rob. We're catching the early train."

Martha sighed. "It's a pity you don't have a place in London. You're always rushing up and down the country."

Joey laughed. "We don't have London money," he said. "Don't worry. Ma won't mind and, if she does, ask Pa. You know you can twist him around your little finger."

Perhaps he was right. Perhaps she should mention it to Pa first, but then all he'd say was 'ask Ma.' Anyway, he had a lot on his plate and she wasn't going to add to it, so she'd have to get round Ma.

She mentioned it at breakfast. Tilly stared at her. "What do you mean, you've been invited to a Christmas Eve party?"

"I told you. Joey and Rob's friend Tubs invited us. Joey said we could go."

"Go where? Is there such a thing as a written invitation? Or was this a rash remark made in the afterglow of too much wine, which has probably already been forgotten?"

"I'm sure he meant it," Martha said, although a sliver of doubt flashed through her mind.

"In which case you'll receive a written invitation. So, no point worrying about it until you do."

There was no answer to that.

Things didn't get any better when she arrived at work. Miss Todd was in a foul mood, which wasn't unusual but this morning it was worse than ever before. She spent half the morning in Mr Bartholomew's office and when she returned, she was in quite a tizz. She called for silence in the office. "I have an announcement to make," she said.

The girls all stopped what they were doing. Martha glanced at Chrissie, who pouted in apprehension. There had been rumours about the business, but Martha had never thought anything of it.

Miss Todd cleared her throat. "The Board have decided that some restructuring will be required in the near future and staffing levels in all departments are being reviewed." She glanced around and swallowed. Then, in a softer voice she said, "It's possible that some posts will have to go." A mutter ran through the office. Martha got a feeling that Miss Todd was looking directly at her. "If it were up to me," she continued, "I'd keep you all on, but, regrettably, it's not. Please carry on." Her distress was evident.

Martha actually felt sorry for her. "What do you think it means?" she asked Chrissie.

"I think it means we're all going to be out a job," Chrissie said.

The rest of the day was spent in silence, each of the clerks' heads bent over their tasks. Martha exchanged occasional glances with Chrissie, but the spirit had gone out of the day, replaced by an atmosphere of resignation.

On her way home she stopped and bought a paper from the news vendor on the corner. If I'm to be out of a job, best start looking, she thought. At the bus stop she opened the papers, searching for the situations vacant, when she saw the headline; *Arsonist Arrested*, above the picture of the burnt-out *Maggie May* that had been in the paper before. Enthralled she read on. She couldn't wait to tell Pa when she got home. I wonder what he'll make of it, she thought.

Chapter Thirty-Three

Monday morning Tilly cleared away the breakfast things, her mind on Martha's announcement about the invitation. The family always spent Christmas Eve together, or they had in the past. Of course, with Joey home now this year would be different. She'd been looking forward to it. She sighed, I suppose they're grown up, she thought. It's not surprising that they want to make their own plans and see their friends. She hoped they'd still want to spend time with her and Sam, but she realised that she could no longer depend on it. She enjoyed Christmas with the family. Trade was slow this time of year, but Sam made an effort and all the boats were suitably decorated for the few trips they did make. They had buskers and carol singers, hot chocolate and mince pies, everyone enjoying the celebrations. She hoped it would be the same this year, although Sam only had the *Martha May* running until the spring. At least, with the new funds in his account, Sam was a bit happier. He still worried about the fall off in trade with the cold weather and the running costs.

"I'm not taking anything for granted," he said to Tilly. "But things are looking up."

In the kitchen Mrs Conway was preparing the vegetables for their dinner. She'd made a list of things she needed so Tilly left her to it and went to the market. On the way back she bought a newspaper to read with a cup of tea before starting on the housework. When she saw the headline *Arsonist Arrested*, with the picture of the burnt out remains of the *Maggie May*, she almost dropped her cup. She couldn't believe what she was reading.

"I'm just going out," she called to Mrs Conway. "Please let yourself out when you've finished."

She grabbed her coat and hat and rushed out to the pier to see Sam. I wonder what he'll make of it, she thought.

When she arrived, she was surprised to see Sam in the cabin talking to Amos Old. He must have seen the paper she still carried in her hand.

"I've heard," Sam said as soon as she walked into the cabin. "Amos came to tell me."

"It seems I owe your man an apology, Mrs Crowe," Amos said. "I wrongly accused him and I'm sorry. I still can't take it in. Lenny Hayes. Who'd have thought?"

"Certainly not us," Tilly said. "I'm as surprised as you are. Why would he do it? What did he have against Sam?"

"Not against Sam, Mrs Crowe. Against Victor Landridge. He must have thought the *Maggie May* was his, as he paid the bills. He lost a lot of money in one of Victor's schemes."

"We saw his name on the investors list, didn't we, Till?"

"I blame myself for letting Victor talk him into it."

"You were on that list too, Amos. You must have lost money as well."

"Aye, I did, but not more than I could afford to lose. Unlike Lenny who put his life savings into it. I wish I'd known. I'd have put him right about Victor Landridge. 'Course I didn't know about the gambling then." He shook his head and stroked his greying beard. "It was a sad day for all of us. I suppose he wanted revenge, but I can't forgive him for what he did. He deserves everything he gets. It'll be end of my yard an' all – my reputation. He had no need to do what he did."

"It wasn't your fault, Amos," Sam said. "Victor was my friend and I believed everything he said." He shook his head and Tilly saw deep sadness in his usually warm brown eyes. "I'll never be able to replace the *Maggie May*. She meant a lot to me."

"Of course she did," Amos said, "and I can only say how sorry I am. I can't do anything about the *Maggie May*, she's gone, and I can't afford to pay owt, but I do want to make amends."

Sam looked doubtful.

"I hear your boy is looking for a yard for his new project. Oil-fired engines in boats, isn't it?"

Sam nodded.

"Well, I have space in my yard now and it's his. Free, gratis and for nothing. No rent. I owe you that much."

Sam looked at him with amazement. "You'd do that?"

Amos nodded. "I hear the boy has ambition. I like that. And, if it does turn out to be a winner, well I'll be in prime position to bid for development rights, won't I?" He grinned.

"That's a most generous offer," Sam said, holding out his hand. Amos shook it. "Least I can do," he said.

As soon as she got home Tilly wrote to Joey telling him about Amos's offer. She thought he'd jump at the chance of a yard on the river. It would be perfect and, better still, he could live at home. While she wrote, she began making plans in her head about redecorating his bedroom. It hadn't been done since he left when he was sixteen. Suddenly the future looked brighter.

Things looked up later too, when Ben called round. He too had read the paper and thought, given that a third party had been arrested for the arson, it might be worth pursuing a claim against the insurance. "We can prove that neither you nor Victor would have benefitted from the fire, neither did either of you have any knowledge of it. I think that gives up a chance."

Tilly hoped that was true.

The lively chatter over the dinner table that evening was about the arsonist, what would happen to him and Joey's good fortune as a result of what he'd done.

The invitation to the Christmas Eve party, addressed to Mr J and Miss M Crowe, arrived in the post next morning while the family were at breakfast.

"I think you should wait for Joey to come home before you open it," Tilly said. "He's coming with Rob to look at the space in Amos Old's yard."

Martha grabbed it. "It's addressed to me," she said, tearing the envelope open. She smiled, although Tilly thought it more of a smirk, as she handed the card to Tilly to read. It read: *Mrs Amelia Trubshaw requests the pleasure of the company of Mr J and Miss M Crowe for dinner and an evening of revelry.* Then there was a date and the address, plus *Cocktail attire*.

"See, Ma. An official invitation. I can go now, can't I?"

Tilly was still reluctant to agree. They weren't their sort of people and Martha was getting sucked into a world she had no place in. "It's Christmas Eve. What do you think, Sam?"

If she'd hoped Sam would say no, she was sadly disappointed. "They just want to have a bit of fun, why not?" he said. He laughed. "Don't you remember when we were young?"

Tilly blushed. He was right. You're only young once. She smiled and handed the invitation back to Martha. "Then you have my blessing," she said. Martha's smile and thanks confirmed that she'd done the right thing, despite her misgivings.

Joey didn't arrive until later that evening. He'd been with Sam and Rob to look over the yard and Tilly could tell he was delighted with it, although not as happy as she'd expect him to be. The subject dominated the conversation over dinner. Harry, who knew the yard well, said it was a great space and Joey was lucky to get it. Sam agreed. "Good of Amos to let you have it," he said.

Joey nodded, but Tilly sensed his agreement was somewhat half-hearted. She tackled him about it in the kitchen, when they were clearing up. "Is there a problem?"

He sighed. "I didn't want to say anything in front of Pa, because I know he's not in a position to help but, to be honest, we're running out of money. Rob's grandfather has put in more than his share. If we don't get a new investor soon...well...we can't afford to carry on."

"Oh." A thousand thoughts ran through Tilly's head, ranging from wondering if she should offer her savings, which would undermine Sam and she'd be reluctant to do it, to whether Joey was intimating that he missed Sir Montague's patronage and was thinking of approaching Lady Thackery. "I'm sorry," she said. "It's one thing we can't help with. Is it so bad?"

Joey shrugged. "Bad enough," he said.

Over the next week, with Sam and Harry's help, Joey and Rob moved their things from Oldham to the new yard. "It'll be an advantage being on the Thames," Joey said. "More chance of trade, more publicity and more well-heeled businessmen."

"No rent to pay will be an enormous help," Rob said. "That's been one of our biggest expenses."

Tilly knew he was being kind, not wanting Joey to feel he hadn't contributed his share.

At the end of the week a letter arrived for Joey. It had Sir Joshua Fanshaw's crest on the front. Tilly guessed what it was. She waited until Rob had left, and the others had gone to bed before she gave it to him. "Oh," she said as casually as she could manage. "This came for you."

He took the envelope. "Looks official." He frowned as he opened it. His brow furrowed further as he read it. He's so like Edmund, she thought as Edmund's face popped into her head, a constant reminder of her past.

"It's from Sir Joshua Fanshaw, Sir Montague's executor. He's looking for any living blood relatives of the deceased." He gazed at Tilly. "Apparently, I'm one. He says that, in certain circumstance, I could have a claim on the estate."

He handed the letter to Tilly. It set out details of a possible claim and the means by which an illegitimate heir apparent could be made legitimate. Anger and trepidation swirled in her stomach. She recalled the conversation they'd had only a week ago about his need for an investor. Would this look like the answer to his prayers? Would he think he can gain the estate and keep his self-respect? A shiver ran down her spine. She handed it back.

"What are you going to do?"

Anger flared in his eyes as he paced the room. He stopped by the fireplace, pausing for a moment in thought. Then he tore the letter into pieces, threw it on the fire slowly dying in the grate and watched it burn. The fire sent sudden sparks up the chimney. "I know what I am," he said, his tone tinged with bitterness that made Tilly's stomach clench. "I don't need anyone writing to tell me and I won't lie to get something I'm not entitled to." He turned and stared at Tilly, an expression of contempt and fury on his face. "If they can't accept me for what I am then I don't want to know them. I don't need their patronage, not at any cost. One day I'll be rich, Ma. I'll make you proud and I'll do it by my own efforts, not by taking something that doesn't belong to me."

Tilly's heart swelled with love, pride and relief. A broad smile stretched her face. "Your father was an honourable gentleman," she said. "He'd have wanted you to be true to yourself. He'd have expected nothing less."

Joey grinned, his anger replaced by fondness. "What would I want with a landed estate anyway? No, let Grasping Jasper have it. I have my freedom, good friends, and the prospect of a good life. If our project comes off, I'll be rich in my own right. Riches honestly gained."

Tilly hugged him. "Thank you," she said. "I'm so proud of you and your father would be too." The wave of happiness that engulfed her lasted almost to Christmas Eve.

Chapter Thirty-Four

The weeks before Christmas Martha spent her evenings making gifts for the family, thankful for the use of Ma's sewing machine. She made an embroidered bag for Katy, a shirt in his favourite colour for George, a short waterproof cape for Harry and a larger one for Pa. She made a heavy-duty workman's apron for Joey with lots of pockets for the tools he worked with building the boat he was working on with Rob. She bought her mother a pair of kid gloves to go with the new hat she was trimming for her.

Every day at the office the atmosphere was one of trepidation. The only bright spot was the weekly visit to the Dog & Duck where the music and company drove away all thought of what might happen. Not that they didn't discuss it. Tony didn't appear at the pub again, but some of the other senior clerks did and they were just as worried as Martha and Chrissie. Martha wondered whether the collapse of Victor's firm and his death had anything to do with it, but she kept the thought to herself.

Shortly before Christmas Martha was leaving work, her mind on what she would do for the evening, when she saw Tony waiting for her. It had been nearly a month since he'd left the office. "Hello, stranger," she said, startled to see him. "What are you doing here? I thought your father had found you somewhere better to work."

"I'm pleased to see you too," Tony said. "And I'm really pleased to see you looking so well."

He offered his arm. Martha ignored it. "So, what are you doing here?"

"I heard they were laying people off. I thought, if you were one of them, I might be able to help."

Martha couldn't afford not to hear more. "Help? How?"

"Like I said, my father owns a shipping company. It's a little way down river and further to travel, but I know you're a good worker. If I asked him, he'd take you on doing pretty much what you're doing here. What do you think?"

"You'd do that?"

"I know I treated you badly. It's my way of saying sorry."

Martha nodded. She was surprised and warmed by his thoughtfulness. "It's very kind of you, but I'll have to think about it."

"Up to you. Offers there if you want it."

Now Martha felt bad. "Sorry if I sounded ungrateful, it's a kind offer but, well..." She bit her lip not sure whether to say any more. It was a hope more than a firm prospect. "I haven't told anyone, not even Ma and Pa, but I'm hoping to work with my Uncle Ben. He's the solicitor who helped in the search for Victor Landridge. I told him about the possibility of being let go and asked him if he had any vacancies in his office. He said that if I lose my job here, he'll be happy to take me on. To be honest, it'd be a lot more interesting than typing up shipping manifests all day."

Tony smiled, a look of relief on his face. "That's good. I felt awful about the Victor Landridge thing. If it doesn't work out with your uncle, you can always come and see me." He handed her his card.

"Thank you," she said, delighted at the warmth in his voice. "You're forgiven."

It had been a difficulty year, the fire on the *Maggie May*, Sir Montague's death, Victor's death in recent memory, but despite the difficulties Tilly was determined to give her children the best Christmas ever. Sam worked hard all year and she thought he deserved a few days off to relax and enjoy himself. She wondered about Harry, too. Taciturn like her father, he didn't say much, but Sam said he had his eye on a girl in the bakery. She'd invited him to a candlelit carol service on Christmas Eve.

In the days leading up to Christmas Katy and George made paperchains to hang in all the rooms. Katy made paper cutouts and George made colourful boats to hang on the tree that Sam provided. They went out and collected holly and laurel to make wreaths which Tilly tied with huge ribbon bows and hung around the house.

On Christmas Eve morning the smell of baking filled the house. Every Christmas the family helped make up hampers for the men who worked on Sam's boats. On Christmas Eve they'd take them round, wishing everyone health and happiness for Christmas and the New Year. The whole family enjoyed the tradition and, thanks to Ernest Harcourt's generosity, this year's hampers would be fuller than ever. Leonora had sent a couple of crates of beer for the boys which were added to the hampers. Mrs Conway had cooked the Christmas puddings and rich fruit cakes several months ago, but still had mince pies, pork and game pies to make.

Once the pies were ready Tilly packed them into the hampers for Sam to load into the buggy he'd borrowed for the occasion. Sam, Tilly, Martha, Katy and George, dressed in their warmest clothes went to the pier, where Harry waited between sailings with the crew.

They all helped handing out the hampers, seeing the smiling faces of the crew, their camaraderie, deep affection and respect for each other and Sam. They joined the men in the salon for drinks afterwards, tea and coffee for Tilly and Martha, and beer and spirits for the men. Tilly noticed a couple of the lads chatting to Martha, and even Katy had an admirer in one of the younger lads. It was always a joyous occasion, with much fun and laughter and, by the time they left to go home, Tilly's face was warm with smiles and good wishes, but not as warm as her heart.

By evening Martha was a dither of nerves, unlike Joey who was full of confidence. He'd made a special effort to polish his shoes and brush his hair. He wore black tie and tails and smelled of citrus and sandalwood. Who's he trying to impress, Martha wondered. She hoped the dress Ma had made for her seventeenth birthday would be suitable. The purple taffeta decorated with flounces, frills and lace wasn't as glamourous as her ball gown, but Joey assured her she looked perfect.

In the cab Joey explained to her that Amelia was Tubs' grandmother, who'd brought him and his sister up.

"His father was in the military and often out of the country," he said. "Tubs was called Trubs, because of his surname, until it got shortened to Tubs. His actual name is Albert Trubshaw."

"I'm not sure I can call him Albert," she said.

Joey laughed. "No. Me neither."

The address was in an older part of town where the houses were substantial, but not ostentatious. Set back from the road each house had an impressive driveway and a small front garden. An atmosphere of faded gentility permeated the whole area. An elderly butler opened the door and they stepped into an elegant hall. A Christmas tree adorned with shiny baubles, ornaments and decorations stood in one corner. Swags of ribbon with garlands of holly, laurel and winter jasmine hung around the walls giving the room festive cheer. He took their coats and showed them into a reception room, similarly decorated, where Tubs greeted them.

"Come in and meet the rest of the party," he said, handing them each a glass of sherry. "We're very informal here, so please make yourselves at home." He looked at Martha and his lips twitched into a smile. "You look wonderful," he said. "I'm so glad you could come."

Rob came over and said hello too. An unexpected flush of warmth filled Martha when she saw him. Joey glanced around until he spotted Abigail, then excused himself to go and speak to her.

"He's not pining for Ellen then," Martha said, seeing the way the wind was blowing.

Rob laughed. "You know Joey. Never lets the grass grow under his feet."

Martha nodded but inside her heart turned over. I hope he doesn't hurt her, she thought. Men are so careless with their affection. Tony's face flashed through her mind.

Mrs Amelia Trubshaw, the hostess, appeared just before the gong went for dinner. A silvery lady in a silvery dress, Martha thought she look ethereal. She drifted in on a cloud of lavender perfume, the curls of her white hair dotted with diamond pins, her bearing majestic, despite her obvious frailty. Wow, Martha thought, what an amazing lady.

"Grandmama, you must meet Martha and Rob," Tubs said by way of introduction. "Martha is JoJo's sister. As you can see, she's the good looking one of the family."

Mrs Trubshaw laughed. "Please call me Amelia," she said. "Mrs Trubshaw sounds so formal. You must sit next to me at dinner. I do find the men's conversations difficult."

The dinner gong sounded, and Tubs offered his arm to lead his grandmother in. Martha took Rob's offered arm and followed them. The rest of the party consisted of a man called Jacob, who'd been to school with Tubs, his fiancée, Emily, Tubs' sister, Clarissa, and her husband, Giles. Joey offered his arm to Abigail and they came in last.

Over dinner, which consisted of three courses, Amelia asked Martha about her father and her life on the river. Tubs had obviously briefed her about her guests. After the soup, but before the main course she glanced down the table to where Joey sat next to Abigail. "I believe that young man talking to my granddaughter is your brother," she said.

"Indeed, he is," Martha replied, her heart sinking in case she'd heard about his behaviour at the ball.

"Dear Abigail," Amelia said. "Such a treasure. She's had a hard life, you see. Her parents died young and she was sent to an aunt. Terrible woman. Drank, and she beat her. Dougie, Albert's father, rescued her and brought her here." She glanced at Martha. "We're very fond of her."

Martha smiled. "I can see why," she said. "She's easy to like."

"Hmm. Your brother's very handsome, isn't he? I can see why Abigail is so attracted."

"Is she?" Martha knew she was, but feigned surprise.

"Oh yes. She may not know it herself yet, but she's definitely smitten. I hope he treats her well."

I hope so too, Martha thought, recalling Tubs' comments at Theo's party.

After dinner the ladies retired to the drawing room for coffee while the men had port and cigars. Amelia took a seat on one of the large, overstuffed sofas by the fire. The others found seats on the sofas or armchairs grouped around her. Martha sat next to Abigail. A maid brought in a large pot of coffee and one of tea. Cups and saucers were laid out on the sideboard. Martha noticed the grand piano upon which a collection of photographs in silver frames stood.

The ladies chatted among themselves while they drank their tea and coffee. Amelia was keen for Clarissa to tell them about a recent trip she'd made to America. Their lively chatter moved from one subject to another. During one conversation Martha admired the grand piano.

"I used to play," Amelia said, "but not so much now. Clarissa can play, but of course Albert is the real pianist. You should ask him to play something."

"Thank you, I will," Martha said, eyeing the instrument. How wonderful to play it, she thought.

When the men joined them, they played various parlour games. Martha found herself paired with Rob for some of the games, while Joey made sure he partnered Abigail. Then, during a break Martha asked Tubs to play the piano. "Your grandmother said you were the pianist in the family," she said.

Tubs grinned. "Good idea. It's time we had some music." He took his place at the piano and began to play. Amelia was right, he was very good, Martha sat entranced while he played Beethoven and Brahms. Then he changed the tempo and played some jazz which had everyone gasping.

"Your turn," he said, when he'd finished. "Jojo said you can play."

Martha, emboldened by the company and the wine she'd drunk at dinner, took her place at the piano and played a couple of classical pieces. Then she played some songs from the musicals and everyone joined in. Abigail joined her and they played some duets, then Clarissa managed a simple melody.

At eleven o'clock Amelia announced that it was time for a light supper and a buffet was brought in, then, over hot chocolate and spiced buns, with Tubs at the piano, they sang carols by candlelight. Martha thought it magical.

Later, as they were putting on their coats she heard Tubs say to Joey, "I'm sorry I can't offer any financial help, but I'll put the word out."

"Thank you," Joey said. "I've invited Abigail to come and look around the yard. I expect you'd like to accompany her."

Tub looked surprised. "Indeed, I would," he said. "I can't wait to see this project I've heard so much about."

Martha guessed it was Abigail Joey hoped to impress with the invitation, not Tubs. She asked him about it on the way home.

"I like Abigail, she's a marvellous girl," he said, "but I'm not in a position to offer more than friendship. I've sunk everything I have into this project with Rob. I believe in it, Martha. Rob's a genius and it'll revolutionise riverboat travel. We're not the only ones working on the idea of oil fired boilers in boats, so we need to get ahead of the game."

Martha shrugged. "Does she know that? I hope you're not just leading her on."

He glared at her. "I'd never do anything to hurt Abby. I thought you knew me better than that." They travelled on in silence for a while. "What about you and Rob? He's keen on you, you must have realised that."

Martha suspected that was the case, but wasn't sure how she felt about it. "I don't know about that," she said. "I like him as a friend, but..." She didn't know what to say. She liked Rob, but it wasn't his face that appeared so regularly in her dreams.

Chapter Thirty-Five

Christmas morning Tilly glanced out of the window and saw the world turned to white. Flakes of snow drifted silently down coating everything in its path. Tilly shivered in the cold, but excitement fizzed inside her for the day ahead when the whole family would be together.

Despite their late night, Joey and Martha were up early enough on Christmas morning to attend the church service before breakfast. Katy and George had been awake since dawn playing with the presents Father Christmas had brought them.

They walked to church together, George kicking his way through the few inches of snow and Joey and Harry attempting to play snowballs with the light covering. Tilly nodded to the neighbours as they went in, a swell of pride filling her chest and stretching her lips into a smile. She enjoyed the church service, the carols, the sermon, the music, all lifted her heart. The celebration of the birth of Christ brought new hope. Perhaps things would be better next year, she thought.

Over breakfast, which Tilly prepared, Mrs Conway having the week off, everyone talked about what they hoped for the coming year. Tilly asked about the party Joey and Martha had been to, hoping to find out who was there. Concern for her children didn't stop just because they were grown up. The fact that Martha might soon lose her job was another worry. Even Ben's offer, kind as it was, didn't change the fact that Martha was of an age to be thinking about her future and a family of her own. Her involvement with Joey's friends worried Tilly. "Did you have a nice time?" she asked as casually as she could manage.

"It was marvellous," Martha said and went on to talk enthusiastically about the house and the dinner, the music, Tubs playing the piano and what a lovely time she'd had. Nothing she said put Tilly's mind at ease.

"Joey's invited them to see his boat at the yard," Martha said, tucking in to her bacon, eggs, sausages and grilled tomatoes.

"Really?" Sam sounded surprised. "I wouldn't have thought they'd be interested."

"They're not," Martha said. "It's Joey who's interested. In Abigail Abbot."

Joey shot her a look that would melt lead.

"Sorry," she said, eyes wide with innocence. "I didn't know it was a secret."

"I invited them as Tubs is putting the word out that I need investors. He knows everyone. It's business."

Tilly and Sam exchanged glances. "Good luck to you," Sam said. Tilly could see how upset he felt about not being able to finance Joey's project himself. "So, Katy and George, tell us what Father Christmas brought you," she said, in an attempt to change the subject.

George piped up first with a list of his new toys, books, games and treats. Having done as she'd hoped Tilly sat back to enjoy her scrambled egg and bacon. It didn't stop her worrying, though.

After breakfast Martha helped her clear the things away.

"So, I take it that this Abigail is the girl Joey's keen on?" Tilly asked when they were in the kitchen. "Really keen, I mean."

"I think so, but he won't say anything until he has something to offer."

He sounded just like Sam before he proposed, Tilly thought. He too had waited until he had something to offer. She was pleased that Joey had learned some things from Sam. The thought made her smile. Of all her children Joey was the one she worried most about. He may look like Edmund, but she saw some of her own father in him; his mule-headed cussedness, fierce independence, his determination not to be beholden to anyone, his temper too. A temper born of the frustration of a man who lived his life his own way, forging his own path, just like Da. A bit of a loner as well, not one of the crowd. She sighed and hoped it would turn out right for Joey. Despite, or more probably because of, the privileges afforded to him by Sir Montague, things hadn't always been easy for him.

Once the breakfast things had been cleared away Martha played with Katy and her dolls, George read one of his new books while Harry, Joey and Sam went out to clear the snow, although from the shouts and laughter Tilly guessed they'd found more fun in playing with it.

Later, after a sumptuous Christmas dinner of goose with all the trimmings, followed by Christmas pudding and mince pies, Tilly, Martha and Katy cleared up while the boys sat around a blazing fire, smoking cigars, drinking port and putting the world to rights.

For the rest of the afternoon, they played parlour games or read books. Sam had bought Tilly some of the latest books and she'd given him a new pipe and tobacco pouch. The smell of pipe tobacco reminded her of Christmas past, her pa and life on the river.

By the time Tilly fell into bed that night she was exhausted but happy. "It's been a good day, hasn't it?" she said.

"Wonderful," Sam said.

"Do you think the children are all right? I worry about them."

"I know you do, but they're fine."

She gazed into his eyes and saw the worry there. "I'm sorry about the *Maggie May*," she said. "Your first boat."

He nodded. "I know. But if the insurance pays out, who knows there may yet get to be another *Maggie May*. It might even have an oil-fired engine."

His grin spread to his eyes and Tilly's heart swelled with love for this man she'd married.

Chapter Thirty-Six

At the end of December Martha was laid off. Chrissie's job was safe. Martha guessed that the fact Victor had recommended her for the job in the first place had something to do with the choice, although Miss Todd insisted it was last in first out.

"I hope this doesn't mean I won't see you again," Chrissie said. "You'll still come to the Dog & Duck on Wednesdays, won't you? We'll still be friends."

"Of course, we'll be friends," Martha said as she packed up her things before leaving the office for the last time. "Best of friends, always."

She glanced around as she left the office. She'd be starting work at Crowe, Rutherford and Hayes, solicitors the following week. Ma hadn't been that keen on the change when Martha told her about it.

"Are you sure?" she said. "It's a very small office. Wouldn't you prefer to work in a larger establishment where there are more people your age and more prospects?"

Martha knew exactly what she meant by *prospects*. She meant more eligible young men. Since making a fool of herself with Tony and how he'd betrayed her, Martha wasn't inclined to want to meet any *prospects*. She'd vowed never to trust any man with her heart again.

"Uncle Ben said he'd been impressed with the way I used my initiative," she said. "He was sure I'd be an asset to the office. He said I had potential."

"I'm sure he's right," Ma said, "but the work will be similar to what you're doing now, typing, filing, general office duties. You won't be going out looking for villains like you did before."

"I know that, but it's what I want to do, Ma. I want to give it a try anyway." To Martha's mind it was a new beginning and she hoped to put all the hurt and disappointment of the past behind her.

Eventually Tilly agreed she could give it a try, although Martha could see her disappointment at the lack of *prospects*.

The trip to the boatyard happened in the New Year. Frost lay on the ground and a bitter wind blew, rattling the masts of the boats on the river.

Martha noticed how nervous Joey was during breakfast. He kept looking at the clock and left to get everything ready as soon as he'd finished eating.

He'd mentioned that Tubs had come through with a new investor.

"Who is it?" Martha asked.

Joey shrugged. "No idea. He didn't say. But at least we can now pay for materials, parts and the wages of a couple of men working on the boat. Amos has been a great help, even allowing us to poach two of his best boat builders."

Tony's remarks about his father being well off and possibly interested in investing in Joey's venture crossed her mind, but she quickly shrugged it away.

Sam and Harry had both expressed an interest in seeing Joey and Rob's progress, when they heard about the tour Joey had offered to Abigail and Tubs. They agreed to meet them at the yard later, both having to be at the pier early to help get the *Martha May* ready for the Saturday trippers.

Martha dressed in her warmest clothes. She wasn't interested in the boat, her interest lay in talking to

Abigail. She hoped to find out more about her, after all, if Joey was interested, Abigail could end up as part of the family.

When she arrived Sam and Harry were already there. Rob greeted her with a grin on his face. "I'm so glad you came," he said.

"It's good to see you again." She realised as she said it that she actually meant it. Things always seemed easier when Rob was around. She didn't know why she hadn't noticed it before.

Sam and Harry were obviously impressed with the boat, walking around it, asking questions as they did so. Tubs and Abigail arrived just as Joey began explaining the mechanics of the engine.

"So, this is what all the fuss is about," Tubs said, eying up the boat perched on stretchers in the yard. "It's bigger than I thought it would be."

Martha just thought it looked huge. They never looked that big on the water.

"It's small compared to Sam's boats," Joey said. "This one's more for ferries and small parties. It's a prototype so this is only thirty-five foot. We're looking at a fifty to a hundred horsepower engine. The same engine capacity would work on much larger vessels, even up to sixty foot."

Sam's eyes widened in incredulity. "Really," he said, his tone one of disbelief.

"No point in wasting all that energy on something too small to be of any use," Rob said. Soon the men were talking together about horsepower, fly wheels, propellers, hulls, keels, rudders, gunwales, carrying capacity, compression points, cylinders, pistons, rotors, gasoline, waterproofing and other things that Martha neither knew nor cared about.

"I didn't know you were interested in boats," she said to Abigail as they stood watching the men.

"I'm not," she said, "but Jojo sounded so enthusiastic, and he wanted me to see it, so, here I am."

"Yes, Joey does have a way of making people do exactly as he wants."

Abigail laughed. "On this occasion, yes. But I'm not naive. I do know about his temper and how he is. Albert has enlightened me as to his background and I was at the ball, if you remember. That must have been awful for you. I'm sorry I wasn't much help."

"It was a shock. I don't blame Joey. I'd have punched Theo Delahaye if I could, for what he said. He deserved it."

"Yes, he did. Albert's known Theo for years and he told me that such behaviour was quite out of character. I don't know what could have got into him."

"Too much rum and Joey making eyes at his sister."

Abigail smiled. "You're probably right."

"I know I'm right. He went to great lengths to tell me how inappropriate any relationship between them would be. Apparently, the Crowe family are not suitable to mix with people of his class and breeding."

"Oh, surely not?" Abigail looked genuinely surprised.

"I just thought I'd mention it, in case your cousin harbours similar notions."

Abigail pulled herself up to her full height, a look of disgust on her face. "I can assure you that any companion or friend I choose will be perfectly acceptable to Albert's family. I like Jojo. Like him, I've been an outsider. I know how it feels not to be accepted. I wouldn't do that to anyone." She glanced at Martha. "Not even to a Crowe."

Martha smiled. She'd liked Abigail from the moment she met her but liked her even more now.

After a couple of hours of talking about the boat and their project, Joey and Rob said they would be running trials on the river over the next few months.

"We aim to launch in summer," Joey said. "I hope you'll all come to the launch party. I'm inviting everyone who's anyone on the river, all the local boat owners. Once they see what we can do the orders will be flooding in."

Sam was obviously impressed. "I can see the benefit. A lighter boat, but with the same capacity and increased reliability. Not sure about the cost though."

"It'll be more expensive than a wooden, coal-fired, steam powered boat, but it'll last longer and run more efficiently, so you'll make up the cost in the long run."

"What about manufacture? Who's going to be putting these boats together?"

"That's where Amos comes in. We'll be sourcing parts from all over the country. The metal hulls from steel works, engines, waterproofing, et cetera from different manufacturers. He's going to convert his yard to assemble our boats and furbish the shells to individual specification. That way production time is cut to a minimum, and customers get exactly what they want."

Rob grinned. "Now you can see why I have Jojo as a partner. He's the boat builder, I'm just the mechanic."

"Well, it sounds as though you know what you're doing and good luck to you," Sam said.

"Quite the entrepreneur," Tubs said, shaking Joey's hand. "I have to congratulate you. I didn't think you could do it, but you have."

Martha had never seen Joey look so pleased with himself.

Chapter Thirty-Seven

Over the next few months, Rob and Joey worked tirelessly on the project, running trials on the river, adjusting and tweaking the boat's performance. Joey travelled all over the country talking to suppliers and manufacturers. He sought out companies that used the canals and rivers to transport their goods and spoke to their transport managers. He spoke to boat owners on rivers as far afield as Northumberland and Abergavenny. When Sam cautioned him to learn to walk before he tried to run, he said he had to think big or not at all.

"That comes from having friends with wealth and entitlement," Tilly said. "He has the confidence and self-belief only available to people who move in such elevated circles."

Sam laughed. "If that's the case, then I'm glad," he said. "He deserves success. I wouldn't begrudge it to anyone who's worked as hard as him and Rob."

The launch of the prototype was planned for June when the weather would be good and the river conditions fair. Joey had invited everyone who was anyone on the river to come and watch. There would be a short naming ceremony and then the family and investors would be invited to board the boat for a short maiden cruise along the river.

Rob and Joey talked about who should christen the boat. Rob suggested Jojo's mother might like to do it, but Joey had other ideas.

"I know who I want to do it," he said.

Six months later the day of the launch dawned bright and clear. June sunshine streamed through the windows of the breakfast room. Joey had risen early, unable to contain his excitement. "Today's the day, Ma," he said to Tilly as he ate his bacon, egg and sausages. "I can't wait to see you all there. If this goes well who knows where we'll end up." He grinned, his eyes shining with enthusiasm.

"I hope it goes well for you," Tilly said. She knew the passion, time and effort that had gone into it. She felt for him with every fibre of her being.

He left as soon as he'd eaten. Tilly put on her best summer suit. Sam and Harry also dressed in their best, for once forgoing the early morning trip to the pier to see everything was ready for the Saturday trippers.

"Jock can manage. I wouldn't miss this for the world," Sam said, his voice filled with pride.

Martha too had dressed in her best. "Joey wouldn't say what they've named the boat," she said, "but I think I can guess."

"Could be anything," Harry said. "I like the name Endeavour. After all it's been one long one."

"I'm not sure you can name a boat after Captain Cook's ship," Sam said with a laugh. "No. I think it'll be named after one of the saints. That's quite usual. It's said to bring good luck."

"You named your boats after your closest family," Tilly said. "I've no doubt Rob and Joey will want to do the same."

The sun shone from a clear blue sky, reflecting on buildings and dancing like diamonds on the water as the family made their way to Old's Yard where the launch would take place. Tilly feared her new straw hat which was extravagantly embellished with satin roses, ribbon and lace as the light wind would be stronger downstream.

Katy wasn't sure what all the fuss was about, after all her pa had launched three boats. George skipped along, keen to get to the yard. His interest lay in the mechanics of the boat he'd heard so much about. "Do you think it will be very noisy, or smelly?" he said. "I've heard engines throw out a lot of smoke."

Katy kept asking who'd be there, would she see anyone famous?

When they arrived at the gates of the yard, they were each greeted with a glass of champagne. Tilly was surprised to see so many well-dressed people there. Most river folk didn't worry too much about sartorial elegance. They stood around chatting while more people arrived, stretching out along the riverbank.

She saw Ben in the crowd. "Hello. I didn't know you were coming."

"Joey invited me," Ben said. "I am his solicitor."

"Have you seen Rob or Joey?"

"No. But I don't expect they'll be long."

Sure enough a few minutes later a bell sounded and the gates of the yard opened to reveal the boat on the slipway, ready to launch. Ropes and lines held the boat in place and a wooden platform had been set up at its bow. They gathered around as Rob and Joey came out followed by Lawton Matherson, Tubs, Abigail and Theo Delahaye.

Tilly's face crumpled into a frown. Cold fury filled her. "What's he doing here?" she said.

"Must be an investor," Sam said. "Or he's a friend." She recalled that Sam knew nothing about Theo's remarks about her, only that Joey and he had had a falling out while drunk. If he'd known she was sure things would be different. For one thing, Theo would walk with a limp, if he could walk at all, and his ability to father children would be severely impaired. She smiled at the thought.

"Looks like the gang's all here," Martha said.

Tilly sighed. Theo Delahaye was the last person she wanted to see.

Joey mounted the steps to the platform, followed by the others. He began by thanking everyone for coming. "I especially want to thank my family for their unquestioning love and support through the years," he said. "For their encouragement and for allowing me to dream. Ma, Pa, this is for you." He raised his glass. "Tilly and Sam Crowe." Everyone drank to Tilly and Sam. "Then I'd like to thank my backers, Lawton Matherson and Theodore Delahaye, who made the dream possible."

Tilly felt sick. She glared at Ben. "Did you know?"

"Know what?"

"About Theo Delahaye being an investor."

Ben nodded. "Tubs introduced him. Asked me to keep it confidential, so of course I did."

Tilly wasn't convinced about Theo's motives. What's he after, she thought. Another way to have power over Joey?

Joey went on to thank everyone who'd worked on the boat, especially Amos for the space to operate and giving so freely of his unrivalled experience in boat building. He spoke about the debt he owed to Rob and how hard he'd worked over the past year. "He's the brains behind it," he said. "And the driver. He kept me going. When my faith faltered, his never did. He's too modest to take the credit he deserves, so, I ask you all, please raise your glasses to Rob Matherson, genius, mechanic and friend."

Everyone raised their glasses to Rob Matherson.

Rob blushed. Joey indicated that he should step forward, but he shook his head and stepped back. "Now we come to the important part," Joey continued. "Abigail, please."

To everyone's astonishment Abigail Abbot stepped forward. She picked up the bottle of champagne which was tied to the bow of the boat. The material covering the name of the boat was pulled away and a gasp went through the audience as she said, "I name this boat *Abigail Grace*. May God bless her and all who sail in her." She threw the bottle against the boat's metal bow. Two men standing at the top of the slipway cut the ropes and, as the bottle smashed christening the boat, the *Abigail Grace* slid quietly into the water. Everyone clapped, raised their glasses and drank to the *Abigail Grace*.

"Well," Tilly said. "What do you think of that?"

"Well, it floats," Sam said, sounding relieved.

Once the boat was stable on the water they were invited aboard. Tilly saw Joey talking to several men in suits, who had gathered around. They too were invited aboard.

"Must be potential customers," Ben said.

The boat was smaller than Sam's paddle steamers, but there was still plenty of room with a long cabin in the middle and decks fore and aft. Rob escorted some of the visitors to the engine room below. Two of the boat builders from the yard were also on board, pointing out the boat's features. Tilly saw Amos, puffed up with pride talking to one of the businessmen. Glasses of champagne and canapes were being served in the cabin by two lads from the yard, suitably dressed for the occasion. It was all very jovial and a party atmosphere prevailed. Thankfully the river was calm and the sun shone.

Tilly took a seat on the fore deck where the sun warmed her face. Sam, Ben and Harry wandered around the boat while Martha chatted to Abigail. They'd become friends since she and Joey had been stepping out the last six months.

Lawton Matherson joined Tilly. "Mrs Crowe, good to see you again."

"And you, Mr Matherson."

"Aw, no need to be so formal. I'm too old for that."

Tilly laughed. "Lawton," she said.

"May I say how charming you look. That's a very nice suit you're wearing."

"Why thank you." Tilly recalled his old-world charm.

"You should be proud of Jojo," he said. "Him and Rob. They've done well."

"I am proud of him," Tilly said. "But I believe your boy Rob was the brains behind it."

"Aye, but it's Jojo who's pulled it all together. He's a good lad."

Tilly smiled. "They're both good lads. They owe you a vote of thanks for the initial investment."

"Aye, investment being the operative word."

"What do you think of the boat?"

"I'm no expert," he said. "I'll judge it by how many they manage to sell. It was a business decision."

Tilly doubted that. His affection for Rob reflected in his face when he spoke of him and she heard the pride in his voice.

They sat for a while enjoying the breeze in their faces and the scenery passing by. Then Lawton went to get something to eat. "I suppose I'd best do my bit and entertain the prospective purchasers," he said. "But it's good to see you again, Tilly."

Tilly enjoyed the ride, smoother than the paddles and quieter, although the thud of the engine could be heard even on the fore deck. She walked around the boat, admiring the workmanship in the cabin. The panelling and fittings were polished teak and mahogany. You've done them proud, Amos, she thought. She took a glass of champagne and a bite to eat. After about an hour they turned around to head back to the yard. It had been long enough for prospective deals to be made, and everyone Tilly spoke to said they were impressed. She sat on a bench on the aft deck, enjoying the view looking out over the stern. She knew nearly every inch of this stretch of the river, so it felt like coming home.

Joey was showing the businessmen around. Tilly heard him tell them they could have the boat furnished to their own design. Harry took to the cockpit to see how the boat was steered. Katy, who'd spent the afternoon between the fore and aft decks leaned on the gunwales. George on the other hand, full of curiosity, had climbed up on the stern rail to watch the wake as they travelled along.

They'd been going for about another half hour when the engine noise stopped and the boat began to drift. A murmur of discontent went round the boat. "Don't worry," Joey called out as he rushed down to the engine room. "Soon have it fixed."

They waited for a while, slowly drifting in the tide. Joey was back on deck, reassuring people that everything was in hand, while Rob sweated in the engine room trying to fix the fault.

"Does this thing have any sort of anchor?" Sam asked, looking dismayed for the first time that day.

"Of course it does," Joey said and went to see if it needed to be put down. As minutes ticked by the murmur turned to mild panic. Tilly saw Joey's hopes and dreams drifting away. People were milling around and, while Tilly sat there, Theo Delahaye came out onto the deck.

Tilly turned her head away, not wishing to engage with him. She was about to call to George to get down from the rail which he'd climbed onto, when the engine must have sparked into life and the boat jumped forward. The sudden jolt sent George flying from the rail into the water.

Horrified, Tilly screamed and a man standing next her yelled out. To Tilly's stunned amazement, Theo stripped off his jacket, climbed over the rail and dived into the water after George. Tilly's eyes widened, her throat constricted, she could hardly breathe. A sickening wave of terror washed over her, nausea rose to her throat. She heard a scream, then realised it was hers. Katy burst into tears while a panicking Abigail tried to comfort her. Shocked passengers shouted and ran forward to stop the boat, while it moved further and further away.

In the pandamonium that followed, someone must have got Rob to cut the engine because it died again, but the boat kept on drifting away. People, still reeling from the sudden lurch forward of the boat, hung on to the nearest object to keep their balance. It took a while for them to realise what had happened.

"George, George," Tilly and Martha were screaming. "Help, help, someone help!"

Tilly's heart stuttered when Sam appeared from nowhere, stripped off his jacket and dived in after Theo and George. She watched in horror as she saw their heads bobbing about, looking for her son. Her heart pounded like an out of kilter engine as Theo and Sam dived under the murky water again and again. Then Martha saw something and pointed, yelling out. Theo was first to the spot where George had appeared. He managed to swim over and grab him and, with Sam's help, haul him back to the boat.

Willing hands reached out and pulled them aboard. One of the lads from the yard laid George on the deck and pumped his chest until he gasped, coughed up the water he'd swallowed and started breathing again.

"Thank God," Sam said. He turned to Theo standing next to him, river water puddling at his feet. "We owe you his life," he said, shaking his hand. "I can't thank you enough."

Theo shook his head. "Lucky I was near, that's all."

Joey wrapped George in some tablecloths. Tilly took him into the cabin, rubbing his arms and legs to get his circulation going again. His face was marble white.

"Give them some room," Joey called out pushing back the crowd that had gathered around them. "We'll be back in dock in fifteen minutes. Please get ready to leave the boat."

"Thank you," Tilly said. Joey bent down to where she had George laid on a bench. "Is he all right?"

Tilly and Martha rubbed George's arms and legs as colour gradually returned to his face.

Tilly glanced up to see Sam and Theo standing nearby. "Thank you, thank you, thank, you," she said. "You've saved his life."

Chapter Thirty-Eight

Back at the boatyard Joey ushered the people off the boat. One of the lads from the yard found some clean dry clothes for George who appeared rather subdued after his tumble. Sam too changed into borrowed workman's overalls. They weren't much, but at least they were clean and dry. Theo politely refused the somewhat tattered clothes offered to him and sent a lad in a cab to collect a change of clothes from his home.

The after-launch party was being held in a local hostelry where a buffet lunch had been laid out ready.

"It's been a really exciting day," Tilly said, "and I'm glad it's gone so well for Joey, but I think I'd better take George home. He's had quite an ordeal."

Sam hunkered down beside him. "Do you want to go home, son?"

George, tears in his eyes and still shivering, jumped up and threw his arms around his father's neck, hugging him tightly. Sam stood, holding him close. "I'll take you home," he said. "I could do with a change of clothes."

Martha wanted to go to the party, so Tilly stayed with her. Katy went home with Sam and George, after saying goodbye to Joey.

In the upstairs room of The White Hart public house, Tilly chatted with some of the people she knew from the river. Everyone seemed optimistic about Joey and Rob's prospects, saying what a good job they'd done and what a difference the boat would make. She saw Martha chatting to Rob. She was surprised to see Tubs and his grandmother chatting to Mr Matherson. After a while Theo returned, having changed out of his wet clothes.

Tilly's heart faltered when she saw him. She owed him her son's life. She screwed up her courage and went up to him. "I want to thank you again," she said. "Your quick action saved my son's life."

Theo shrugged, making light of it. "Any trained naval officer would have done the same," he said.

Tilly wasn't sure that was true. "Thank you all the same." She paused in thought. She'd rushed to judgment of a man she hardly knew. "I fear I owe you an apology. I have thought ill of you and I see I may have misjudged you."

Theo's eyebrows shot up. "Not as badly as I misjudged you, Mrs Crowe. It is I who should apologise to you. I behaved abominably, something for which I am profoundly sorry."

"You were drunk and let your feelings run away with you. It happens."

"You are very kind to say so."

"If you thought so badly of Joey, why did you invest in the project?"

Theo shrugged. "Tubs assured me of its potential, added to which I wanted to right a wrong. I felt partly responsible for Jojo's predicament, although, I seem to have done him a favour. I've never seen him in such high spirits."

"You're not responsible for Joey's behaviour. That, I fear is something beyond even your control." As she said it she wished she hadn't. It sounded resentful and grudging.

Mirth tinged Theo's smile. "As are many things, Mrs Crowe. Unfortunately."

He nodded as he bid her good day. Martha was still talking to Rob. Theo joined them. Tilly sighed, a remembrance of lost youth and fated optimism filled her.

A short while later Sam returned, having changed into a suit. "Joey asked me to come back," he said. "I think he wants to say something."

Sure enough, Joey stepped up on the small platform at the end of the room and tapped his glass to call for attention. "Ladies and gentlemen," he said. "I have an announcement which I intended to make earlier, but things got a little out of hand." Several people chuckled and some merely murmured their agreement.

"Thankfully I have been assured by my father that my young brother, George, is none the worse for his escapade and is now happily tucked up in bed with a book." A ripple of approval went around the room. Sam nodded in confirmation.

Joey went on, "Earlier today I proposed to the most wonderful girl in the world and I'm delighted to say she agreed to marry me. The name of the boat may have given something away, but please raise your glasses to my fiancée, Miss Abigail Grace Abbot."

Everyone cheered and raised their glasses. Martha, Rob and Theo cheered the loudest.

Later that night, as they were getting ready for bed, Tilly asked Sam what he thought about it.

"It's a good start," he said. "But it's only a beginning. There's a long way to go before it comes to anything. And a lot of hard graft, but I'm sure they're both up to it."

Tilly frowned, puzzled. Then realisation dawned. "The engagement, I mean, not the boat."

Mirth danced in Sam's eyes. "Oh that," he chuckled. "The same."

Tilly laughed. "Stop teasing," she said and punched him lightly on the arm.

"Oh, that means war," he said. He grabbed her, pulled her down on the bed beside him and kissed her all over.

The next morning breakfast was a somewhat muted affair. Joey had stayed over with Rob, his lodgings being closer to the workshop. George, fully recovered from his misadventure, ate well, wanting to go over the park and sail his collection of boats.

"It's such a lovely day," Tilly said, "it's a shame to waste it staying indoors. I could make us up a picnic."

"I thought I'd go and have another look at the *Abigail Grace*," Martha said. "There were so many people on board yesterday I didn't get a proper look."

"Can I come?" George said. "I want to see the boat again."

"No, you can't," Martha snapped. "In fact with your penchant for falling in I don't think you should go to the river at all."

"Aw, Ma," George wailed.

"It's all right, she's teasing," Tilly said. "I don't believe it's the boat she wants to see at all."

Martha blushed.

"Can I go, Ma. Can I?"

Tilly smiled. "Not to see the *Abigail Grace*, but we could take a trip on the *Matilda May* if you like. I know Pa would be glad to see you and you can spend the day helping out."

"And me," Katy said. "I can help Pa too."

So it was settled. Tilly, Katy and George would take a trip on the river, while Martha went to see Rob and

Joey at the boatyard. Tilly made up a picnic she could take. "I expect they could do with it after yesterday," she said.

Relieved to be able to go alone, Martha put on her hat and coat to walk to the yard. Normally it wouldn't be open on a Sunday, unless they were busy, but Rob had mentioned that they'd be working there going over what they had learned from the launch.

She enjoyed the walk. The sun shone in a clear blue sky. Church bells sounded in the distance, carried over on the lightest of breezes. Walking by the river she breathed it in, as she always did. She couldn't imagine being anywhere else. The river was so much part of their lives.

When she got to the yard Rob was on his own, going over some drawings set out on a board propped on the table against the wall. "Hello," she said glancing around. "No Joey?"

Rob stopped what he was doing and turned around. "He's gone to see Abigail. It seems they've a lot to talk about."

Martha laughed. "Oh, of course." She pointed to the drawings. "Anything I can help with?"

He shook his head. "I'm just trying to work out why the engine faltered yesterday. It's most unusual and we can't have it happening again." His face creased into a look of deep concern. "I heard what happened to George. I'm so sorry. I hope he's all right."

"He's fine, thank you. Quite recovered. It was his own fault for climbing on the rail."

"Even so."

Martha walked around the workshop. "So this is where the magic happens," she said.

"I don't know about that. This is where the work is done, if that's what you mean."

Martha continued walking around. "Did you know about Theo investing?"

Rob looked bashful. "I did. I also heard about his bravery diving in the river to save George. It was a heroic thing to do, risking his own life."

"I doubt it was much of a risk," Martha said. "We swim in the river all the time, especially in summer."

Rob smiled. "So, he's not your hero, then?"

Martha shook her head. "He's quite good looking though, wouldn't you say? And...er...eligible."

Rob shrugged. "If you like that sort of thing. He can be controlling and manipulative, too."

"Yes, you said before. Then why allow him to invest in your business?"

A look of shame and embarrassment filled Rob's face. "Okay, maybe I got him wrong. Maybe I was mad at him and a bit drunk myself. Maybe you should forget what I said."

Martha brightened. "I like a man who's big enough to admit when he's made a mistake," she said. She continued walking around the yard. They fell into silence, until Rob said, "It's good to see you again."

"You too."

"Can I take you out to lunch?"

Martha indicated the basket she carried. "I've brought a picnic."

"Great," he said. "A picnic over the park then?"

She nodded and he offered his arm, which Martha took. You're hard work Rob Matherson, she thought, but I'll get to know you better yet.

Over the next week Martha went more and more often to the yard. Rob and Joey worked on the boat while she helped out in the office. She'd do some filing and paperwork. "Jojo's good," Rob said. "But he's not the most organised man on earth."

Martha was glad to help out.

She thought often of Theo, his face appearing in her dreams. She recalled his ease and elegance, but it was nothing compared to Rob's anxious gentleness, his selfless dedication and commitment. Ma had said that one could easily be blinded to a man's faults by his ease of manner and superficial charm, but compassion, a willingness for self-sacrifice and putting others first were a greater mark of a man's character.

The more she got to know Rob, the more they laughed together and found things in common, the closer they became.

Thoughts of Theo faded as her affection for Rob grew.

Chapter Thirty-Nine

Spring 1899

Tilly couldn't remember the last time she'd felt so nervous. She wasn't nervous for herself, but for her son. She hadn't felt at all nervous at her own wedding, it was one of the happiest days of her life, but now Joey was getting married. She liked Abigail. She'd got to know her over the last months of their engagement. She even liked her grandmother, Amelia, finding they had much in common. But, on his wedding day, all her thoughts were of Joey.

She recalled the day he was born, in an upstairs bedroom in a friend's house in the country. She didn't miss those days. Then she thought of Edmund, but his face seemed faded as she tried to recall it. All she could think was that he was so very young, hardly a man at all. Joey was a man now, perhaps the man Edmund would have grown into. Would he have been proud of his son? Of course he would. Tilly was proud of him, so was Sam. How lucky she was to have Sam. She thought of their wedding. It wasn't as grand as Joey's would be but the love between them was as great.

As she got ready, she glanced in the mirror. She'd aged a little, but then hadn't everyone? She adjusted her hat, a confection of straw, lace, ribbons and flowers, and stared at her reflection. She chuckled and thought of the long limbed, skinny girl with the dirty face she used to be. Tilly Thompson, you've done well for yourself, she thought and chuckled. She'd do Joey proud.

He'd asked if she would mind if he invited Lady Thackery and his Aunt Deborah. Joey was her great-grandson after all.

"I owe it to Sir Montague," he said. "For all he did for me."

Tilly didn't mind. Lady Thackery had replied warmly, wishing them every happiness and sent a large cheque, a silver tea service and a canteen of cutlery for their new home. She said she hoped they would visit in the summer. Tilly wasn't sure how she felt about that, but they were his family, so it was fitting.

Theo Delahaye had been invited too. Unfortunately, or perhaps fortunately given what Tilly saw as his inappropriate interest in Martha, an overseas posting had made it impossible for him to attend. He'd sent an exquisite, ornately decorated dinner service as a wedding gift. Tilly smiled at the memory of Joey saying they'd think of him every time they sat down to dinner.

Sam called up to her, worried about being late. "Coming," she called, tweaked her hat one more time, and went down to join him.

Sam smiled and offered his arm. Handsome in his morning suit over a gold brocade waistcoat, her heart blipped as it always did when she saw him. They would see Harry, acting as usher, Martha, chief bridesmaid, Katy also a bridesmaid and George, a page boy, at the church.

"Ready?" Sam asked as the carriage arrived. Tilly nodded. Sam squeezed her hand. "Big day," he said, his face beaming with pride. She saw the love in his eyes and took a breath.

"Ready," she said as jumble of memories of the many other occasions she'd relied on Sam's strength and fortitude ran through her mind.

Outside the church an old oak tree cast its shadow over the path, lined with bluebells in abundance, scenting the air. The guests mingled, chatting and laughing. Sunlight filtered through the trees dappling the grass. Harry, looking as dashing and handsome as his father, ushered them into the church.

Inside the church candles flickered, lighting up the floral arrangements of primroses, violets and wild roses that adorned the pews. Tilly and Sam walked, heads held high, to the front and took their seats.

Martha, dressed in a gown of pink silk, the neckline edged with satin roses, fixed the headdress of fresh orange blossom into Abigail's auburn curls. "You look beautiful," she said.

Abigail's smile would have lit up the whole street. She stood and twirled in front of the long mirror. Her white silk dress, embroidered with pearls, shimmered in the sunlight streaming through the window. "Will I do?" she said.

"Of course, you'll do. You look wonderful. Joey's a lucky man." Martha meant it. Abigail's eyes sparkled like diamonds, her face bright with excitement and happiness.

"Are you nervous?" Martha asked.

Abigail shook her head and held out her hand. "Steady as a rock," she said. "I'm looking forward to it." She twirled again to look at her reflection in the mirror. "You'll be next," she said, grinning at Martha.

Martha blushed, her cheeks pink as her dress. "Not me," she said. "I'm too young to settle down, or so Ma keeps telling me."

"I thought you and Rob..."

Martha shrugged. "He'd be more interested in me if I had pistons, gaskets and valves." That might be true at the moment, she thought, but given time...

Abigail laughed. "I don't believe that. Don't worry, your turn will come, once Rob realises what a gem you are."

Martha smiled. "I'm happy as I am, thank you." That was true, she was. She wasn't ready to settle down yet, and neither was Rob, but when he was, well, she'd be waiting.

Katy called up the stairs that the carriage had arrived. Abigail took a breath. "This is it," she said. Martha nodded, butterflies fluttered in her stomach. "You look amazing," she said.

"Thank you."

Martha smoothed Abigail's dress and train and together they went downstairs.

Amelia gasped when she saw her granddaughter. She kissed her cheek, with tears glistening in her eyes. "Beautiful," she said. "Just beautiful."

Martha rounded up Katy and George, and together they walked to the waiting carriage, golden sunlight shining down on them. A perfect day, Martha thought.

When they arrived at the church the organ notes rose to a crescendo, signalling their arrival. The congregation stood and Abigail walked down the aisle on Tubs' arm, carrying her bouquet of wild roses, bluebells and violets, the train of her dress flaring out behind her.

Martha, Katy and George followed, the girls each carrying a posy of primroses.

Joey stood, nervously waiting. Rob, his best man stood beside him. He turned his head as his bride walked towards him. Martha saw the deep love in his eyes.

The service was both solemn and uplifting. As they each said their vows, the congregation sat in reverential silence. Rob placed the ring on the open Bible to be blessed. When the vicar pronounced them man and wife Joey kissed his bride to the cheers and applause of everyone present. The organ sounded and they walked back down the aisle, man and wife together united by love until death.

A photographer took their pictures, and the guests showered them with rose petals as they climbed into the carriage for the journey to a local hotel for the reception.

"Lovely service," Tilly said to Sam as they made their way to the reception. When he nodded and smiled Tilly knew that he too was remembering their wedding.

The wedding breakfast of soup, pheasant with all the trimmings, and an elaborate dessert of fruit meringue and cream was served in an upstairs room. After the meal Tubs stood and thanked everyone for coming. He spoke of Abigail's beauty, talent and forgiving nature, making everyone laugh when he said he wasn't so sure of Joey's. He toasted the bride and groom. When Joey stood to make his speech there was no mistaking the deep love and affection in his eyes. He said how happy he was and how he intended to spend the rest of his life making Abigail happy. Not everyone heard Tubs say, "You'd better, mate," but Tilly did.

Everyone raised their glasses to Abigail, the bride. Rob's speech was light-hearted and made everyone chuckle. When he raised his glass to toast the bridesmaids, Tilly noticed that he looked directly at Martha, who blushed. A sliver of hope slid into her heart.

The newlyweds opened the dancing. Sam took Tilly onto the floor, deep love in his eyes. In his arms Tilly's heart swelled. This was the man she loved more than life itself, the father of her children, who brought her son up as his own. "What are you thinking?" she asked.

He grinned. "One down, four to go," he said. He spun her around into a whirl of love and joy. Tilly laughed. It had been a wonderful day.

THE END

About the Author

Kay Seeley is a talented storyteller and bestselling author. Her short stories have been published in women's magazines and short-listed in competitions. Her novels had been finalists in The Wishing Shelf Book Awards. She lives in London and loves its history. Her stories are well researched, beautifully written with compelling characters where love triumphs over adversity. Kay writes stories that will capture your heart and leave you wanting more. Often heart-wrenching but always satisfyingly uplifting, her books are perfect for fans of Anna Jacobs, Emma Hornby and Josephine Cox. All her novels are available for Kindle, in audio, paperback and in Large Print.

Kay is a member of The Alliance of Indie Authors and The Society of Women Writers and Journalists.

If you've read and enjoyed this book, please be kind enough to leave a review so other readers can enjoy it too.

Why not sign up to my monthly newsletter for the latest news about my writing, free short story and a glimpse into the past with my historical jottings. Sign up here: I'd love to hear from you. https://kayseeleyauthor.com/

Acknowledgements

I couldn't have written this book without the support and encouragement of my family and writing friends. I particularly want to thank my daughters Lorraine and Liz for reading it and their helpful suggestions. Thanks also go to Helen Baggott for her valuable assistance and Jane Dixon Smith for the wonderful cover. Mostly I'd like to thank my readers for their continued support and encouragement. Hearing from people who've read and enjoyed my books makes it all worthwhile.

Thank you.

Contact Kay through her website:
https://kayseeleyauthor.com/

If you enjoyed this book, you may also enjoy Kay's other books:

Novels

The Water Gypsy
Troubled times for Tilly (Water Gypsy Book 2)
The Watercress Girls
The Guardian Angel

The Hope Series
A Girl Called Hope (Book 1)
A Girl Called Violet (Book 2)
A Girl Called Rose (Book 3)

Fitzroy Hotel Series
One Beat of a Heart
A Troubled Heart
A Heart full of Hope

All Kay's novels are also available in Large Print

Box Sets (ebook only)
The Victorian Novels Box Set
The Hope Series Box Set

Short Stories
The Cappuccino Collection
The Summer Stories
The Christmas Stories

The Water Gypsy

Struggling to survive on Britain's waterways Tilly Thompson, a girl from the canal, is caught stealing a pie. The intervention of Captain Charles Thackery, saves her from prison. The bitterness and resentment among the other staff leads Tilly into far greater danger than she ever thought possible. Can she escape the prejudice, persecution and hypocrisy of Victorian Society, leave her past behind and find true happiness?

The Watercress Girls

Annie knows the secrets men whisper in her ears to impress her. When she disappears who will care? Who will look for her?

Two girls sell cress on the streets of Victorian London. When they grow up they each take a different path. Annie's reckless ambition takes her to Paris to dance at the Folies Bergère. When she comes home she takes up a far more dangerous occupation.

The Guardian Angel

When Nell Draper leaves the workhouse to care for Robert, the five-year-old son and heir of Lord Eversham, a wealthy landowner, she has no idea of the heartache that lies ahead of her. Robert can't speak or communicate with her, his family or the staff that work for his father. Can Nell save him from a desolate future, secure his inheritance and ensure he takes his rightful place in society?

The Fitzroy Hotel Stories

One Beat of a Heart

One Beat of a Heart, is all it takes to change a life forever.

Clara Fitzroy, spoiled and entitled, refuses to conform to convention. Her reckless behaviour has devastating consequences and an ill-judged liaison threatens to destroy everything she's hoped for. Daisy Carter, the hotel housekeeper, has problems of her own. A family relationship brings grief and heartache and a well meaning action ends in disaster.

A Troubled Heart

Verity Templeton, eighteen and fiercely independent, travels to London with her aunt for the season.
Then she meets Brandon Summerville, the handsome, arrogant, wealthy man about town Charlotte is in love with. Will she be able to resist his obvious charm?

A Heart full of Hope

When Charity Browne arrives at The Fitzroy Hotel on her way to a country house party, she knows there's more to the invitation than a weekend in the country. Sparks fly when she collides with dashing Jack Carter, the hotel housekeeper's disreputable brother. What happens when two worlds collide?

The Hope Series

A Girl Called Hope

In Victorian London's East End, life for Hope Daniels in the public house run by her parents is not as it seems. Pa drinks and gambles, brother John longs for a place of his own, sister Violet dreams of a life on stage and little Alfie is being bullied at school. Silas Quirk, the charismatic owner of a local gentlemen's club and disreputable gambling den her father frequents, has his own plans for Hope.

A Girl Called Violet

Violet Daniels isn't perfect. She's made mistakes in her life, but the deep love she has for her five-year-old twins is beyond dispute. When their feckless and often violent father turns up out of the blue, demanding to see them, she's terrified he might snatch them from her. How far will Violet go to protect her children?

A Girl Called Rose

Set against the turbulent years of The Great War, A Girl Called Rose is a deeply moving story of young love, heroism, sacrifice, human weakness and the enduring strength of family ties. Can first love survive long separation or will Rose discover that her heart belongs to another?

You may also enjoy Kay's short story collections:

The Cappuccino Collection
20 stories to warm the heart

All the stories in *The Cappuccino Collection* are romantic, humorous and thought provoking. They reflect real life, love in all its guises and the ties that bind. Enjoy them in small bites.

The Summer Stories
12 Romantic tales to make you smile

From first to last a joy to read. Romance blossoms like summer flowers in these delightfully different stories filled with humour, love, life and surprises. Perfect for holiday reading or sitting in the sun in the garden with a glass of wine.

A stunning collection.

The Christmas Stories
6 magical Christmas Stories

When it's snowing outside and frost sparkles on the window pane, there's nothing better than roasting chestnuts by the fire with a glass of mulled wine and a book of six magical stories to bring a smile to your face and joy to your heart. Here are the stories. You'll have to provide the chestnuts, fire and wine yourself.

Please feel free to contact Kay through her website www.kayseeleyauthor.com She'd love to hear from you.